"Try to say my name, but say it very slowly. D-a-v." He watched as the tiny construct's mouth moved more slowly than before, but the squeak was still unintelligible.

"Try it again. This time drag the word out very, very slowly. D-D-D-a-a-a-a-v-v."

"Dv."

"You *can* talk, can't you?" Dav exclaimed. "You just speak so quickly we couldn't understand you."

Wherann nodded, chittered, and tried again to slow his words.

"Dgn. Dgn. Dgn-dgn-drgn."

Dav had been looking down at Wherann, trying to understand what the construct was trying to say. The trail turned sharply, and suddenly he understood the warning.

Dragon!

A blue dragon stood right in front of him.

First Quest™
Books

Son of
Dawn

Dixie McKeone

SON OF DAWN

Cover art by Paul Jaquays.

Interior Art by Terry Dykstra.

First Printing: May 1995
Printed in the United States of America.
Library of Congress Catalog Card Number: 94-68137

9 8 7 6 5 4 3 2 1

ISBN: 1-56076-884-3

TSR, Inc.
201 Sheridan Springs Road
Lake Geneva, WI 53147
United States of America

TSR Ltd.
120 Church End, Cherry Hinton
Cambridge CB1 3LB
United Kingdom

To my daughter,
Captain Davon Lee McKeone,
the definitive lady warrior.
I needed two characters
to show her courage,
integrity, sense of purpose,
and great heart.

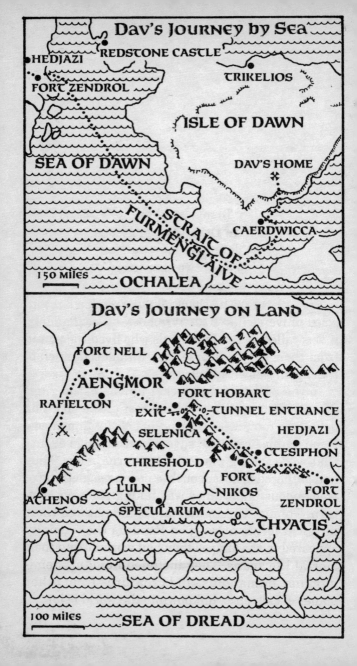

Prologue

Early Spring, 993 AD

High above the world of Mystara circled a moon-sized universe never seen by mortal eyes. Pandius, it was called by the Immortals who lived there, and from their lofty universe they influenced much of the life on the world below.

In the center of this pocket universe, the great dome of Pandius dwarfed the rest of the city. The dome was filled with a gathering of the Immortals. None had been called, save by the strange events that were taking place on the world below. They had gathered spontaneously, knowing something of tremendous importance was taking place on Mystara. Though the Immortals could change their physical forms at will, on Pandius they usually appeared in the shapes they had worn during their mortal life spans. They included humans, demi-humans, humanoids, and creatures from other planes of existence, unknown to the world below.

1

Dixie McKeone

By tacit agreement, they had taken their places for a formal council. The hierarchs sat in the center. Behind them, ranged according to rank, were the eternals, empyreals, celestials, and temporals on their individual tiers, and above them the initiates. Perched far above the rest and overshadowing all were the four Immortal Dragons, the luminescent Pearl, the gleaming Opal, the glittering Diamond, and the three-headed Great One, ruler of all dragons.

They were gathered to witness a battle taking place at Castle Qain, in the Blackheart Kingdom on the Alphatian Continent. A gathering of twelve wizards had turned into a battle of power.

Bolts of energy tore into great granite blocks. Some ricocheted down the passages, killing the hapless servants who were foolish enough not to flee. Seven of the twelve wizards had already been destroyed, their bodies littering the passages and chambers of the tower. Now the surviving five threw all their power into protecting themselves while trying to kill each other.

Four of the survivors appeared to be concentrating their efforts against Reddican, the owner of Castle Qain, but they also hurled potentially fatal spells at each other. Each wore two or more bejeweled pendants on golden chains.

On Pandius, the Immortal Djaea, a heirarch from the Sphere of Matter, rose with regal poise. Her form was that of a mature and lovely woman, her mouth tightened in a thin line. Her searching gaze took in the crowded tiers of the dome.

2

"Who can tell us what caused this battle?" she asked, her voice carrying to the vaulted roof.

In the highest tower of Castle Qain, its owner, Reddican, fell to the combined power of the wizards Chalmis and Orvan. Reddican lay sprawled in the passage, staring with lifeless eyes. Chalmis hurried forward and removed the jeweled pendant from around his neck. With Orvan, he retreated down the corridor, searching for the other two wizards.

The Immortals watched as a young female servant peered out from one of the chambers, crept down the passage, and cringed as she saw the body of Reddican. After a moment, she knelt, touched his face, then his hand, and finally pulled his cloak aside. When she saw the gaping wound, she shuddered and her eyes grew moist. Then she retreated back the way she had come.

"Easir, a bond servant," Valerias informed the others. "She's carrying a child by Reddican." Romance and passion were the main interests of the beautiful Immortal Valerias, so she made it her business to know the father. All the Immortals knew a new life stirred in Easir's body, though her pregnancy was not far enough advanced for a mortal to recognize it.

But the citizens of Pandius soon lost interest in the servant. Chalmis and Orvan had come upon Melina, whose powers were formidable. She carried five identical pendants, which swung from her wrist on golden chains.

Acting together, the two male wizards cast a

3

shrinking spell. Melina partially deflected their
spell, but she wasn't able to completely escape it.
She screamed as her left leg, arm, and the left side
of her torso shrunk, compressing her internal
organs and twisting her body grotesquely. Her
backbone broke in a series of loud snaps, and in
seconds the life went out of her eyes.

Chalmis and Orvan raced down the passage
after the pendants that lay glittering on the stone
floor. Orvan, the younger of the two, was several
paces ahead of Chalmis when the older wizard
stopped, raised his hand, and sent a stream of fire
arcing toward his companion's back.

While Orvan screamed and twisted in the fire,
Chalmis carefully stepped around him and picked
up the charms. He checked the chamber beyond,
from which Melina had appeared, and saw the
young wizard Lavar lying facedown on the floor.

Chalmis waited until the fire that consumed
Orvan died away. Then he pulled the two pendants
from the other wizard's charred neck and hurried
toward the circular steps that led to the keep and
out of the castle.

Odin, the most powerful hierarch in the Sphere
of Thought, rose to his feet. His tall, broad-shoul-
dered frame was stooped with age. He leaned on a
staff, and around the crown of his tattered hat flew
his two constant companions, the ravens Hugin
and Mugin.

Odin searched the faces of the Immortals. When
he spoke, his voice was soft, but every ear heard
him clearly.

"Twelve of the most powerful wizards in Blackheart have gathered for some purpose unknown to most of Pandius," he said slowly. "I repeat, unknown to *most* of Pandius, since wizards are the most closely watched of all mortals, yet their activities have been hidden from our eyes. This speaks of a conspiracy to conceal their actions, and it could only have been accomplished with the aid of Immortals."

Odin searched the minds of the black-robed, mummy-shrouded Thanatos; red-headed Loki; Alphaks the Elegant; Masauwu, who dressed in silk and jewels; and several others from the Sphere of Entropy.

"Could it be that the self-proclaimed protectors of Alphatia have been neglectful in their duties?"

The fiendish Immortal Alphaks smirked, his fangs bared in a grotesque grin. His horned head and shoulders shook with mirth. The whip he always carried in his right hand quivered as if its many tails were alive.

On the tier below Alphaks, the feathered serpent Atzanteotl frowned. Below his elven face, his plumed coils writhed in irritation.

"Why are they fighting?" Odin asked in a voice that demanded an answer.

"We're watching ambition betraying ambition," Thanatos said, shrugging off Atzanteotl's glare, as if saying there was no longer any need for secrecy. "Reddican had decided to rule Mystara, beginning first with Blackheart and then the continent of Alphatia." Thanatos spoke easily, proud of his part in the conspiracy. As one of the most powerful of the hierarchs, he had no fear of his peers. His tattered wings rustled in his glee. His skull face, half hidden beneath the layers of his death shroud, grinned at the assembled company.

"He convinced the others to share Mystara with him," Thanatos continued. "They were attempting to increase their strengths by absorbing each other's spells in the pendants. According to Reddican, they could then overpower other wizards and absorb their magic as well."

"But there's very little magic in those baubles," Djaea objected.

"What there is, is shielded from mortal detection, but you're right. It amounts to very little," said Atzanteotl, the elven-faced serpent. "Because the pendants are shielded, the others had just learned Reddican had drained the power of their crystals for his own use."

"But all this is impossible," jackal-headed Pflarr spoke up. "What you're suggesting is against the laws of magic."

"Against the laws of magic on Mystara," Atzanteotl agreed with a sly smile. "But Reddican has a pendant from another plane. He used it to convince them his theory of combined power was valid. A little sleight of hand, a smooth tongue, and their greed and ambition did the rest."

"And he used their power to enhance his own," Thanatos laughed, the hollow sound echoing throughout the dome. "They worked hard to place their fates in his hand."

Djaea stared at Atzanteotl. "This charm of Reddican's came from another plane? Which one?"

"I have no idea. Does it make any difference?" Thanatos shrugged, rustling his wings again.

Djaea, who hated ignorance and sloppy thinking, glared at the hierarch of entropy and was about to chastise him when Odin spoke.

"And now Chalmis has all the power in his possession?"

"Not at all," the trickster Loki chortled. "Chalmis does not have the planar charm."

"The real pendant is so well protected it has no magical emanations whatsoever," Thanatos replied. "And it is not one of the jeweled pendants he has stolen."

"Then Lavar still has a chance," Djaea murmured. The fifth wizard was only stunned. Chalmis, in his haste to leave the castle, hadn't checked the fallen wizard closely.

"But where is the real pendant?" Djaea asked.

Thanatos shrugged. The rest of the assembled Immortals watched as the female, Easir, entered a small storeroom filled with cast-off clothing, bedding, and a broken table. She counted the stones along the rear wall, first up three rows and then across from right to left until she reached the ninth. She pushed against the upper-left-hand corner of the stone, at the same time applying pressure to the one above it. Suddenly the ninth stone swiveled, revealing a small cavity.

She reached inside and pulled out several small bags made of thin leather, filled with fine gemstones. She laid them carefully on the broken table and picked up a discarded tunic. Ripping strips from the tattered garment, she used them to tie the bags around her waist beneath her gathered full underskirt.

"She's a thief," Atzanteotl laughed.

"Is she?" Odin asked. "Reddican is dead. He left no heirs save the child she carries. Is it stealing to take what belongs to her unborn child?"

Back in Castle Qain, Easir arranged her full skirt to hide the concealed leather bags. She tried to close the stone in the wall, but something blocked it. She reached inside and pulled out a two-inch disk made of a silver-white metal. A leather thong had been threaded through a small hole near the edge. Easir inspected it for a moment.

"So that's where he put it," Atzanteotl chuckled.

"She doesn't know what it is," Thanatos snarled. "She holds the fate of Mystara in her hands and doesn't *know* it."

"The fate of Mystara?" Djaea was on her feet again, along with half the assembled Immortals. As one being, they turned to watch Easir. She finished her examination, shrugged, slipped the thong over her head, and promptly disappeared from the sight of the Immortals.

"What happened?" A chorus of murmured questions filled the dome on Pandius. Up on the highest tier, all four dragons gave voice to their dismay. The Great One roared with all three of its dragon-like heads.

Odin stared at Atzanteotl. "Have you shielded

those magicians so they could create a magic that has power even over us? I ask you again, what planar laws govern this thing?"

Atzanteotl ruffled the feathers of his coiled body and refused to answer. His elven face was creased in a frown. For once, even Thanatos found no pleasure in the havoc he had helped to create. He rustled his ragged wings, took a grip on his scythe, and disappeared. He was soon followed by Atzanteotl, Thanatos, Loki, and several others from the Sphere of Entropy.

The Immortals from the four other spheres soon followed them. In moments, Castle Qain filled with searchers who appeared from nowhere, further frightening the terrified servants who had survived the battle.

On Pandius, The Great One flew down from the upper tier to consult with Djaea and Odin.

"The human female disappeared from your sight also?" He spoke with his center head. Above it, the other two looked at each other as if each expected the other to have some explanation for the strange occurrence.

Odin and Djaea nodded.

"If this magic of Reddican's can block our sight, what other powers might it hold over us?" The Great One asked.

"I don't know," Djaea replied quietly.

"Neither do Atzanteotl or the others who aided him," Odin said. "They were as startled as we were."

The other three dragons flew down to join the group on the floor of the great dome.

Dixie McKeone

"Do we dare leave such a weapon in the hands of a mortal?" asked the luminescent Pearl.

"We'll take it from her fast enough," Diamond replied as smoke escaped from his nostrils.

"No one can take it from her until she's found," Djaea said. "At least, since she doesn't know what it is, she won't be tempted to use it."

"It might be best to leave it with her," said Tiresas, the Immortal bard. "There are parts still to be played that have not yet been imagined, even by my farseeing companions."

The rest of the Immortals turned their attention to Tiresas. His gift of prophesy surpassed all others, but his method of delivery surprised them. For once, he had spoken plainly rather than hiding his meaning in song or verse. He had seen into the fate of the woman and the pendant and thought it important enough to make his message clear.

But the decision was not theirs to make. Hours later several other Immortals joined the first ten who had begun the search for the servant. For more than a month, they combed Alphatia and the islands beyond, but Easir had dropped from Immortal vision.

* * * * * *

Kaldmont 28, 993 AD

In the city of Trikelios, on the eastern coast of the Isle of Dawn, few lights burned to illuminate the predawn darkness. In the imposing residence built by the pirate Dolsor Curan and occupied by his crippled son and heir, one light gleamed through the cracks in a shuttered window.

Withis Curan leaned over a bed carved of oak and covered with the finest linen. By bending forward, he emphasized his twisted back and the unsightly hump on his left shoulder, but the lovely Easir's eyes could no longer see him. Beside her slept her newborn child.

With a gentle finger, Withis closed the lids of Easir's eyes and wiped away his tears that had fallen on her ashen face. Even while he mourned, he thanked the Immortals for the few months of happiness they had shared.

He knew she no longer heard him, but he repeated the promise he had made.

"I will keep your secrets, my love, and love the babe as though he were my own son. Since I cannot name him for his real father, I will call him after you. In the ancient high elven tongue, 'Easir' means 'fate.' I will call him 'Davonin,' which means 'destiny' in the same language."

Withis removed the thong and the disk of white metal from around her neck and put it on the child, reknotting the old leather strip so it would fit around the tiny neck of the infant.

Chapter 1

Struth the Shaker

Like most orcs, Assag Growlbelly and Bigmaw
Crookfang hated humans. They considered human
wizards the worst of the lot, but their leader, King
Thar of Oenkmar, had ordered them to serve
Struth the Shaker. The orcish king had formed an
alliance with him and wanted him protected.

Assag wanted protection from the wizard as he
and Bigmaw crouched in the fissure of the cave,
hoping to escape the wizard's attention, but knowing they must not leave until he dismissed them.
They had already learned of Struth's tendency to
vent his anger on anyone present, and he was often
angry.

Assag wondered if Struth's bad temper didn't
arise from the terrible wound to his arm. The wizard had been wounded in the great war that had
ended only months before. Humans, elves, and
halflings of the continents of Brun and Alphatia
had killed themselves off at a great rate. Even the
orcs of Oenkmar had surfaced from their under-

ground domain and did their share of killing and pillaging. It had been a great time, Assag remembered, but then he thought sourly of their defeat when they were driven back underground.

Best not to think of that. Instead, he wondered why the wizard hadn't healed his arm. Struth was always busy, either using his power or resting when he had worn himself out with his spells.

Assag was fascinated by the wizard's power. He watched as Struth sat on a rickety bench, working slowly, fashioning a clay *obeah*, a tiny figure used in magic spells. The old wizard attached stubby wings to the roughly humanoid shape, which stood about four inches high.

"And now for the blood," Struth muttered as he pulled a thin, wicked-looking knife from beneath his cloak and pricked his own right arm. As the blood flowed, he held the wound over the figure and the clay reddened.

The wizard began his incantation, and Assag clapped his hands over his ears to keep out the strange words. The chamber darkened, and fell whisperings seemed to come from the walls.

Then, before Assag's startled eyes, a thin black mist filled the air, partially obscuring the torches embedded in the cracks of the walls. Slowly the mist gathered itself into a cloud that grew steadily blacker and smaller as it hung over the *obeah*. Then it dropped to cover the tiny figure.

The condensing blackness formed into a tiny human-shaped figure with a dark gray body and arms and legs as slender and graceful as a young elf's. Its head resembled a bat with huge eyes and tiny, pointed ears. As Assag watched in frightened fascination, it spread large, delicate wings and rose to hover above the lumpy earthen figure on the table. The clay *obeah* was pale gray again; the blood had disappeared.

Struth nodded in approval, then rose and signaled the orcs that they were free to leave. He turned toward the inner chamber and his make-shift bed. The little construct folded its wings and lay down on the table to sleep.

Assag and Bigmaw crept out of the cave. They had served Struth long enough to know his strength was drained by his spells, and he always slept after using his magic.

After nearly two weeks had passed, Assag was certain it had taken tremendous power to create the construct, since Struth had been sleeping almost constantly. Occasionally they saw the tiny winged creature, but often it slept as well.

One sunny afternoon the orcs were outside the cave roasting a haunch of venison. When the outer crust was crisp and half blackened, Assag cut two large slabs from the half-roasted haunch. Bigmaw bit into his portion, swallowed it without chewing, and spat on the ground.

"Augh, too fresh," he complained. "Not fit for anything but humans."

"You willing to go hungry until it rots?" Assag asked. "Better eat while Struth sleeps. No telling what he'll want when he's up and about again."

Bigmaw grunted in agreement as he chewed

vigorously. "Bringing in dirt to make that little monster was none of our orders from Thar."

An hour later they were dozing when Assag heard heavy footsteps tromping on brittle twigs and someone pushing through the bushes on the hillside. The steps were coming from the north, probably some of his people, but it was best to be prepared. He and Bigmaw jumped to their feet and stood with their axes held ready.

Moonbane and Garflaw Unglad emerged from the thick brush. Brothers, both were huge, even for orcs. Moonbane, the meaner of the two, sneered at Assag.

"You challenging me?"

"No. Got orders to be ready for enemies. Could have been elf scum or human crud trying to sneak up on us." Assag carefully laid his axe aside.

"Meat's half cooked," he said, pointing to the fire. "Too fresh, but it's cooked." After their journey, he suspected the new arrivals would rather eat than fight.

Moonbane and Garflaw finished off the haunch of venison and came to sit in the entrance of the cave. They pulled off their boiled leather helmets.

"Things ain't going according to plan," Moonbane said. "Looks like we'll have to try again to get some high-muckety elves."

"What happened?" Assag asked.

"The raiding party was supposed to pick up some real high-muckety shadow-elf scum, and they done it, got two whelps. . . ."

"Them little elves was dressed fine as—as—"

Garflaw groped for a description as he pulled two small white silk cloaks from beneath his weskit and handed them to Assag, but Moonbane cut off his description.

"Word is them little ones was just what was wanted, and Rovag, as led the raiding party, got a whole load of them jools the shadow scum thinks so much of."

"Then why is it bad news?" Bigmaw asked. Assag wondered too.

"On the way back, that rebel Korshnid ambushed Rovag and his troop when they was leaving that cursed forest. That half-elf scum—"

"Rovag is half-elf?" Bigmaw asked, his pig eyes wide in surprise.

"Watch your mouth!" Moonbane threatened. " 'Course he wasn't. He was my cousin, wasn't he? I was talking about Korshnid. That one's tricky enough to be half-elf, even if he ain't. What self-respecting orc would have trolls and goblins and kobolds all in one group? Got to have elf blood." Moonbane glared to make sure the others understood his outrage. Then he went on.

"Anyway, Korshnid killed most of our party and took them elves. Only Studgad got back alive, cuz he was hanging back to see if they was being followed. Near as we can figure, later on Korshnid had some hard fighting with a patrol of Darokin filth. Wouldn't have known it was him as fought 'em, 'cept as Vigwin was killed and his body left to rot. 'Course, you knew Vigwin was Korshnid's brother and traveled with him, didn't you?"

Assag and Bigmaw nodded. That was old news.

"Korshnid took them elves clean away, off down the Streel River, he did," Garflaw said with relish, finishing the tale of bad news. "Nobody knows what happened to 'em after that."

"It's time we was getting back to Oenkmar," Moonbane said, grinning. "You can pass along the news to that wizard you look after."

"You was sent. You tell him," Assag said, not wanting to bear bad news to the wizard, but Moonbane had already delivered his tale and wouldn't stay around to repeat it to Struth.

"Got to get back and see if Thar has more messages he wants sent," Moonbane said with a grin. "Never shirk your duty."

"I don't understand," Bigmaw complained when the brothers had disappeared into the distance. "Never could figure why they wanted them jools the Shadow Elves like so much. They break all to pieces onct they's brought to the surface."

"Don't get that part myself," Assag replied. " 'Less they just took 'em to make the elves mad, treasuring them things like they do. Goes along with stealing some of the high-born—driving them to war." He fingered the cloaks, which were both rather small. The fabric was soft, silky, and intricately embroidered.

"But if we want to fight 'em, why don't we just go in and fight?"

"The plan is to make the Shadow Elves fight Darokin," Assag explained. "Rovag was to take a couple of them high-nosed human Darokin warriors down in the tunnels and kill 'em, making it look like the humans took the elves. I figure Rovag took care of that part, since they got the elf scum and the jools afore Korshnid caught up with them. Now them elves'll think Darokin done it. Let them fight each other, see. Then, when they've killed off each other and there ain't so many left, we can take over part of both lands."

Bigmaw stared at his friend admiringly. "You're smart enough to be a chief, Assag, you know that?"

"Ain't my idea," Assag admitted, though he enjoyed the compliment. "Heard Struth and Thar making the plan—mostly Struth, though Thar didn't take much convincing, seeing how he feels about that stinkin' scum from Darokin."

"What I can't figure is what we want with Darokin. All that sun . . . ugh," Bigmaw said as he picked at a small tear in his leather coat.

"Can't say as we want it so much as to get back at that Darokin scum that pushed us back underground in the war. Think that's mostly what Thar wants."

Bigmaw sighed. "Ain't likely we'll see no war now. Korshnid took care of that when he grabbed them Shadow Elves."

"There'll still be a war, but that ain't what concerns me. We're stuck with telling Struth what happened. He could boil our brains."

"Who's to say we know anything about it?" Bigmaw asked. "Ain't nobody heard Moonbane tell us. We could wipe out his tracks, bury them little capes, and pretend he was never here."

Assag turned to stare at his friend. "You know, you ain't *always* stupid."

Just beyond Bigmaw's shoulder, Assag saw Struth's little construct crouched on a boulder staring at them. It had heard every word. The wizard had told them the little creature would be his eyes and ears. Assag just hoped the spy had been listening when Moonbane and Garflaw told their tale.

* * * * *

Struth the Shaker lay on his makeshift bed of dried grass and half-cured hides. He cursed his wounded body and his lack of strength. Months earlier, he had been injured in the final stages of the war between Alphatia and Glantri. The fighting had spread to include most of the lands of eastern Brun before it had ended with the sinking of the continent of Alphatia. In the last major battle, Struth had been one of the thousand wizards from Alphatia who had attacked their prime enemy, Glantri. The numbers had been one too many for Struth, who had been severely wounded by an inexperienced Alphatian mage fighting at his side.

He had barely managed to escape from the battlefield into a cave in the Broken Lands. Months had passed in a blur of pain so great he was unable to concentrate on his healing spells. He would have died if he hadn't been able to subjugate two orcs, who brought him food and furs to keep him warm. Struth had slowly begun to heal himself, but his depleted physical strength reduced his power until his healing spells were weak and only partially successful. Slowly, working a little at a time, he had healed all his wounds except for the repeated flare-ups of infection in his left arm.

But even while his body was mending, his mind was active. The orcs had brought him news of the war, so he knew Alphatia had sunk beneath the sea. He cared little for Alphatia and even less for Blackheart, the kingdom of wizardry on the lost continent, but his castle was gone. That enraged him. His mind turned to finding a new home, and at the same time taking his revenge on the countries on the continent of Brun that had helped to destroy his comfort.

He saw no reason why he shouldn't succeed. He had little to fear from other wizards. The most powerful of each nation had been prime targets of their enemies and were almost all destroyed.

He knew, too, that many of the countries on Brun were weak, ravaged by the recent war. The peasants would be dissatisfied because their rulers would raise taxes to fill their empty treasuries. The disruption of orderly life and general unrest would give him an opportunity to establish a power base and the beginnings of a new order.

But even though he might be the most powerful wizard left on Mystara, he knew he couldn't stand alone against the armies and the combined remaining forces of magic. He needed allies, an army of allies.

That was when he had thought of Thar, King of Oenkmar. The orc king had been soundly defeated when he tried to increase his own domains and was still angry about it.

Struth met with the orc king and promised Thar an opportunity for a killing spree of looting and pillaging that had the orc drooling down his fat chest.

The wizard had already worked out a plan by which they could outrage the proud Shadow Elves and make it appear that Darokin was to blame for killing their people, taking some captive, and, at Thar's suggestion, stealing some strange crystals the elves seemed to value above their lives.

The Shadow Elves hated and distrusted all other races because for centuries they had been denied land on the surface of Mystara. Darokin feared these strange elves, who had cursed the forest within their borders and had driven out the elves of Alfheim.

The two nations would be at war within months. Struth and the orcs would wait until the battles had decimated their numbers, and then they would move in and take over large parts of Darokin and Aengmor.

Struth had already decided he would make his home in the city of Corunglain, located at the forks of the Streel and Vesubian rivers. He would have the Broken Lands, with armies of trolls, orcs, kobolds, and goblins, at his back. They could easily subdue the humans of any city they selected. With the two rivers as his highways and an army behind him, he could widen his domain as he chose.

Days of exhaustion had followed his teleportation to the orc kingdom and back. He had been forced to rest and build up his strength for two weeks after creating the construct, but he considered the little creature worth the effort. He would never have learned about the high-born elf children if the construct hadn't overheard the orcs. The wizard had smiled when Bigmaw and Assag concocted their feeble plan to keep from bringing him the news.

They were right, of course. Struth had been enraged when he learned the renegade orc had taken the kidnap victims, yet perhaps the damage wasn't as bad as the orcs thought.

Assag had made an important point. If the orcs kidnapped the elves and stole the jewels, then it was safe to assume their leader, Rovag, had killed the two captive Darokin soldiers in the tunnels. The elves would find the bodies, so the proof of Darokin's involvement had been planted. The outrage would throw them into a frenzy.

Struth was less certain about the jewels. Thar had said the Shadow Elves treasured some sort of worthless crystal. Struth was certain the orc king had lied about the value of the stones, wanting to keep the treasure all to himself. Well, let him. Struth had no time for anything but his war.

He sat up on his bed and shouted for Assag and Bigmaw. He took a brief moment to enjoy the fear he engendered in the orcs before ordering them to bring him the capes that had been taken from the elves.

He dismissed them and fingered the white, silken cloth, then muttered a simple incantation.

Fatigue washed over him again, but his spell worked. He turned his head to the southeast and sensed the rocking of a boat, accompanied by a feeling of fear and helpless captivity. Even as those feelings reached him through the cloth and the spell, he could sense that the distance between the cloaks and their owners was widening.

With a more powerful spell, he might have learned who held the Shadow Elves captive and why, but that didn't matter as long as neither Darokin nor Aengmor knew where they were.

The elves would be enraged, and Darokin would soon learn their country was blamed. Struth smiled, his black eyes gleaming with pleasure. He'd have his war, he'd have Corunglain, and one day he'd have his revenge against Glantri and possibly the rest of Brun.

Yes, death rode the winds, and Struth was lashing it to greater speed. He threw back his head and laughed.

The evil sound echoed through the caverns. Outside, the orcs shivered.

Chapter 2
The Journey Begins

Dav Curan knew he was silhouetted against the skyline, but he paused and turned in the saddle, taking a long look behind him. He was gazing back on the Great Escarpment of the Isle of Dawn. The escarpment was a trackless wilderness populated only by wild animals, monsters, and humanoids. Dav had spent all his remembered life there in a sheltered valley, its only entrance protected by magic. He had expected to remain there, studying with his scholarly stepfather, Withis, helping to grow the crops that fed them and hunting on the escarpment.

Ten days ago, however, Withis had been bitten by a viper, and Dav's life had suddenly changed. Loneliness and a promise to continue his studies had brought him out of the valley. He was on his way to Caerdwicca to take passage on a ship to Specularum in Karameikos, the closest port to Luln, where he would study with Amslothe Verdon, a respected scholar and an old friend of Withis's.

24

Son of Dawn

As if reminding Dav of his duty, Wikko, the larger of the two mules, started down the path that led to the sea plain below the cliffs of the escarpment. Milstin, the other mule, followed, and Eidor, Dav's horse, fell into line behind them. In the distance, a golden thread of beach separated the green plain from the Bay of Caerdwicca.

The animals knew the trail. They had made the annual trip to Caerdwicca for supplies with Withis for years. Dav had visited the small rustic seaport only three times in his life, the last time more than two years ago. When he was a small child, he had been too young for the dangerous trip. Then, after their last servant died, he had stayed behind in the valley to take care of the stock while Withis went to purchase supplies.

Dav was taking a dozen large cat-skin furs to trade at Caerdwicca. They were prized for their soft, thick, intricately patterned fur. His own cat-skin coat rested on the back of his saddle. He had dyed his doeskin shirt and trousers to match so when he hunted on the escarpment, they provided a camouflage that approached invisibility.

He was a tall, rangy youth, still coming to terms with a sudden spurt of growth during the summer. He looked out at the world with black eyes, deeply set in a face that was beginning to show angular lines. His deep tan hid the natural paleness of his skin.

A homemade longbow hung over his right shoulder and just behind his left was a quiver of expertly fletched arrows. The collar of his shirt almost hid the hilt of a large hunting knife.

Dixie McKeone

The weapons he carried were a necessity on the escarpment, and they might prove to be just as important in Caerdwicca. His two sturdy mules, the horse, his extra clothing, and the bundles of furs strapped to the mules' backs could attract robbers in the small pirate port.

His shirt hid a multipocketed vest filled back and front with Thyatian emperors, the metal coins a legacy of his wealthy stepfather. Even less likely to be noticed were the bulges on the inside of his wide, shabby belt, which held an even greater wealth in gemstones. A small purse attached to his belt made it seem as if he carried his money in plain sight.

Although he carried the weight of two inheritances from two fathers, he tried to keep the gems and coins from his thoughts. He would have traded them gladly for the knowledge that the gentle old scholar he had buried ten days earlier had really been his father. He was still too wounded with the revelation to think about it logically.

Dav reached the plain just before sunset. The next morning he began his journey beneath a cloudy sky and a cold wind. He hunched down in his coat and tried to drive away a sense of loneliness, sharpened because it was his birthday. He was sixteen and alone. The next day would be Nuwmont the first, the first day of the year 1010, which he mentally marked as the beginning of his new life. By midday, he reached the shore, and his fascination with the waves drew him out of his dark mood.

As he traveled, the strip of soft sand became spotted with boulders. Late in the afternoon, he approached a huge outcrop of stone. It extended halfway up the beach and well out into the sea. From a mile away, it looked like a gigantic loaf of bread and reminded him of his hunger.

From his three trips to Caerdwicca with Withis, he knew the rock was split by a wide longitudinal fissure. The break was nearly ten feet wide and filled with a stretch of dry sand, a perfect place to make his camp.

As Dav rode into the shelter, he saw three men crouched around a small driftwood fire. They jumped to their feet and pulled their knives when they saw him. Their clothing was ragged and none too clean. All wore wide, intricately tooled belts that were peculiar to Hattia, a large island off the southeastern coast of Brun, part of the Empire of Thyatis.

"My apologies if I startled you," he said. "I'm just seeking a place to camp for the night."

The best dressed of the Hattians stood on the far side of the fire; he also appeared to be the most intelligent of the three. He relaxed and slipped his knife back into its sheath.

"Well met, stranger. You'll forgive our caution, but these are dangerous times."

Very bad times, Dav thought, if three armed men react so sharply to the appearance of a lone traveler.

"Lertin, get more wood for the fire," the leader ordered a tall thin man, whose beard was parted by an old scar down his cheek. "Cust, you go with him," he said to the shorter, heavyset man. Cust's face and beard had human features, but his thick back and legs and long muscular arms were huge, orcish. As the others left the rock cleft, their leader smiled at Dav.

"You traveling alone?" When Dav nodded, the smile widened. "You're welcome to join us, especially if you want to add that meat to the stew." He pointed to the carcass of a rabbit that Dav had brought down with an arrow that afternoon.

"You're welcome to share it." Dav untied it from the saddle and handed it to the Hattian before he dismounted. He unsaddled the horse and partially unloaded the mules. The Hattian helped him, and they exchanged names.

Gorval, the leader of the Hattians, said they were also travelers, sailing around the island to Trikelios. He questioned Dav, and the youth felt no hesitation in telling the Hattian that he was on his way to Caerdwicca to trade his furs. To admit he planned to take passage to Specularum would be admitting he carried gold for his fare.

While they talked, Dav finished unloading the mules. When he was finished, Gorval led him toward the small fire. Dav took a seat where the Hattian indicated, with his back to the beach. Gorval moved around to the other side of the fire, and as Dav's eyes followed him, he saw movement just inside a second fissure that branched off from the first.

Four people sat huddled together for warmth. They wore wrist shackles and were chained together. Their gray homespun clothing identified them as bond servants. The two adults, a man and a woman, seemed resigned. A boy, nearly as large as Dav, stared at him with the vacant eyes and the open, wet mouth of a half-wit. The golden-haired girl, who looked to be about twelve, stared at him with a sudden hope he couldn't understand.

Gorval saw the direction of Dav's gaze and shrugged. "We're transporting criminals." His shoulders sagged and he lowered his head. "It isn't a pleasant job, but it has to be done."

Dav had never seen anyone chained, and it shocked him. He also sensed the lie in Gorval's explanation. The two adults were too spiritless to be criminals and the others too young.

He was trying to work out his feelings when the girl started talking to him with her eyes. She threw darting looks at him and then back over his shoulder. She flinched as if she were about to be struck from behind, but there was no one behind her.

There was no one behind *her!*

Dav rolled to the side just in time to avoid the blow of a heavy length of driftwood. By the time the heavy cudgel struck the ground, throwing up sand and dust, Dav was three feet away, scrambling to his feet. Just as he straightened, a strong arm clamped his elbows to his sides, and he felt the cold edge of a knife at his throat.

"It's still you'll be," said Cust, the short, stocky Hattian. Across the fire, Gorval was slowly rising to his feet, his smile triumphant.

Enraged, Dav dropped to his knees and arched his back. Cust's own grip helped to flip the stocky man over Dav's head. The Hattian landed on his back across the small fire. He lay half stunned for a moment, then screamed in pain.

Dav jumped to his feet and backed away before the others could react. Gorval leapt forward and rolled Cust out of the fire. The leader left the burned man writhing in the sand while he pulled his knife.

Some peripheral part of Dav's brain was taking note of the girl's activities. She urged her three companions to their feet. What could she do? The others seemed too meek to help. He was too intent on Gorval and Lertin to give any more attention to the prisoners.

Cust moaned and cursed. Eidor neighed, reared, and then galloped out of the fissure. The mules sidled and brayed in agitation, but they stood their ground.

Dav drew his own hunting knife from its concealed sheath. Knowing he was trapped in the fissure, he backed toward the wall of the rock, only to find his path blocked by Milstin.

"Get out of my way," he ordered the mule, but Milstin refused to move, and Dav couldn't spare the time to coax him.

He warned himself to be careful. Orcs and animals he had fought on the escarpment were strong and quick, but slow thinkers. Now he faced humans.

While Dav waited with his back to the mule,

Gorval stood with his legs slightly apart, watching the young scholar with narrowed eyes.

Lertin had backed away from the fire, well out of reach, blocking the exit from the fissure. Dav couldn't face one without turning his back to the other.

Lertin crept forward, the driftwood club in his left hand, his knife in the other. He stayed close to the eastern wall of the fissure, forcing Dav to turn away from Gorval.

As Dav turned, he reached behind him and grabbed Milstin's short mane. Urging the mule to move with him, he blocked Gorval's approach while Dav faced Lertin. When Dav released him, Milstin stood his ground. Knowing the mule's tendency to kick, Dav stayed well away from the mule's hindquarters.

Lertin frowned at the mule but pressed on. "Think you're smart, eh, boy?" he muttered.

Lertin feinted with the knife and swung the club. Dav ducked but took a glancing blow on the shoulder. Pain shot down his arm. He lunged with his knife and drove the Hattian back a few steps, gaining a moment to look over his shoulder and locate Gorval.

The Hattian leader, blocked by the mule, gave all his attention to the struggle between Dav and Lertin, so he hadn't noticed the captives sneaking up behind him.

Lertin moved in again and swung the wooden club. Dav ducked, nearly falling under Milstin's front feet in his scramble. He heard a sickening thump as the club came down on Milstin's rump, and the mule brayed in pain and lurched. Already off balance, Dav was knocked sprawling.

He fell on his back, caught between the mule's forefeet and Lertin's shuffling boots. He saw Lertin's blade descending toward his midriff, but Milstin was faster than the Hattian. The mule's big head jutted forward and caught Lertin's arm with his big flat teeth. The Hattian screamed and dropped the knife. He struck at the mule again with the club. Milstin increased the pressure on the Hattian's arm until Lertin dropped his second weapon and pushed at the mule's head with his free hand. In his struggle, he kicked Dav in the side.

Dav rolled in a backward somersault and came to his feet just as Milstin freed the Hattian. Lertin stumbled back and made his second mistake. He was just close enough for Wikko, the second mule, to get in a good kick that sent the man sprawling.

"Good move. You can have him for dinner," Dav said to the beast as Lertin scrambled to his feet and lurched away up the beach. Dav turned, ready to take on the Hattian leader, who was still being kept out of the fight by the bulk of Milstin's body.

Gorval crouched on the other side of Milstin, staying just out of reach of the sharp hooves and flat teeth. He was still unaware of the prisoners who crept up on him, moving slowly to keep the chains from rattling.

The girl led them. She had armed herself with

the only weapon available, a short length of broken, rotted tree trunk some twelve inches in diameter and several feet long. It appeared to be water-logged and almost more than she could lift. Gorval had been using it for a seat. Dav wondered what she thought she could do with it.

She showed him.

When Gorval started forward, she swung. She could only raise the weight waist-high, but she gave him a sound crack on the right elbow. Fortunately he was caught in midstep and off balance. He fell to his knees and dropped his knife.

Dav tried to push by the mule, but Milstin, still angry at being struck, refused to budge.

"Will you move your stupid rump?" he shouted at the mule, who merely brayed back at him. He shoved ineffectually at the beast. Meanwhile, the girl had ruthlessly jerked on the chain, pulling the half-wit boy and the woman forward. She tripped the boy, who fell against Gorval. As he tumbled, he pulled the woman down with him.

Fine! By the time they finished falling over each other, someone could be dead, Dav thought. He pushed again at the beast, then gave up and dove under the animal's body as Gorval pushed the woman and the boy off. The Hattian rose and reached for the girl, who threatened him with his own knife. She was just out of reach, but he caught the chain and jerked it to pull her toward him.

But Gorval had not fully considered the result of his action. He had grabbed the chain between the girl and the half-wit. When he yanked the girl toward him, the half-wit was pulled forward too. The boy tripped over the driftwood, stumbled into Gorval's back, and all three went down in another heap.

Dav leapt forward, helped the boy to his feet, and rolled the suddenly still body of Gorval off the girl. The blade of the knife was buried to the hilt in the Hattian's chest, heart-high.

"He—he fell on it," the girl said, staring at the body as if she couldn't believe it.

At the end of the shackled line, the man was helping the woman to her feet, seemingly oblivious to anything but her. She ignored him and gazed at Dav.

"Are we *your* prisoners now?" she asked timidly, glancing at the knife in his hand.

Dav stared at her, too startled by the question to answer immediately. The suggestion brought fire to the girl's eyes and a wary look from the man.

"I don't want any prisoners, not you or anyone else. I wouldn't know what to do with them," Dav said. "As far as I'm concerned, you're free."

"Free? Really free?" She stared at him in disbelief. The worshiping look in her eyes, half hopeful, half doubting, made Dav uncomfortable. He slipped his knife back in his neck sheath to remove its threat.

"I can't give you a certificate, but it's none of my business what you do."

"Thank you," she said softly, then stepped forward and caught his hands. "Thank you . . . oh, thank you!"

Dixie McKeone

"Thank yourself," the girl snapped. "Thank Adoc and the mule. All this character did was pull a stunt that could have gotten him killed. I never saw anyone so clumsy and stupid in a fight!"

Chapter 3

Unexpected Company

Dav stared at the girl, feeling as if she had slapped him. Who did she think she was? A dirty ragged urchin who wore a copper bond servant's bracelet under the shackle on her left arm.

"It worked," he shouted at her. Needing a release from his anger, he turned on Cust, who had stopped writhing on the ground and crouched by the wall of the fissure.

"Get out!" he snarled at the injured man. "Get out, or I'll put a knife through you. Better still, I'll let *her* do it!" He pointed at the girl.

Milstin had moved away down the fissure. Cust looked warily at the prisoners, Dav, and the body of Gorval. He sidled by the mule and stumbled out of the crack in the rock. Dav followed and watched as he limped off down the beach. Lertin joined his companion, still holding the arm Milstin had bitten.

Dav watched them as they headed north. He tried to calm his disordered thoughts before turning back into the sheltered area.

Dixie McKeone

By the time he joined the prisoners, they had found Gorval's keys that hung around his neck on a thong and were using the smallest one to unlock their shackles. Dav watched as they massaged the sore, chafed skin where the metal cuffs had rubbed against it.

He scuffed around in the sand and found Cust's knife and gave it to the man. After removing the blade from Gorval's chest, he cleaned it and handed it to the girl. Her face paled as she took it. Lertin must have picked up his blade, Dav decided. He couldn't find it in the sand.

The woman thanked him again, chattering aimlessly in her relief and reaction to her fear. As she babbled on, she told him the names of the prisoners.

Dav watched and listened. The man, Vorchal, was twice Dav's age, so the youth expected him to take charge. But when Vorchal had assured himself that the woman, Reris, was unharmed, he stood looking around as if he didn't understand much more than Adoc, the half-wit boy.

Dav's jaw tightened in frustration. The last thing he needed was to be saddled with four people who had no idea what to do with themselves. He had made a promise to Withis and refused to allow himself to be sidetracked.

They stood around the campfire as if they had never seen one. Dav doubted if any of them had ever spent a night away from civilization. He clenched his jaw, telling himself he didn't owe them anything else, but he could get them through until morning, he decided.

"It's too late to leave here and search for another campsite tonight," he said, putting Reris to watching the stew and Vorchal to cutting up the rabbit. Dav took Adoc with him to gather driftwood to keep the fire burning through the night.

As he and Adoc returned with their last load, Vorchal and the girl, who was called Leanna, appeared from the dimness of the second fissure. They drew two small, struggling captives forward. Dav recognized them by their white skin and hair, large, pointed ears, and slanted, pale blue eyes.

Shadow Elves.

Shadow Elf *children*, he amended.

"We knew they were keeping someone else locked belowdecks," Leanna said.

Dav's skin prickled with excitement when he saw the children. He felt as if he were seeing a legend come to life. Nearly three thousand years before, the elves of southern Glantri had fled a catastrophe. He couldn't remember exactly what it was, but many of the elves had escaped below ground and were forgotten by most of the surface dwellers.

Two years before, Dav and Withis had heard about the mutation of the trees in the Canolbarth Forest in Alfheim. There were also rumors that the Shadow Elves were moving to the surface again. Dav knew from experience that by the time news from Brun reached Caerdwicca, it was usually too garbled from retelling to be fact, so he had discounted it. Now he was seeing the proof standing in front of him.

He couldn't guess their ages. If they had been human children, he would have thought the boy was about four years old and the girl eight or nine. They wore filthy Hattian cast-off clothing, probably discarded by Lertin and Cust. The sleeves and pant legs covered their hands and feet.

When Leanna and Vorchal brought them closer to the light of the fire, Dav noticed that a deep violet pattern of swirls covered the elf girl's forehead and curved down on her cheekbones, framing her eyes. The pattern was intricate and concentric, the painstaking work of a true artist, Dav thought. Above the collar of the loose, ragged shirt, a similar design trimmed the sides of her neck in a delicate tracery.

The elven girl saw the three people waiting by the fire and seemed to realize there was no longer any hope of escape. She stopped her struggling, but her glare showed her spirit.

"The great Kanafasti will turn your bones to water and boil them in your flesh!" she threatened, speaking in her own language. "You will die in the molten lakes! My father will lead our people to search the world for you. You will suffer a thousand deaths."

Dav's training in the old languages included the Shiye-Lawr, Vyalia, and Alfheim dialects. Apparently the Shadow Elf dialect had not diverged far from Shiye-Lawr in the three millennia they had lived below ground.

He laughed at the haughty, ragged little elf. Then he translated the threats while Leanna and Vorchal drew their captives forward.

"They have killed the evil one," the boy said when he noticed Gorval's body, awe and fear plain in his eyes. His voice was a high treble and his features softer than the female's. His face was bare of any markings.

"It is always so with the surface vermin, who have no loyalty to anything but their evil and their greed," the female replied. She tried to maintain her bravado, but she looked uneasily from the body of the Hattian to the others.

Two more to look after, Dav thought, and the female would not be pleasant company.

"Stop worrying. No one's going to stick a knife in you," he told them, using the Shiye-Lawr tongue. Both elves stared at him as if his ability to understand and speak to them was sacrilege.

"And you might thank us for freeing you from the Hattians." His irritation fell away as he noticed they were trembling with cold. "Come closer to the fire," he suggested.

Vorchal took the order to mean he should release the elves, but Leanna still kept her grip on the girl's arm.

"You can't just turn them loose. They'll run away. We'd better shackle them," she said.

Her suggestion made Dav angry. "You liked being in irons so much you don't want to deprive them of the pleasure?"

Leanna stood her ground. "Isn't this the Isle of Dawn?"

"What's that got to do with putting them in chains?"

41

"They're *Shadow Elves*. They'll escape the first chance they get. If what I've heard about the Great Escarpment is true, they wouldn't last the night."

"I'll talk to them."

"And what makes you think they'll listen?"

"Some people can stop using their mouths long enough to hear what's being said," Dav snapped. He took the elf girl's arm from Leanna's hold and led her over to the fire. The same intricate design on her face was abbreviated on the back of her hands, he noted.

While Dav was talking to the elves, Vorchal inspected Milstin's rump, apparently checking for injuries, and then he and Adoc dug a hole in the sand farther up the beach. They dragged the dead Hattian away to bury him.

Dav told the elves where they were and how he and the other prisoners had killed Gorval and driven the others away. The elves acted as if they didn't hear a word Dav said, but when he described Milstin's part in the fight, the elf boy was too fascinated to maintain his pretense. He stared at the mule.

"Is that a horse?" he asked.

"Erian!" the girl hissed. "Do not lower yourself to speak with these humans."

"I just wanted to know if it was a horse," he muttered, hanging his head.

"It's a mule," Dav said. "In a way, it's like your friend there. When it's scared, it wants to fight."

Erian peeped at Dav from under his lashes and smiled, a male-to-male understanding that traversed political, cultural, and philosophical boundaries. Dav grinned back at him.

Hoping he could keep the elves from running away during the night, Dav told them about the Great Escarpment. He described some of the creatures that lived on the heights and occasionally came down to the plain. Erian peered into the darkness as if he expected to be attacked at any moment. Dav hoped he had scared them into believing him.

Leanna set Vorchal and Adoc to cleaning spoons and trenchers she had found on the Hattians' boat. By the time they were finished, the stew was ready, but Dav could hardly eat it. The rabbit was tender and good, but the vegetables were dried out and tough. The others chewed without complaining, apparently too hungry to care.

They ate in silence until the pot was empty. When their stomachs were full, they sat around the fire, and Dav learned they had all been captured on the beaches of Brun.

Vorchal and Reris were bonded to neighboring landowners, and they had slipped out for a stolen evening together. Adoc was mute, but he had painfully followed the conversation and pulled a handful of shells from his pocket, apparently explaining why he had been on the beach.

"I was gathering driftwood for the cook fires," Leanna said. "The Hattians just sailed along the shoreline and caught anyone they could overpower. Since you were alone, they decided to take you, too, I guess."

Dixie McKeone

"But why?" Dav asked.

She shrugged. "Once you're in chains, you can be sold anywhere slavery still exists," she said.

They were sitting in a ring around the fire. Vorchal's and Adoc's backs were to the mules. Wikko edged closer and stretched his neck to breathe on Adoc's hair. The half-wit jumped, startled, but when he saw the mule, he reached up to rub its soft nose, his mouth widening in a delighted smile. Dav remembered Vorchal's concern for the mules. He suddenly knew he had the answer to one of his problems.

He had dreaded selling Eidor, Wikko, and Milstin. They were more like pets than property. He had considered turning them loose, but they would be safer with new owners than in the wild. He had thought about taking them to Brun, but they would hate the confines of a sea voyage, even if he could find a ship that would take them.

Dav knew the animals would be happier if they could live in the valley; the freed prisoners wouldn't want to return to their bondage, he decided, so perhaps they could help each other.

"Suppose you could make a home here on the Isle of Dawn," he said. He told them about the protected valley just half a day's ride into the Great Escarpment. He described the surrounding area and how they could avoid the dangers if they were careful. In his grief over Withis, he had forgotten to empty the storage bins, so they were filled with the autumn harvest.

"Take care of the house, the furnishings, and the

44

animals. The four of you can live there as long as you look after each other. Just remember that I'll be coming back one day, and I expect to find everything in order. If not, I'll personally take you back to your masters." As long as they stayed within the protection of the valley, they'd have a better life than they would as slaves, probably better than their late masters.

Withis had been the crippled son of a wealthy pirate. When he left Trikelios to live the life of a scholarly hermit, he took his luxuries with him. Dav's threat might protect the inlaid tables and silver lamps that Withis had cherished, and keep Vorchal and Reris from mistreating the half-wit and Leanna.

Naturally the girl had other ideas.

"Not me," Leanna spoke up. "I'm taking the Shadow Elves back to Brun."

"I'll take them back," Dav said, saddling himself with a responsibility he begrudged. He had known he would accept it since he had seen the lost, frightened look in the elf children's eyes. Their pain scoured against the still tender wounds of his own grief.

"I'm on my way to Karameikos. Alfheim isn't that much farther away." In the pressure of the moment, he had forgotten the name the Shadow Elves had given the blighted forest of Canolbarth. He swore at himself, knowing the girl would use his slip of memory against him.

She did.

"I'm taking them back to *Aengmor*," she insisted.

Dixie McKeone

"At least *I* know where they belong." Leanna pointed at the girl. "She wouldn't be that haughty unless they were highborn. If they are, they're worth money, and I'm collecting it."

"Now, why should I have expected anything else from you?" he asked. "I don't buy and sell people, and I don't allow it if I can stop it."

"I wouldn't sell anyone, but I *am* after the reward, and there will be one. I can tell that by the way they're dressed."

"Yes, I noticed their priceless clothing," Dav replied.

"Why are they wearing those rags unless their own clothing was so expensive it was worth selling?" she asked.

Dav kicked himself for walking into that one.

Leanna studied Dav for a moment. "If you learn how to handle yourself, you could come along and I'll give you half of what's left of the reward after I buy back my certificate of bondage. That's what *I'm* after." When he didn't immediately accept, she shrugged. "Or stay here, for all I care."

For a moment, Dav was too angry to speak. If he learned how to handle himself indeed!

"Three children?" he scoffed. "How old are you? Twelve? Would you take them, or would they take you? And I suppose you just happened to be carrying enough money to buy ship's passage for three while you were picking up driftwood."

"I'm half a year from fifteen, and I don't need passage money. I know how to sail the boat. We'll go back the same way we came."

"That's ridiculous." Dav stood and brushed the sand from his trousers. "You're too small to be fourteen. Even if you are, you couldn't sail that boat alone, and you can't teach the elves to help you because you don't speak their language." While Leanna bit her lip and worked on an answer, he rose and went back to the bundles of furs. He passed out enough cat skins so they could all sleep on the dry sand in comfort and then suggested they keep watch in shifts.

"You can have the first watch while you're thinking up an answer to my last question," Dav said to Leanna as he rolled himself in his fur. He closed his eyes, but he could hear the soft sounds of the others as they prepared for sleep. They made him aware of his loneliness following the death of Withis.

In minutes, he was asleep. He awakened to find Vorchal shaking his shoulder.

"The elves are gone," Vorchal said. "I just turned my back for a minute to look up the beach and make sure the Hattians hadn't come back. . . ."

"The boat!" Reris shouted and pointed.

Dav turned to look and could see the silhouette of the mast as it began to move.

By the time Dav was on his feet, Leanna was up and had grabbed a burning brand from the fire. She disappeared through the split in the rock that led to the boat. While he ran along behind he raged at her, at the others for letting the elves escape, at the elves, and at himself for not allowing Leanna to shackle their feet. Their fear and their desire to escape made them a danger to themselves. If he had known people were so much trouble, he would have stayed in the valley.

In the dimness, he careened into an outcrop, banging his left shoulder, and fell sprawling. By the time he was on his feet again, Leanna was out of sight.

With a mental "thank you" to his dead mother, he reached inside the neck of his tunic and pulled out the light charm she had bequeathed him at her death. A small hole in the white metal disk was threaded with a leather thong so he could wear it as a pendant. He rubbed the charm between his hands, and it began to glow. It lit the passage ahead, and he sprinted into the light. In seconds, he was out of the fissure and running along a tumble of wet boulders made slick by the sea spray. The night fled in front of him, and the rocks of the natural harbor stood out as if it were daylight.

Less than thirty yards from the fissure, he saw the boat. The female elf was on the deck and had partially raised the sail. The wind caught it, and the vessel strained at the stern mooring line that Erian was attempting to free. Both elves wore the cat-skin furs like long, awkward cloaks. They had somehow fastened them at their necks.

Leanna had reached the boulder where the stern line was tied and pulled the boy away. She used her foot to push the line down for a more secure hold and then leapt aboard the boat. She dashed for the halyard to drop the sail.

Dav jumped from boulder to boulder, concentrating on the boy, who was still trying to free the stern mooring line. As Erian looked up, he saw Dav approaching and stopped. He raised both hands and pushed at the air. Dav could see his lips move, but the wind blew away his words. Then the child went to work again on the rope, but stared in disbelief as Dav continued toward him.

Suddenly the strands parted, and the elf just managed to grab the end of the rope as it flew through the air. The child was jerked off the rocks. He arced out over the waves and went splashing into the sea, still clutching the rope. The cat-skin fur spread out behind him, and as he hit the water it closed over him like a shroud. And it would become a shroud, Dav thought. The child would never be able to swim with the weight of the fur pulling him down. Aboard the boat, the elf girl screamed.

Without hesitation, Dav dove into the sea. He told himself he was a fool. The way the boat leapt away when the rope was released, he could never reach the boy. His hope renewed a little when, after the first spurt of pent-up force, the boat steadied. It still moved forward, carried along by the current close to the shore.

As Dav swam with powerful strokes, he felt the weight of the vest that held his coins. He had forgotten it when he dove in after the child. How could he possibly manage the elf in the heavy fur as well as himself and the extra weight he carried?

The light charm glowed even under water, and

beneath him he saw the child kicking feebly, still holding to the rope. Dav dived, grabbed the boy around the waist, and pulled him to the surface. The child was worn out from struggling, but when Dav attempted to free the leather thong that tied the heavy fur around his neck, the elf struggled, attempting to push the human's hands away.

"We'll never make it with that weight!" Dav shouted, but the boy ignored him. He understood the child's feelings. The few stories of the City of Stars that had reached the surface of Mystara told of the intense heat deep in the earth. Erian had spent weeks on the surface world in flimsy clothing, cold and miserable. He wasn't giving up his fur and was too young to understand it could mean his death.

At the stern of the boat, he could see Leanna and the elven girl as they hauled on the line. Dav and Erian were still ten feet from the stern when suddenly Leanna shouted and the elf girl screamed. They hauled desperately on the rope.

A creeping fear, colder than the water, crept up Dav's backbone. He looked around, frantically trying to pinpoint the danger.

The boat was out beyond the breakers. The swells, slightly ruffled by the wind, rose and fell in a gleaming reflection of moonlight. A little less than fifty feet away, a spot of velvety blackness seemed to suck up the moonlight. Around the edges, he could see ripples of disturbed water as the blackness approached.

His light charm was still glowing, and he saw

the reflected gleam of two bulbous eyes and a huge mouth rimmed with sharp teeth. He could just barely see the creature's tentacles as it rapidly closed the distance. From Withis's lore on the monsters of Mystara, Dav recognized a decapus, an aquatic predator with ten suckered arms and a voracious appetite.

With one hand holding the rope and the other arm around the elf child, he would be unable to use his knife, an inadequate weapon against such a monster, but the only one he had.

Chapter 4

Confrontations

Erian had also spotted the decapus. He began to whimper and tremble.

"Get behind me," Dav told the child, trying to hide the fear in his own voice. "Hold on to my shoulders. Hurry!"

Erian worked his way around Dav, clutching the human's shoulder with one hand and the rope with the other.

The decapus drew steadily nearer. They could smell its fetid breath as its four-foot body expanded and contracted with its breathing. It paused in the water, its eyes blinking against the glare of the light charm.

Dav was surprised when a shower of snowflakes and glittering foot-long crystal shards sailed over his head and struck the decapus in the eyes and mouth. The monster roared, sending another waft of stinking breath toward Dav and the boy as it drew back. The short, glittering ice spears melted in the water.

52

Using the few seconds of respite, Dav hauled himself and the child along the rope until they were nearly touching the boat.

"It's coming!" Erian whimpered, his voice fluttering with fear.

Leanna and the elf girl reached down and pulled the child aboard the boat, but the decapus was too close for Dav to climb to safety. He swung around and pulled his knife. Two tentacles reached for him. He struck out at the first, just barely nicking the tough hide. The second wrapped around his left leg and began to pull. The force of the decapus would have jerked him free of the rope, but a third arm caught his left arm and hand, wrapping around the line as it gripped him. His joints and muscles screamed. He felt as if he were being pulled in half.

With a force of will he didn't know he had, he drew his body into a knot, stabbing at the tentacle wrapped around his leg. The long arm whipped away, but another grabbed him around the waist.

Dav stabbed at the tentacle around his waist, but he was tiring from his struggle against the slowing effect the water had on his movements as well as the monster that held him.

A tentacle whipped around his right arm and prevented him from using the knife. Another wrapped around his chest. He watched helplessly as the open mouth of the decapus came nearer, opening, preparing to devour its prey. The gaping mouth was only inches away when a long iron-tipped pole whacked the monster on the head. The decapus jerked back in pain. Dav felt as if his legs and arms were being yanked off his body. Then the pole struck again. It caught the decapus in the mouth, breaking off two teeth.

Two tentacles lashed out at the pole. One had held Dav's right arm. With his knife hand free once more, he stabbed at the body of the creature just as Leanna struck a third time with the pole. The sharp iron tip pierced its left eye.

Suddenly the tentacles whipped away.

"Climb!" Leanna shouted. "If it dives and comes up under you, I can't do a thing."

Dav didn't need a second invitation. He clamped his teeth onto the handle of the knife and climbed the rope. From above, hands pulled at his shirt, his shoulders, his arms.

He hit the deck scrambling and jumped to his feet. Leanna held the tiller with one hand and the pole in the other, and Dav gripped his knife as they stared over the stern of the boat. The swells rolled peacefully. Then they saw the decapus rise to the surface again, twenty feet behind the boat.

"Will it try to climb in after us?" she asked him.

"I don't know." He kept watch for several minutes. The boat continued along the shoreline, but the creature disappeared into the darkness in their wake.

"I guess it's had enough," Dav said. "But we'd better watch for it when we turn back."

"We can't turn back," Leanna said. "Like it or not, we're on our way."

"We're not going anywhere on this boat!" Dav

shouted. "Now, turn it around and take us back to the rocks."

"I can't take us back." Leanna's announcement echoed with a combination of defiance, triumph, and sincerity.

"You were going to sail it all the way to Brun, and you can't even go back to the camp?"

Leanna shook her head. "I can sail it before the wind, and I can tack against it. I can even lower the sail and steer it onto the beach, but I know I can't take it in to those rocks, especially at night. I doubt if even Gorval would have tried it after dark." She paused for a moment, giving him a chance to take in what she had said. "I couldn't do it in the daylight."

Dav thought about the waves crashing against the giant boulders and knew she was right. Her defensive expression did more to convince him than her words.

He glared at the elves. In saving Erian, he had left his weapons behind, along with his clothing and the furs he meant to sell in Caerdwicca. His left hand burned. The livid red spot where a sucker on the decapus's tentacle had drawn blood was clearly visible in the moonlight. The wound reminded him he had also lost his pouch of healing herbs.

His hand went to his waist. The old belt was secure, and the weight of the vest full of coins had nearly dragged him under. He really didn't need the money from the furs. He could afford to buy other clothing.

He was still irritated with the elf children, but Erian was shaking with cold. The boy stared up at him, afraid of his anger.

Leanna obviously knew how to handle the boat, so he took Erian below, tugging the boy along behind him when he resisted. When he reached the main cabin, he wondered if they wouldn't be more comfortable on deck. The bulkheads curved up from narrow bunks, piled high with dirty bedding and old clothes. The narrow table and two benches bolted to the middle of the floor looked as if they hadn't been scrubbed in years. At the far end of the room, a brazier rocked in a metal frame that kept it upright in rough weather. Ashes had spilled out of the top and lay scattered on the floor. He wrinkled his nose at the stench and wondered how anyone could live in such filth.

The elf girl appeared in the doorway, carrying two rolls of cat-skin furs. The little monster had stolen them! Then Dav wondered why he was outraged. Just minutes before, he had been angry because he had lost all his belongings. He spared a moment to wonder how she managed both rolls when it was all he could do to carry them. Then he realized she wasn't actually touching them; she was using a levitation spell.

He turned to the boy, and in the light of the charm, he saw why he had been unable to free the child of the fur. The girl had cut strips of hide from the edges and worked them through slits. He turned to her and saw that she had a third strip tied around her waist. Tucked inside it was Lertin's knife, the third Hattian blade Dav had been unable to find.

The girl had been clever to find the knife, make good use of it, and then escape while the others were supposed to be watching over them.

Dav cleared off the cleanest of the bunks, stripped the child of his wet clothing, and wrapped him in a dry fur before putting him on the bunk. As Dav turned, he found the elf girl staring at him in wonder.

"You saved my brother. You could have left him to be killed by the decapus and escaped danger yourself, but you saw that he reached safety first. Why did you do this, human?"

"How many times must I tell you we are not your enemies? And my name is Dav Curan. You don't need to tell me I'm human. I know it, *elf girl.*"

He met her stare until she dropped her gaze.

"I am Calenderi," she said. "I allow you the knowledge of my name because you saved my brother, but mark what I say, hum—Dav Curan. You will suffer boiling in the molten lakes if you harm us. And we will not be locked in that filthy place again." She pointed to the small door that led to another compartment in the bow of the vessel.

"I ought to," Dav retorted. "I should have let Leanna put you in chains." He stood glaring at her for a moment and then shrugged. What was done was done. By the time they returned to the rocks, the others would be on their way to the valley.

Calenderi tried to outstare him, but her eyes kept shifting to the door at the end of the cabin.

She held on to her courage, but her trembling betrayed her. He pitied her, but he also admired her courage.

"I'm not locking you in," Dav told her more softly. "You can't get back to Aengmor alone, and if you want my help, you'll do as I say." He left them in the comparative warmth of the cabin and returned to the deck, tucking the light charm back inside his tunic. The glow immediately left it.

* * * * *

On Pandius, Ranivorus blinked. The Immortal patron of the gnolls stretched and mentally felt his being. Nothing seemed to be amiss, but he had felt that same sickening lurch, a pull on his resources had come again. It was always so when the power of Reddican's charm was put to use. The deepseated fear that always accompanied it clung to his mind for several minutes, then disappeared.

Not that he had lost his Immortal power, but the drain was unsettling, always accompanied by the fear that whatever pulled on him could have drained him. Could it? Putting that strange power to the test might be worse than worrying about it.

The Immortals would meet again. They would send out more searchers to find Reddican's charm. And again the seekers would return with nothing to report. It had happened before. He knew it would happen again.

* * * * *

When Dav came on deck, Leanna watched him warily as he walked toward the stern and took the seat beside her.

"I'm not going to argue about going back," he said and watched her relax. "The elf girl—her name is Calenderi—just thanked me for saving Erian's life," he said. "I didn't thank you for saving mine, but I *am* grateful. Can I help with the steering? You'll need to show me what to do—that is, if you don't think I'm too stupid to learn."

He couldn't forget her remark immediately after the fight with the Hattians. Still, she had saved his life. He gave himself a mental kick for being petty and was summoning an apology when she beat him to it.

"I'm sorry I said that. It wasn't true." She gave him a small smile. He realized he was seeing her for the first time without anger. Her expression was softer, a little vulnerable. In a way, she reminded him of the elf girl down in the cabin. Both were putting on a show of bravado to hide their fears.

"You see, we had no hope of escape until you arrived. Then it was like—like we suddenly had a chance. I knew when you said you were alone that they'd try to capture you, too. I knew you'd fight and we might have an opportunity to help you overcome them, or maybe we could get away."

"Between us, we won," Dav reminded her.

"But when they attacked you, I realized you weren't a trained fighter, and I was so angry—not really at you, but at the Immortals."

"I'd never fought with another human," Dav said, "but you couldn't have done any better than I did. Probably not as well." That was unfair. She was smaller and not as strong, but he was beginning to believe she was older than her size indicated. She might be fourteen after all.

"*Of course* I could," she said, as if he were foolish to doubt it. "I was raised in mercenary camps. I *know* how to fight. My best friend was Soranar, an old soldier who trained the new recruits. Since all he knew was battle, our games were always with the wooden weapons he made for me."

As she talked, he learned her history. Her mother had been a camp follower who deserted her before she could remember. Her mercenary father, Challathan, provided a home for her only because his commander, Colonel Kalian, was an honorable man and insisted Challathan should take care of his child. After the colonel's death, her father sold her into bondage to cover his debts. Dav could hear her bitterness in her voice. When she looked up at him, she saw and resented his sympathy.

"At least it was better than being kept a prisoner in the wilderness," she said, comparing her life to Dav's.

The accusation was so unjust, it took a moment before Dav realized she was referring to him. He was just beginning to understand what a wonderful childhood the old scholar had given him.

"I wasn't a prisoner," he explained patiently. "We just shared responsibilities. I can't complain about my life."

After a few minutes, she shook off her resentment and showed Dav how to handle the tiller and the partially raised sail. After an hour, she praised him for his ability to learn, as if attempting to make up for her earlier insult.

"Together we can sail the boat to Brun, all the way to Athenos and maybe part of the way up the Streel River, to Tavaro, as close as we can get to Aengmor in the boat," she said.

"No."

"You mean we can't sail up the Streel?" She seemed disappointed. "I'm sure it's navigable. It's a long way to Aengmor from the coast, but—"

"I mean I won't help sail this boat to Brun."

Sailing was simpler than Dav had expected it to be, but the wind behind them was light, and the moonlight allowed them to see the shore. On the open sea, they could face problems neither could handle. Few ships braved the oceans in winter, and the storms were more than usually harsh that year.

"I suppose you just happen to be carrying enough money to buy passage for four?" she quipped, throwing his own sarcasm back at him. "Have you any idea what it would cost? Maybe as much as two hundred gold pieces."

"I doubt it's that much, but if it is, I can still pay it," Dav said, thinking she must be exaggerating. If she wasn't, his hidden vest would weigh a lot less.

"Oh." Leanna sounded as if someone had punched her in the stomach. She gazed at him with awe.

"And we'll be safer aboard a larger ship with experienced seamen."

Leanna grudgingly agreed. "When we get the reward, I'll pay you back for my fare," she said. "I'll even pay half the fare for the elves, if there's enough left after I buy back my certificate. That comes first, before anything else."

"Agreed. That comes first," he replied. Just thinking about how close he had come to wearing chains helped him to understand her intense desire for freedom.

While they talked, the sun rose and they had a better view of the shore. Beyond the sand, a grassy plain, occasionally interrupted by copses of trees, stretched back to the cliffs of the escarpment. They raised the sail and the boat plowed ahead, pushed by a freshening breeze, but it was still midmorning before they saw Caerdwicca in the distance.

Leanna turned sullen again as she warned him of her lack of experience in docking, but Dav had already decided they shouldn't sail up to the pier. Caerdwicca was a haven for pirates.

They found a deep creek a mile east of the town and moored the boat just inside its mouth. Leanna went below to change her ragged skirt and shift for equally ragged pants, tunic, and jacket. Dav covered her copper bondman's bracelet with a bandage of cloth torn from a shirt. Then he explained their plan to the Shadow Elves, but Calenderi objected.

"You will sail this boat," she ordered. "Then we will not suffer the company of more humans." She turned a haughty gaze on Leanna. "In the future, you will serve us decent food, and you can clean this filthy cabin." She waved a hand at the cluttered, dirty compartment.

Leanna hadn't understood a word, but after her time in bondage, she was quick to scent an order. "You tell that arrogant little cave monster that whatever she wants done she can do herself!" she snapped, glaring at the elf.

Oh, great, Dav thought. He wasn't about to translate for either of them.

"I won't put up with impudence," Calenderi declared. "If she doesn't behave with respect, you must beat her."

"Wait just a minute," Dav said, stepping between the two females, but they sidestepped him and continued their face-off.

"I'm no one's slave anymore," Leanna shouted at the elf.

"I will have you fed to the dragons for your insolence," Calenderi threatened.

"Stop it!" Dav shouted in Thyatian and Shiye-Lawr, pushing Leanna toward the door of the cabin. He grabbed the key and followed Leanna to the deck, locking the door after him. He knew he risked losing any trust he had built with the elves, but they might try to steal the boat again.

The flimsy shacks on the outskirts of the town gave way to sturdier wooden buildings as they neared the center. The only stone building sat on a rise overlooking the rest of the community. Leanna had forgotten her anger as she looked around the town and up at the squat stone structure.

"That's the home of Baron Uthgaard McRho-maag," Dav said.

"Why are the shops closed?" Leanna asked. "And what do those banners say?" She realized she had just revealed the fact that she couldn't read and bit her lips as if she could pull her words back again.

"Nuwmont the first," Dav said, reading the wording on the flimsy cloth that fluttered in the wind. "They're welcoming the year 1010. We won't be able to buy our passage today." He should have remembered the holiday, since the day before, Kaldmont 28, had been his birthday and the last day of the year.

"We can at least get some food," Leanna said and threw him a worried look. "Do you have enough money for that and our passage?"

"I think I can manage," Dav replied.

"You keep a total of what you spend, and I'll pay you back out of my reward," she said, leading the way into the largest tavern.

The rush-covered floor was crowded with tables and benches filled with holiday celebrants. On the left wall two spits turned large rounds of butchered meat in the huge, open fireplace. Smoke from the fire escaped out into the room and hung like a cloud above their heads, hiding the open beams of the raftered ceiling. More than thirty people were eating, drinking, laughing, and talking.

Dav found the noise exciting, confusing, and deafening. Leanna led the way to a table halfway down the long room and he followed.

Son of Dawn

Two hunters in doeskin clothing shared a table with three sheep herders, recognizable because of their gray-white woolly vests, and five seamen. One sailor was telling a tale about battling a giant sea squid, and the others were interrupting, adding details.

Dav and Leanna shared the empty bench at the end of the table. A stout woman in a grease-spotted apron, with strands of hair escaping her braids, stopped next to Dav. She carried a tray with mugs of ale and small loaves of bread, about eight inches long and half as wide, filled with thick slabs of meat.

"Seats is for them as is buying," she said. "We got ale and meat rolls."

Dav bought two of each. His first experience with ale was not as pleasant as he had expected, but the bread was fresh and crusty, and the meat tender and succulent. The hunters sang a lusty song that attracted the attention of the entire room. When they finished, the seamen called for more ale and treated the impromptu entertainers.

"I might take up hunting—that is, if I get to Karameikos," said a tall, lanky seaman. "And if I can find the right bait to catch an elf." His friends laughed and nodded.

"Just put salt on its ears," the sheepherder sitting next to Dav remarked, and the others laughed louder than Dav thought the joke deserved. The sheepherder glanced at Dav, who looked stunned.

"Ain't you heard? Old King Telemon's young son and daughter's been took right out of Aengmor.

They say them Shadow Elves is as mad as can be and threatening to fight all of Brun. Be worth a few coins to catch 'em and take 'em back."

"Might be worth more to sell 'em to Mauntea or Stefan," the lanky seaman put in. "One or the other might be glad to get 'em as hostages."

Dav worked out the implications. Corwyn Mauntea was president of the Darokin council. After the recent war, Darokin could hardly afford to fight another, so they might value hostages to keep the peace. Karameikos hadn't suffered as badly, but since all her allies had been weakened, King Stefan would stay out of trouble if he could. Dav knew few of the details of the war that had raged across the continents of Brun and Alphatia, but his historical studies had given him an insight into the politics that often followed major conflicts.

"Emperor Thincol might pay more." Another seaman nudged his companion. They both grinned but didn't elaborate.

Dav knew Thincol Torion was Emperor of Thyatis, but he didn't understand the implication of the remark.

The conversation was interrupted by a shout of anger from the next table. A swarthy hunter threw a glass of ale into the face of a shopkeeper. The hunter dove across his own table after the townsman, toppling him and the others who shared the same bench. They tumbled across the narrow aisle between the tables and upset the bench at Dav's table, throwing four of the seamen to the floor. The table rocked. Dav and Leanna grabbed their heavy mugs and food and tried to scoot their short bench back out of the way.

"Fight!" shouted a herder and knocked one of the hunters sprawling.

The sheepherder on Dav's right jumped to his feet, grabbed Dav's arm, and pulled him up. The herder drew back his fist.

Chapter 5

A Watcher in the Shadows

Dav pulled away from the sheepherder. "Why do you want to hit me?" he demanded. "What have I done to you?"

The herder frowned at him as if Dav had lost his wits. "But it's a fight," he said as if Dav should have understood. "You never been in a tavern brawl, boy?"

Dav shook his head. He didn't understand why he should want to fight someone he had laughed with a moment before. Leanna slipped off the bench and crawled under the table. He saw her scuttle from the shelter of their table to the next.

The sheepherder insisted Dav remove the small purse at his waist and grip it tightly in his right hand. It would keep him from breaking his fingers when he threw a punch.

"You ready?" the herder asked, and Dav, uncertain what to do, nodded. The herder swung, but he had drunk more ale than Dav. Dav ducked and knocked the man to the floor.

"You got the idea," the herder mumbled as he struggled to his feet.

Suddenly Dav felt ready to go back and take on the decapus. He could do anything! With a yell, he charged a grunting group of six who seemed intent on wrestling each other to the floor. He rammed them, using his shoulder and his side, and they all went over in a heap. Somehow Dav ended up near the bottom of the pile.

Pain shot through his leg as someone stepped on his left knee, and another booted foot nearly crushed the fingers of his right hand. He lost his hold on his purse. He scrambled across the floor and grabbed it. The stout woman who had served their meat rolls gave a scream and sat down hard on top of him. The breath went out of his lungs in a whoosh. He thought his rib cage had collapsed.

When she rolled off his back, Dav staggered to his feet, half stunned. He backed away from a wild-eyed seaman, who laughed and swung wildly. His swing connected, and Dav was knocked backward out the door. Dav grabbed at the doorframe, but only succeeded in turning himself around so he fell on his face in the muddy street.

He got to his feet and brushed at the mud. Leanna slipped out the door, carrying the jacket she had worn when they entered the tavern. He caught the aroma of fresh bread and venison wafting from her bundle.

"I've got enough meat rolls in here to feed us for a day or so," she said.

"But you didn't have any money," Dav said.

"They were too busy to notice."

"I hope they don't come looking for us. That's all we need."

Dav ached all over. Added to his injuries in his fights with the Hattians and the decapus, his left knee was stiff, every breath made his ribs hurt, and the fingers of his right hand were swelling.

Leanna was too absorbed with getting out of town and Dav with his aches and pains to notice they were followed by a small, slender auburn-haired man in a green coat. He stayed well back and in the shadows of the trees until he saw them board the boat. He smiled and found himself a hiding place in the bushes nearby.

Calenderi was angry because Dav had locked them in the cabin. She was even angrier when, after eating a meat roll, she learned the date was Nuwmont the first, a traditional day of fasting for the Shadow Elves.

She admitted they were the children of the Shadow Elf king and understood the implications of their value as hostages. She expected her father and her older sister, the Radiant Princess Tanada-leyo, to go to war over the kidnapping.

"And because they took the soul chr—" Erian began.

Calenderi dug her elbow into the boy's side, silencing him with a sharp look.

"Because they took what?" Dav asked.

"It is a matter of honor that our father rescue us," Calenderi said, ignoring his question. "It would shame our nation if he did any less, and it would make our enemies believe we are afraid to avenge wrongs done to us."

"But will he be fighting the right people?" Dav asked. "I find it hard to believe that humans went hundreds of miles down into the City of Stars to steal you away."

"We were not in the deep caverns. We had traveled up near the surface," the elf princess said. "Our father was sending us on a visit to Aengmor to learn what surface life is like. A troop of orcs attacked our escort and killed them." She frowned. "There was a great deal of confusion, and something strange happened. There were two Darokinian soldiers with the orcs, but when I first saw them, their hands were tied. Then later I saw their bodies, but they didn't fight our people. I didn't understand it."

"How could you be sure they were from Darokin?" Dav asked.

"The orcs who captured us took us to the surface, where another group of orcs, goblins, kobolds, and trolls attacked the first group and killed them all," Erian said.

Dav thought the child was embellishing the story.

"Then all those monsters fought with some humans," Erian added, and Calenderi nodded.

"Through the trees, we could see a town beside a large river when the humans attacked," Calenderi said. "I'm sure it was the Streel River, so we had to be in Darokin. The two who were killed in the passages by the first orcs were dressed exactly like the patrol that attacked Korshnid's band. That's why I was sure the humans in the tunnel were from Darokin."

"That mean orc, Korshnid, killed the first orcs and the humans and took us a long way down a big river. Then he sold us to Gorval," Erian said, determined to finish the story.

Leanna had been waiting for Dav to translate, but now she raised her head suddenly.

"Did he mention Korshnid?" she asked. "He's the leader of a group of outlaws made up of different humanoids. They're hunted by everyone on Brun, even their own people." But Leanna was more concerned with the journey back to Aengmor. "We don't dare take them aboard a passenger ship," she said. "The seamen were right. Several countries would pay a good price for those elves to use them as hostages. We'd lose them to the pirates in minutes."

"What did the seaman mean when he said Emperor Thincol would like to have them?" Dav asked.

"Aengmor is in a strategic position," Leanna replied. "It's close to the borders of Glantri, Rockhome, Ylaruam, and Karameikos, and it's inside Darokin, a perfect place from which to launch an invasion on any of its neighbors. If he could force an alliance with the Shadow Elves, he'd be in a strong position. There's a rumor he wants to conquer the provinces that once looked to Alphatia for protection, but it's still a rumor."

"Then we can't trust anyone," Dav said quietly. As a child, he had dreamed of great adventures. This one was a little more than he wanted.

"Certainly we can't trust pirates," Leanna said. "Our best chance is to take this boat."

"We can't do it. What would we do if we were caught in a storm on the Sea of Dread?"

"We won't go out on the Sea of Dread," Leanna explained. "We'll work our way south along the coastline of the Isle of Dawn and then north to Redstone before we go out on the open sea."

"We'd be weeks just traveling north," Dav said slowly. Still, if he remembered his geography lessons, they should be able to cross the Western Sea of Dawn in a couple of days.

"But it's safer," Leanna reminded him. "In fact, it's the only way we could do it."

"I suppose safer is better than not at all," Dav said. "We still might arrive in time. King Telemon will have a long way to come."

"How far?"

"Legend says they have huge cities more than six hundred miles down inside the world. I doubt if they can come straight up. They'd have to travel many miles for every mile of ascent, I'd guess. And if it's that far down, King Telemon may not have even received the news yet." Dav knew he was being optimistic, but he was hoping they could reach Aengmor in time to prevent a war.

The elves had been watching Dav and Leanna as they talked, but little Erian had been growing steadily more concerned. He reached out a trembling hand and laid it on Dav's knee.

"You won't sell us, will you?" Erian asked, his eyes wide with fear.

"If you do, my father will feed you to a dragon," Calenderi threatened.

"To the first pirate I see," Dav joked, and immediately regretted his remark. His anger at the princess was no excuse for frightening Erian.

"Of course we won't sell you," he told the child. "We've been discussing the safest way to get you home. But you must help us keep your identity a secret. Lots of people are searching for you; we can't fight them all."

"You want us to hide?" Erian asked. He moved closer to Dav, as if seeking shelter.

"Then we will take this boat," Calenderi said with her customary decisiveness.

"The only way we can take this boat is with your help," Dav warned. "If you don't do your share of the work, we can't make it."

"Work? Like a servant?" Calenderi stared at him, shocked and outraged.

"I'll work," Erian said. "I want to go home."

Dav didn't expect much help from the elves, but the threat might make the voyage easier. At least it could reduce Calenderi's arrogance.

Dav found a ragged piece of parchment, the remains of a sea chart, and using a stick of charcoal, he made a list of their needs while Leanna and the elves made suggestions. Leanna's were practical and to the point. If he had listened to Calenderi, he would have filled the ship with delicacies and golden plates.

They needed food and water for the journey. Because the Shadow Elves suffered from the cold, they needed charcoal for the small brazier in the main compartment, which doubled as a source of heat and cook fire. The food would wait for the next day when the stores opened for business again, but the boat was well supplied with water casks that could be scrubbed and filled.

"This filthy place must be cleaned," Calenderi insisted and put out a hand as if she would touch the table that was bolted to the floor. She drew back her fingers in distaste.

"You tell her I know just the thing." Leanna smiled, rose, and picked up one of the empty kegs as she left the cabin. Peace reigned until she returned with the keg half filled with wet sand. The elf princess watched as Leanna cut a ragged scrap off one of the cat-skin furs, scooped out a handful of sand and started to scour the table.

"See how it's done?" she asked Calenderi, then handed her the piece of hide.

"I will not put up with this insolence!" the elf princess screamed, but Leanna bowed, laughed, and took the water kegs up on deck.

Dav escaped to the beach and started gathering wood for the charcoal, glad to be away from the two females. He made his charcoal fire within sight of the boat, where he could see Leanna scrubbing casks on the beach before taking them upstream to fill them. When he volunteered to help her carry them back to the boat, he found them full of small pears. The fruit was hard and not very sweet, but it would last through most of their trip. He helped her carry them back on board and found the elves hard at work. The table and benches were spotless. Erian scrubbed at the floor of the main cabin while Calenderi worked in the forward hold. They had thrown the filthy bedding out on the deck.

"I suppose I'll play the servant and wash it after we get water in the kegs," Leanna said. "You can help after you bring in your charcoal."

Dav limped back to the beach, muttering about bossy females.

The next morning, armed with their list, Dav and Leanna returned to Caerdwicca. The town boasted two stores that catered to seamen and hunters. Afraid too large a purchase might attract attention, they decided to make two trips. The first time they circled the town and came in from the west, entering the first shop. They bought half their rations, a longbow and broadsword and scabbard for Dav, a short sword and short bow for Leanna, and quivers of arrows for both of them. Dav picked out some clothing and had Leanna do the same. Her eyes were shining as they made their way back to the boat, once again taking the circuitous route.

"I'll pay you back," she kept saying. "You write down everything you bought. I'll pay my share."

"Don't worry about it. It's still cheaper than passage by ship," Dav replied.

Neither noticed the auburn-haired man in the shadows of the trees as he slipped along parallel to their path and slightly behind them. When they reached the boat, he hid in the shadows, smiling to himself.

Aboard the boat, they changed into their new clothing, hoping it would alter their appearance enough so when they entered the town from the opposite direction, they lessened the chance of being noticed as the same shoppers. They returned to the town and were approaching the second store when Dav paused and pointed at several men who were advancing from building to building, searching inside and out. One man even lifted the top of a rain barrel that stood at the corner of the tavern and peered inside.

"Searching for something—or someone?" Leanna gave Dav a worried glance.

"It couldn't have anything to do with us," he said and led the way into the second store. He had locked the elves belowdecks again, this time with their understanding and permission.

Dav was more lavish in his purchases. The tide was coming in and would be high by the time they returned to the boat. They planned to set sail as soon as they were back aboard. By the time anyone in Caerdwicca became curious about them, they would be at sea.

Leanna had been sparing in her list of what they needed, but Dav had heard the sailors talking of being becalmed, and he had no wish to go hungry while sitting in the middle of the sea. Uneasily he touched the pouch at his waist as he totaled up the price of his purchases. Still, he hadn't spent nearly as much as their passage would have cost.

He chose two pairs of pants and two tunics for each of the Shadow Elves, holding them up to Leanna as if they were for her. Obviously they were too small, but the shopkeeper wasn't about to correct the error and lose a sale.

"Looks like you're planning a voyage," the store-keeper said as he kept a running total on their choices.

"Aye. Thought the same when I was sent for the buying," Dav said, imitating the sailors he had met in the inn. "Didn't say where we was heading, but then he wouldn't, would he?" The "he" could have been one of the pirate captains, and the store-keeper didn't ask questions.

Dav checked the shop's supply of cloth and found some loosely woven black material, cheap and flimsy but exactly suiting a purpose he had in mind. Then he discovered he had to buy two more sacks. The four he and Leanna had brought with them wouldn't hold all the supplies. They stag-gered out of the shop, Dav carrying four large sacks, all heavily loaded. Leanna was bowed under the weight of two.

Dav realized he had attracted more attention than he wanted. Across the rutted, muddy road, a small, slender auburn-haired man in a green coat stood watching. Then Dav remembered he had seen the fellow before, once on the previous day after the fight and again that morning when they had entered the first shop. They didn't need curios-ity from anyone.

Dixie McKeone

The stranger stood at the corner of the inn. Sunlight glinted off his auburn hair as he stared at them, a little smile on his lips. The smile disappeared in surprise as Dav's eyes met his.

They had just reached the road when the burly leader of the searchers stepped into their path.

"Have you seen a short, scrawny fellow with reddish brown hair, wearing a green coat?" the largest of the three asked. He looked significantly at Leanna, who shook her head, and then at Dav.

Of course he had, but they'd passed right by the fellow he'd seen, so the description must have been a coincidence.

The seamen seemed angry, frustrated, and primed for a fight, but not with Dav and Leanna, who continued along the road out of town and took the shade-dappled path to the boat. The day had turned unusually warm, and perspiration stung Dav's eyes as he hurried toward the boat. His discomfort added to his impatience to reach it and set sail.

As soon as they climbed aboard, they dropped the sacks and cast off the mooring lines. Dav poled the boat out from beneath the trees and swung it around while Leanna raised the sail. Dav was careful of the pole. One end was blunt wood with traces of mud on it, showing its use. The other was tipped with a sharp metal point. The design served a defensive purpose as well as the mundane chore of poling.

"There he is!" The shout rolled out over the water, and they saw four men racing along the shoreline. They were pointing toward the boat.

"How did they find out?" Leanna asked as she took over the tiller. "If those elves have been on deck . . ."

"They shouted 'There *he* is,'" Dav reminded her. "They weren't talking about the elves. They're talking about *me*. But what did I do?"

"I don't know, but we'd better get out of here." Leanna caught the wind, the sail billowed, and the boat skipped over the water. As they passed Caerdwicca, they saw seamen scurrying over a vessel, making ready to sail.

Dav carried three sacks belowdecks and returned for the others. He saw a hand reach up over the fantail of the boat and clutch the backboard of the seat by the tiller. He was still staring when a second hand appeared.

Dav pulled his knife and was advancing when a man heaved himself on board. It was the auburn-haired man in the green coat who had been watching them in Caerdwicca. Leanna was so startled she abandoned the tiller for a moment. She glared at him, pulled her own knife, and then edged back to catch the swinging tiller again. Her blade remained in her right hand as she awkwardly steered the boat.

"Who are you?" she demanded.

"Serdic, dabbler in the magic arts, at your service." The stranger ignored their weapons as he bowed to Leanna and then slipped his arms out of the straps that held a wide, flat backpack close to his body. He seemed completely at ease as he took off his finely woven green woolen coat and wrung the water from it. Beneath the outer garment, his forest-green trousers and silken shirt of the same color clung wetly to his skin, showing off muscles that were well defined for so compact a body. His green eyes danced and his grin was infectious.

"You need have no fear of me. I have no intention of harming you. I must leave the area, and you're going my way."

"How do you know which way we're going?" Dav asked, his blade still in his hand.

"You're leaving here," Serdic said, grinning. "That's enough for the present." He sat on the deck and started pulling off his boots.

"And what makes you think we'll take you with us?" Leanna asked.

"Do you want to take me back? Can you afford to?"

Dav and Leanna exchanged glances.

"Convince us we shouldn't hand you over to your friends," Dav said quietly. The man might be bluffing, but he seemed too sure of himself. They should know the worst, he decided.

"People who hide their boats in creeks and take care not to advertise how much shopping they're doing obviously don't want their real business known." He smiled again as if he were enjoying a joke. "While I was in the water, didn't I hear the mention of elves?" He turned to Dav. "Dare I guess you've somehow trapped the quarry that has set all Mystara hunting for them?"

Dav stared at Serdic, trying to keep his face blank, but he wondered why he was taking the trouble. The magic-user was right. They couldn't take him back and risk a search of the boat. He could see the determination in the smaller man's eyes. Serdic would use whatever information he'd learned about the elves to buy his way out of trouble.

"I need help to get away, and you could use my small expertise in sailing," Serdic said. "And in times of trouble, two magic-users are better than one."

"And who's the other one?" Dav asked, wondering if Serdic knew the elves had some magic of their own.

"Only another magician could have seen through my spell." Serdic smiled.

"What magician? What spell? What are you talking about?" Leanna demanded, still upset by their new arrival.

"A little misunderstanding with Jesnow, captain of one of the pirate ships, made it dangerous for me to remain in Caerdwicca. When he sent his crew to search for me, I used an invisibility spell to avoid them." Serdic raised his eyebrows at Dav. "But you saw me as plainly as I saw you. Your power must be equal to mine."

Dav could only stare at Serdic, wondering what he meant.

Chapter 6

Pursued

Serdic's insistence that Dav was a magic-user left Dav speechless. The suggestion was too absurd to deny.

He gazed at Leanna, who returned a speculative look, but neither spoke. She was tacking the boat against the wind, and she had her hands full. Serdic smiled again, his expressive mouth hinting at some humor they could not see.

"You'll doubtless want to discuss the change in circumstances," he said. "I suggest you do so and let me take the tiller."

"You're not touching this tiller," Leanna snapped. "We're dumping you as soon as we're far enough away from Caerdwicca to keep you from giving the alarm."

"Do you know how to sail?" asked Dav, hearing little beyond the mage's offer to relieve Leanna. Their uninvited member might be more of a help than a hindrance.

"When one finds himself in need of escape, one

learns a lot of things." Serdic grinned. "I once worked on a coastal boat much like this. I can make better speed, and we'll need it." He pointed back toward Caerdwicca, where they could see the sleek ship leaving the dock.

"Why are they after you?" Dav asked.

"A little matter of too much ale, the result of a client paying me in advance. It's good business to get paid by a pirate before he sets out on his venture."

"That doesn't tell us what you did," Leanna said.

"Jesnow, captain of the ship now in pursuit of us, and his chief competitor both knew a richly loaded ship would be coming through the Strait of Furmenglaive. Jesnow hired me to put a holding spell on his rival."

"And you got drunk and didn't do it," Leanna said.

"On the contrary, I did my duty," Serdic replied, smiling. "But in my inebriated condition, I confused the ships. Jesnow sailed away from the dock and sat within sight of Caerdwicca for three days."

"It's a wonder he didn't kill you," Leanna observed.

"That's precisely his intention. That's why I suggest you let me take the tiller."

Dav nodded in answer to Leanna's look of inquiry, and Serdic slipped onto the wooden seat. He sharpened the tacking angle, and the deck canted as the boat surged forward.

Dav crossed the deck and hefted two sacks of provisions, sliding on the sloping deck as he carried them below. Leanna brought the last sack.

"You are going to let him stay on the ship?" Calenderi asked as soon as they were in the cabin. Her anger showed in her flashing eyes. Erian was plainly frightened.

"He knows about you," Dav told her. "If we take him back, he'll use that knowledge to save his life. There are more men on the ship following us than Leanna and I could fight."

"I don't like him, and I don't trust him," Leanna said and continued in a voice stifled with a begrudging admission. "But I can't deny we could use his ability with the boat."

"And his help might save lives," Dav reminded her. "We're in a race with a war, and we must never forget it."

When Dav translated for the elves, Calenderi thought for a moment, then nodded. "He will travel with us to Brun."

Dav decided to let the elf make all the decisions that agreed with his. Despite her haughtiness, she was brave and intelligent. While she let them know she was not accustomed to work, she had labored to clean the cabins and had helped store the supplies.

The efforts of the elves had surprised Dav until Erian recited the Immortal Rafiel's "Verse of Food and Cleanliness": *Let your food be pure and clean. Keep also yourselves pure and white before me, and let not your souls be spotted with wrongdoing against me, and I, Rafiel, will guide you.*

If their Immortal insisted they scrub everything

they touched, they should have the run of the boat, he decided.

The night before, Leanna and Dav had washed the filthy sleeping pallets, sleeping furs, and old clothing in the waves, rinsed them in the fresh water of the creek, and spread them on the railings. The clothing had dried in the morning breeze, but the thick pallets were still damp.

When Dav and Leanna returned to the deck, she tested a pallet. Deciding it was dry, she folded it and tucked it under her arm.

Dav frowned at her activity.

"What's wrong?" she asked.

"We're fleeing for our lives," Dav reminded her. "At least for Serdic's life, and the freedom of the elves. We're in a desperate situation."

"And we shouldn't forget it." She tested another pallet and turned the damp side to the sun.

"But instead we're doing *laundry*," Dav complained. "It just seems so mundane."

"What do you want to do, puff on the sail?" Leanna teased. "Only one person at a time can steer the boat."

Dav brought out the needles, twine, and the black cloth he had bought in the shop. He cut and fashioned two sacks, each about fifteen inches square. Then he took them down to the cabin to check his idea.

A few minutes later, he returned to the deck. Idly watching him as he maintained their course, Serdic started and then laughed. Dav was followed by the elves, who wore their new clothing and the loosely woven black sacks over their heads to protect their delicate skin and their eyes from the sun.

"Be careful," Dav warned Erian. "Can you see the ropes on the deck?"

The elf prince nodded, and the corners of the sack bobbed like two floppy ears. Both children turned in Serdic's direction. Then Calenderi tilted her head as if looking behind them.

"The pirates are too far away to see you, but if they get closer, you go below again," Dav said and left them to explore. Erian ran about, poking into everything. Calenderi soon forgot her royal dignity in her first opportunity to examine the rigging and watch the movement of the sails.

Dav sat by Serdic, memorizing his every move as he tacked against the wind. The auburn-haired man was maintaining the distance between them and their pursuers, but the pirate vessel was too fast for the sailboat to outrun it.

"Would it slow us down if I took the tiller for a little instruction?" Dav asked.

"That depends on how much training you need," Serdic replied. He relinquished the tiller but stayed close. Dav felt a moment of fear as the sails luffed and the boat lost headway when he tacked, but when the boom swung over, he felt the power and speed return.

"Not bad for a first try." Serdic clapped Dav on the shoulder and adjusted his hold on the main sheet. For the rest of the afternoon, Dav remained at the tiller. He needed to get his training in good weather. They ate on deck. Then Leanna went below to sleep, and Serdic stretched out on deck near Dav. They were more experienced and would handle the boat during the night.

Dav stayed a constant distance from the shore. The wind strained at the sails. The boat moved faster, but the small galley continued to follow them.

Ten days later it was still just in sight.

They kept themselves occupied to keep from worrying. Calenderi and Leanna were constantly together, arguing and insulting each other as they mended the old Hattian garments, needing the occupation, not the clothing. Both Shadow Elves learned a good deal about the Thyatian tongue, and Leanna was quickly picking up the Shadow Elf dialect.

Dav also learned. Leanna hadn't exaggerated when she said she was an expert with a sword. She not only knew how to fight, but she also was a surprisingly good teacher.

Erian proved to be a good fisherman, though his method was the strangest Dav had ever seen. When Dav was at the tiller, the elf child sat with him and sang strange, wordless songs. Within minutes, the wake would be swarming with fish that seemed to fight for a chance to impale themselves on the boy's fishhook. Erian's successes were a welcome supplement to their diet of dried jerky, hardtack, and pears.

Serdic was the only one without some occupation to keep him busy when he wasn't at the tiller. He became more restive, pacing the deck, watching the ship behind them.

"How far will Jesnow follow us?" Dav asked him. They had sailed around the southern tip of the Isle of Dawn and northwest through the Strait of Furmenglaive. They had reached the Sea of Dread, and the pirates were still following.

"All the way to Alphatia if need be," the mage snapped, speaking of the continent that had sunk only a few months before. Dav understood. No peril would stop the pirate.

"I made a fool of him, and he can't let it pass. He'd lose the respect of his men. If they catch up with us, we should have a plan," he said. The pirate vessel had drawn slightly closer in the last few hours.

Leanna and Calenderi sat close by, sewing.

"Why don't you put another holding spell on him?" Leanna asked.

"He has a magician or a cleric on board protecting the ship. I can't touch it."

"Someone more powerful than you, and you didn't tell us?" Leanna glared at the mage.

Her question brought back Serdic's grin and the mischievous twinkle in his green eyes. For several days, his tension had made him morose.

"And scare you into dumping me off at Furmenglaive or Ochalea? He can't reach us. He's trying, but Dav is holding him off. Together we'll be able to handle his magician."

"Why do you persist in thinking I'm a magic-user?" Dav asked. Serdic's dependence on an ability Dav didn't possess could lead to serious trouble.

"Why do you persist in saying you aren't?" Serdic countered. "It takes magic to hold off magic, and I know you can do that. You're at least as strong as I am, or you couldn't have seen me in Caerdwicca. Jesnow's crew didn't find me until I was close to you and you negated the spell."

Erian knelt on the seat by Serdic as he trailed his fishing line behind the boat and listened.

"You came through the invisible wall I made on the rocks," he reminded Dav.

"My ice spell wouldn't work on the decapus when it was near you," Calenderi added.

"So why keep denying it?" Serdic asked.

"I don't have any magic except my light charm." He pulled out the dull white metallic circle that hung around his neck like a medallion.

Serdic reached out a hand and touched it. He shook his head. "I'd say you've used all the power in that. I don't get any emanations at all."

"Could someone have put a spell on Dav so he's protected from magic?" Leanna asked.

"It's possible, but it would take a master magician, and the cost would be enormous. Besides, that type of spell is dangerous."

"What are the dangers?" Dav asked, thinking Leanna might be onto something. His stepfather had been a wealthy man, and he had taken good care of Dav.

"Spells lose their power as they're used," Serdic replied. "If you relied on it, you could be hiding behind a shield that wasn't there. Very little could harm you, but if you were injured, no healing spell could help you."

Dav remembered his injuries from the fight in the tavern and knew a protective spell wasn't the answer. The magician seemed to give up the idea he could get magical help from Dav. It grieved Dav to learn he had used all the power in his light charm. He'd seldom used it, but it was a gift from his unknown mother and was valuable for that reason alone. He tucked it back inside his tunic.

"The elves have magic," Leanna said.

"We have no magic for fighting, only to protect us," Calenderi said. "Erian cannot help except to create a wall of protection around himself and a few others. That is his only spell. I can levitate and throw missiles, but my weapons are only ice shards."

"But you have other powers. Erian can sing to the fish. . . ."

Calenderi shook her head. "That isn't magic. In the time when the world was new and all elves walked abroad on the surface of the world, they spoke to all living things and the forces of nature. Some of our people are still born with the old talents. Erian can speak to the animals and feel their hearts, though he does not understand their language. The songs of the wind are clear to my ears. It speaks to me of many things." She pointed toward the shore. "It sings now of a creature of great strength that chases a deer. The deer tires and falters. I hear his stumbling movement, his hesitation. . . . He leapt a great distance and stumbled. Claws are scrabbling to stop. The hunter cannot follow and roars in frustration. The deer has escaped."

Her ability fascinated Dav. "That's not magic?"

She shook her head. "It is a skill in some of our people, a leftover from the ancient times. Better so, because a spell must be relearned, but a talent is always there."

They ate their evening meal just before sunset. During the night, they showed no light, always hoping they would lose the pirates in the darkness.

At full dark, Serdic took his place at the tiller. The rest went below, the Shadow Elves to escape the chill of the evening, the humans to sleep.

Dav awoke to hear Serdic shouting. He jumped to his feet, grabbed his sword from beneath his pallet, and careened into the bulkhead when the deck canted sharply to the left. He regained his balance and dashed on deck, thinking that Jesnow had caught up with them.

Leanna ran right behind him, her sword in one hand, her knife in the other.

He expected to see the pirate ship alongside and the deck full of angry men. Instead, he skidded to a halt and stared. His mouth went dry, and a cold knot formed in his stomach.

The wind and the waves had risen during the night. To the south, the sky was black with the clouds of an approaching storm. Pale moonlight still lit the deck and the sea to the north. Less than a hundred yards away, rapidly approaching the boat, was a monster that did its part to name the Sea of Dread.

"A sea hydra!" Leanna gasped.

Moonlight glinted off the scales of eight ten-foot-long necks, each with a dragonlike head nearly three feet long. Two horns sprouted just behind each set of eyes. Eight mouths spread wide, the dark maws trimmed with gleaming, pointed teeth that momentarily froze Dav with fear.

Serdic had left the tiller and stood at the rail, reciting an incantation. A fireball shot out across the water, striking the closest head. It burned with the unnatural heat of magic and fell off the blackened stump of the neck. The sea was lit from below as the magical fire continued to burn as it sank. The creature drew back in shock.

"Get another one if you can," Dav said. "Maybe you can scare it off."

"I only have one other weapon shot," Serdic said. "Then we're on our own. Are you sure you don't have any magic?"

"I said so," Dav answered. He sheathed his sword and reached for one of the long iron-tipped poles. Leanna took the other one.

They stood waiting as the hydra approached.

Chapter 7

Stormbound

The hydra writhed with pain. The remaining seven heads roared in rage, and the creature swam rapidly toward the boat, moonlight reflecting off its fourteen glowing eyes.

"If you have another spell, you'd better use it," Leanna suggested as the sea monster approached.

"Let it get a little closer. I can't afford to miss," Serdic said.

The hydra closed to striking distance; Dav stood poised to fight. His broadsword remained in its sheath. Instead, he held one of the poles that served double duty as a lance. Then he saw Calenderi a few feet away. She braced herself against the rail, hooking one foot around a support post.

"Get back to the cabin!" he shouted at her, but she raised her hands and muttered an incantation. Rapierlike ice shards struck the creature in the eyes and slowed it slightly, but after a moment, it resumed its relentless forward course.

"Get below!" Dav shouted at her once again, but

she stood her ground. He could see her fear. He admired her courage, though it could get her killed to no purpose, since her only weapon was the large knife that had belonged to Lertin. Dav wanted to force her to go belowdecks, but at that moment, the nearest head of the hydra struck at him, the open mouth gaping.

He jabbed at it with the pole, intending to drive the heavy shaft down the hydra's throat, but the boat skipped and he caught it in the left eye, driving the shaft in more than a foot. Its scream overrode the wind as the light died in the creature's right eye. The head hit the railing before the writhing neck jerked it back.

Beside Dav, Leanna poked her pole into a neck but failed to do any serious damage. The head writhed away in pain, but another immediately took its place. Two more heads lashed out toward Serdic at the tiller, but they collided with an unseen wall. They butted against it, but it held. Erian had used his only spell. His wall protected Serdic, but it prevented the mage from using his last magic weapon. The mage rushed up the deck, nearly losing his footing as the boat tossed on the waves. When he stepped beyond Erian's wall, he threw a lightning spell. Another of the hydra's heads burned away.

At first, Dav thought Serdic's spell seemed to go on and on, most of it missing the hydra. Then he heard the roll of thunder, and he realized the other bolts came from the approaching storm. He could see large waves rocking the boat.

Dixie McKeone

Dav struck three times with the pole without any noticeable success, though the hydra grew more wary, attacking more cautiously. He stepped back and dropped the pole on the far side of the low peaked cabin roof, letting it roll off on the port side of the deck. The boat rocked, rising and falling on the waves as if it were alive. He didn't want the pole rolling around under his feet.

With his hands free, he pulled out his broadsword as a head arched up above him and reached for him, jaws gaping, the yellow eyes gleaming as if they were lit from within. He slashed at it with his sword and felt the blade cut into the thick, scaly hide, cleaving the neck nearly in half.

On the other side of Leanna, Serdic slashed away with his sword, fending off a determined attack. He hadn't noticeably injured his attacker, but he kept it at bay.

Another head lashed at Dav, and he swung the blade, but the ship abruptly dropped into a wallow between the swells. The gaping jaws closed on nothing, and Dav's sword clove empty air.

As the boat rose up again, he caught the same head with a glancing blow. Another head darted toward him, but Calenderi and Erian warded it off with the pole Dav had discarded.

"Get below!" he shouted at them, but they ignored him.

The boat suddenly rose on a swell, and Leanna nearly lost her footing. She held her sword tightly in her right hand, the blade pointing up as she braced herself against the raised roof of the cabin.

As the boat rose suddenly, her blade came up under a jutting head, and the blade went straight through the middle of the lower jaw, burying itself nearly to the hilt. She gave a cry of mixed fear, surprise, and triumph. As the hydra's head jerked up, she gripped her sword with both hands. The blade lifted her off her feet before her weight pulled it free and she fell to the deck.

Dav stepped to his left, trying to span the area between the determined elves and Leanna, who slid along the wet deck, unable to rise to her feet.

But the hydra had lost five of its eight heads and had had enough. It drew back, roared defiantly, and swam away.

As the monster disappeared in the distance, Dav hurried to the stern of the boat and struggled to bring it under control. The wind had risen until it was all he could do to run before the storm.

Up near the bow, Leanna and Serdic seemed to be having an argument. Dav stayed at the tiller. Leanna came marching back, Serdic following her.

"I knew something was wrong when I saw that monster," she said, too angry to hear how ridiculous her words sounded. "Hydras don't often come in close to land."

"Well, this one didn't know the rules." Dav was lightheaded after the battle. He felt a need to laugh and joke.

"Yes, it did," she snapped. "We're not hugging the shore anymore. When we went below, Serdic changed course. We've been traveling almost directly west for four hours."

"So we'll sail northeast and get back to the coast in another six hours, maybe less," Dav suggested. The boat skipped across the water at an incredible speed.

"And which way is northeast?" Leanna asked him, looking up at the sky. He followed her gaze and realized the scudding clouds had hidden the moon and the stars.

"We'll be able to tell in the morning," he said.

"What good will it do us? By then the storm will be too strong for us to risk sailing into a cove or a river," she shouted over the growing force of the wind. "Because of him, we'll be riding out this storm on the open sea!"

Behind Leanna, Serdic shrugged an apology. "I didn't know a storm would blow up so suddenly," he said. "I intended to sail west, then turn north, and in the daylight, we'd head back for the shore again. Then Jesnow would be ahead of us."

"I don't think we'll have time to worry about Jesnow," Dav said.

Within hours, his prophecy proved true. The wind kept rising, driving them forward. Dav set the sail and spilled all the wind he could, but they were flying up and down the swells. The night darkened until even the top of the white sail was lost in the blackness. Leanna took the tiller, but after an hour, she had to call for one of the men. She didn't have the strength to hold it.

Dav and Serdic took turns throughout the night, into the next day, another night, another day. Before long, Dav lost track of time.

Leanna said they had fought the storm for five days. Dav took her word for it. The nights were filled with rising and falling in the darkness. The days were worse. The waves often reached fifty feet high, towering over the boat before it rode up the sides to the crests and back down again.

Just after dark on the sixth day of the storm, Serdic shouted an alarm. Dav, sound asleep, awakened when Calenderi shook his shoulder.

"An attack," she said, repeating Serdic's message. "Bring your sword."

Dav stumbled to his feet. This time he followed Leanna as they rushed on deck.

"It's at the bow!" Serdic shouted over the wind. He stayed at the tiller, not daring to let go and risk broaching the high waves.

Dav raced forward after Leanna. In the darkness, they could just make out long, slender tentacles whipping in the air. Dav hacked at one and clove it in half, then another, and another. Leanna did the same, but the monster continued to cling to the boat, although it made no attack on them. Dav paused, reached down, and picked up a piece he had hacked off. He held a supple branch with thin green leaves.

"We're fighting a *willow tree!*" he shouted in disgust. He intended to say more about false alarms and foolish panic and a few other things he hadn't yet worked out when he heard a strange voice.

"Awk! Don't kill me! Don't kill me!"

Dav exchanged looks with Leanna.

"Awk! Wake up, wake up! There are people,

101

people. They are cutting up our tree, our tree."

"Who's cutting up our tree?" a gruff, sleepy voice asked. "Where are we?"

"In front of a boat. Awk, yes, a boat, but they have swords, big swords!"

"Hello the tree!" Dav shouted.

"Hello the boat," the gruff voice answered. "Do you attack anything that gets close to you, or just the vegetation?"

"Sorry. We didn't realize it was a vessel in disguise," Dav answered. His fatigue and relief had made him silly.

"Couldn't you find a more comfortable way to travel?" Leanna shouted.

"We just did—that is, if you've got room for two more."

"Glad to have you," Dav replied, not sure his answer was completely true, but they couldn't ignore victims of the storm.

The tree rocked slightly, and a head appeared, trimmed with a full black beard and topped with a metal helmet. A short, stocky dwarf swung out of the tree and dropped lightly to the deck.

Water streamed off his clothing. He stood about three and a half feet tall. A wicked-looking battle-axe hung from his belt next to a dagger sheath. He bowed.

"Hoganvar Stonetalker, at your service," he said and turned back to the tree, pulling two packs out of the darkness. A sturdy crossbow and a quiver of quarrels were tied to the larger bundle.

"HeyYou! Climb up here! Come on, you three-toed, featherheaded berry picker!" He waited a moment. "If I have to come and get you, I'll pluck your feathers and we'll have *chicken for dinner!*"

The limbs that overhung the deck started to shift, and suddenly, over the wind, they heard a panicked cry from the tree. The dwarf jumped to the nearest thick branch and caught it, bracing his legs against the railing.

"HeyYou! Climb!" he shouted. He sounded as near to panic as a dwarf could come.

"My foot, my foot! Awk, my foot is caught!"

Dav grabbed a limb, trying to keep the tree from floating away. Leanna and the dwarf helped, but all three knew they wouldn't be able to keep the tree from breaking free of the boat. Over the wind, they heard the crack of splintering wood as a limb split. The tree shifted and the boat lurched, as if anxious to rid itself of its restrictions.

The dwarf jumped and grabbed a thick limb above his head. He hooked one arm over it and reached out a hand.

"Throw me our packs," he shouted to Dav. "Hurry! We need our food!"

Dav refused to let go of the tree, condemning the dwarf and his companion to the storm again, but Leanna, more practical, grabbed for the packs. Just as she drew back her arm to toss them up to the dwarf, a pale shadow emerged from the dark branches and flopped to the deck. The dwarf dropped to the deck just as the tree broke free. He ignored the young humans as he rushed to his companion.

"Are you hurt?" he demanded of the feathered

creature who rose uncertainly to its feet and shook its feathered, beaked head. "It's a wonder you aren't," the dwarf raged. "Getting your foot caught . . . of all the idiot things to do. I'd have left you there, you know."

In the uncertain light, Dav first thought he saw a talking bird. HeyYou's head, neck, thin body, and legs down to the third joint were covered with pale feathers. The lower legs and feet were rough skin, and the creature had clawed, three-toed feet, with small spurs at the back. Then, as HeyYou raised an arm, Dav saw that it was feathered, with long, fingered hands. Dav realized he looked at a gyerian. HeyYou had a two-inch advantage in height over his companion.

As the dwarf ranted, Dav grinned. Hoganvar had been willing to jump back into the tree rather than leave his friend, but he refused to admit it.

Dav admired the loyalty, but his quick ear picked up something strange in the dwarf's speech. He had spoken to them in Thyatian, but when he addressed the gyerian, he used dwarvish, a careful, forced Rockhome dialect, but Dav caught the underlying Denwarf-Hurgon. Hoganvar was a refugee from Alphatia.

Leanna sidled over to Dav. "Keep an eye on your purse. Gyerians will steal anything."

"He won't be running away with it," Dav answered, gesturing to the rough sea.

When he'd finished berating his companion, the dwarf turned back to Dav and Leanna. "Let me give you a word of advice. If you ever find a gyerian fledgling alone and helpless, don't feed it. You'll be stuck with it for the rest of your life."

"Come down to the cabin, out of the storm," Dav said and led the way. He begrudged them the shelter of the cabin because of the Shadow Elves, but he couldn't leave them on deck.

When they reached the cabin, Calenderi and Erian stared at the newcomers.

Hoganvar stood at the brazier, warming his hands and observing the elves without being obvious about it. HeyYou stood in the corner, watching avidly as Leanna poured water into two cups. Leanna forestalled the dwarf's questions by handing him a cup of water. He drank it down in gulps and handed it back for a refill. HeyYou took his, tilted his head back, and poured the water down his beak in one short, steady stream. Leanna refilled their cups, and HeyYou would have taken more, but Hoganvar stopped him.

"We'll not be drinking all their water," he told the gyerian. "They may be in short supply."

"We have enough for now," Dav said, only qualifying the statement because he had no idea how long it would be before they reached land.

"Still, it's best to wait a bit before drinking more," the dwarf said. The gyerian clucked and muttered and settled on his haunches by the brazier, fluffing out his feathers to dry them.

"We're grateful for the rescue," Hoganvar said. "We don't mind paying for our passage. We have our own food, but we've had no water since we were washed out to sea. Where are you bound?"

Dixie McKeone

"That way." Leanna pointed toward the bow of the boat. She laughed, and Dav joined her. They both still felt foolish after the attack on the tree.

"We haven't known where we were or what our direction is since the storm began," Dav explained. "We were on our way to Brun." He changed the subject. "What made you take up tree riding?"

"Took passage on a ship out of East Portage, bound for Athenos in Darokin. The storm caught her at the point of the peninsula and drove her aground. We'd just gotten ashore when a flood came down out of the hills." He glowered at the gyerian. "This featherhead picked a tree for us to climb, and it got washed out to sea."

"Awk, only tree, only tree there was," the gyerian muttered.

"East Portage?" Dav repeated. There were no charts on the ship, but he remembered his lessons about the geography of Mystara. "Then we've been blown north. But at sunset last night, I thought we were traveling west."

"Myself, I think the wind has changed," Hoganvar said. "I expected to fetch up on the coast of Brun in a day or so. At least, that's what I hoped." He looked around the snug cabin. "I like it where we are, for the present."

"He should be given some dry clothing," Calenderi suddenly broke in, speaking to Dav.

Hoganvar apparently understood the elf. He dropped his gaze, but not before Dav had seen the renewed questions and speculation. He decided the dwarf should understand their intentions.

"The elves are returning home," Dav said, carefully choosing his words so Hoganvar understood they were not prisoners. "We're accompanying them to make sure they arrive safely." Some safety, he thought as the boat rolled and the brazier rocked in its metal cradle.

"Then you aren't their kidnappers?" the dwarf replied.

"We met them on the Isle of Dawn." Dav saw no reason to keep the circumstances of their meeting, or what they had heard in Caerdwicca, a secret. "They're not for sale as hostages. I've made myself responsible for their safe return."

Dav stared at Hoganvar, making sure the dwarf saw the challenge in his eyes.

Chapter 8

Land Ho!

Dav saw that the dwarf had understood him, so he relaxed when Hoganvar shrugged.

"Just consider us passengers. We'll pay our way."

"If you know how to sail a boat, you can work it off," Leanna spoke up. "Dav and Serdic have had to do all the sailing, and they're worn out."

Hoganvar frowned and shook his head. "Never learned anything about boats. Dwarves don't much like the water."

"We can use my knowledge and your strength," Leanna persisted. "We could do it together."

Dav tried to object, but she overrode him.

"You and Serdic are both exhausted. If you don't get some rest, one of you will make a bad decision and capsize us."

Hoganvar stood up suddenly. "I'd rather sail than swim."

Dav disliked being overruled by Leanna, but he needed some rest, so he agreed. He took a fur into the forward hold and stretched out to sleep. For the first time since the storm hit, he awoke without being summoned. He was still tired, but he knew he had slept for hours. Beside him, he heard the steady breathing of Serdic.

In the main cabin, Calenderi was coaxing a few pieces of charcoal to light from the embers still in the brazier. Erian sat up and rubbed his eyes. The gyerian, already awake, was squatting in front of his open pack, fingering a small hoard of the cheap, gaudy trinkets that gyerians found so irresistible.

Dav ate some jerky and hardtack and took a few swallows of water. Then he went on deck to relieve Leanna and Hoganvar. Leanna looked half frozen, and even the dwarf showed the strain.

"You should have called me earlier," he shouted over the wind, but they ignored him.

"I think the storm is easing up," Hoganvar said as he relinquished the tiller to Dav. "Or maybe it just doesn't seem as bad when I'm not clinging to a tree."

When Dav took over the steering, he agreed with the dwarf. The storm still tore at them, but he thought it might be missing a few teeth. He kept looking back over his shoulder. The sky behind him and over his left shoulder was definitely lighter. He wondered if he was seeing the dawn sky, which meant they were traveling west southwest, or clearing weather.

While he was wondering about it, Erian slipped up on deck. He sat by Dav for a few minutes and then jumped to his feet.

"Land!" he shouted, pointing directly ahead.

Dav stared at the indistinct gray line on the horizon. To human eyes, it was only slightly darker than the heaving sea. They watched for several minutes before he accepted the evidence of his eyes. By then, he knew the storm was driving them straight toward the shore.

"Get Serdic," Dav said, knowing only the mage might have enough skill to bring them in to a safe landing. When the magic-user came on deck, he already wore his backpack that held his spellbooks and his few clothes. Dav relinquished the tiller to him.

"Try to pick a soft spot," he told the mage.

"Not that I'll have much choice," Serdic said, staring into the gloom of the stormy morning.

Dav stayed with Serdic while the others remained below and packed their supplies. A sudden squall of heavy rain obscured their vision. They couldn't even see the front of the boat. Dav went forward, hoping to call back a warning to Serdic, but suddenly a huge boulder seemed to rise out of the water just to their left.

For a breathless moment, Dav thought they would hit the boulder dead on, but a wave carried them past it, missing it by inches. The boat slipped by a second rock to starboard, but then their luck ran out.

A pair of huge boulders jutted up like teeth directly in front of the bow. Three feet of the narrow bow passed between them, then struck. Dav heard the tearing of splintering wood. The railing he gripped for support gave way, and he pitched over the bow.

He felt the graze on his hand as he reached for the boulder on his left, but he landed well beyond it. He fell into the waves, and the surf dragged him toward the shore. He found the bottom and tried to stand. His head popped out of the water when the undertow pulled his feet from beneath him and swept him toward the depths.

Dav tumbled in the swirling water. He felt sand under his hands before he spun up again, turned head over heels, and rushed along with the raging undercurrents. His eyes stung from the churned sand. His lungs felt as if they were collapsing from want of air.

When his hand struck a boulder, the only solid thing in his tumbling world, he grabbed at it. He skinned his fingers but managed to hold on. By strength of will, he pulled himself up on its slick surface until his head was out of the water.

Twenty feet away, he saw the boat as a swell raised the stern, turned it sideways, and dropped the small craft on its side. Over the roar of the waves, he heard the scream of tearing wood. The others were tumbled off the deck. HeyYou's pale, feathered arms spread wide as if he were flying over the water. Calenderi tumbled overboard near him. Dav lost sight of Serdic, Leanna, Erian, and Hoganvar, but he might be able to help the others. He dove back into the liquid maelstrom, knowing he had little or no chance of finding them in the strong undercurrents.

He wondered how he expected to help anyone else when he couldn't control his own direction. Then Calenderi washed against him. He caught her around the waist and felt himself grabbed from behind. An arm flopped over his shoulder, and feathers covered his face.

The undertow carried them into deeper water, but Dav felt sand under his feet. He straightened his legs, pushing with all his strength, and they shot to the surface.

Dav gasped, gulping air into his burning lungs. They were facing out to sea, and the fast current swept them toward a jagged boulder. Hitting it could mean broken bones if they weren't killed. He put out a hand in hope of softening the impact when he heard the gyerian gasping.

HeyYou sneezed.

A deafening roar stunned Dav with sound, and they were catapulted out of the water, flying over the waves. They tumbled back into the shallow surf and washed up on the beach.

"What—what happened?" Calenderi asked. The elf princess stared at him with wide eyes.

"I—I don't know." Dav looked around, half expecting to find some magician standing on the shore, but they were alone. He'd sort out the mystery later, he decided.

He spotted Leanna, Erian, and Hoganvar clinging to the roof of the cabin, but they had reached a dubious safety. Smoke poured from the cabin. The brazier had been upset in the wreck.

Serdic swam toward shore and staggered out of

the waves. He was gasping and retching from the salt water he had swallowed.

"Dwarves can't swim," Serdic gasped as he fought to catch his breath. "And I doubt the little elf can make it on his own."

"Hoganvar's pack, awk, Hoganvar's pack," Hey-You gibbered and waded into the surf to pick up the pack that had washed ashore. Dav watched absently as the gyerian pulled the pack out of the water. Then he noticed the rope attached to it, along with the crossbow.

Dav was wondering if they could make use of the weapon and the rope somehow, but just then a huge wave lifted the remains of the boat and brought it crashing down on the rock, tearing it apart and hurling the others into the sea.

Dav splashed back into the waves again, swimming hard for where Leanna, the dwarf, and the elf child had disappeared. As he was lifted by a wave, he saw that Hoganvar and Erian were clinging to a section of broken spar and Leanna was holding on to one end of it, kicking furiously, trying to move it toward shore. Dav saw her expression of relief when he swam up beside her to lend assistance.

Hoganvar and Erian did their best to help, but they were all exhausted by the time they reached the shallows and splashed ashore.

When the dwarf could finally speak, he raged at HeyYou. "Why couldn't you have been with me when you sneezed?" he demanded.

"When he *sneezed?*" Dav didn't understand.

The dwarf glared at him. "Not many things

under dragon size can stand up against a gyerian's sneeze. He blew you onto shore. Not *me*, the one who saved him when he was a fledgling, who fed him and looked after him."

"Awk, found your pack! Found your pack, I did." HeyYou pointed at the dwarf's belongings. "Want a denarius. Should get a silver piece. Did a good job, a good job!"

"Let *him* give you a denarius. You saved *his* life."

"I'll give him a gold piece if you two will find us some shelter," Dav snapped. They were all tired, wet, and cold. He saw no point in standing in the rain while the dwarf and the gyerian argued.

The waves were flinging the debris from the boat onto the shore, and along with them came the sacks of supplies and the packs that had been left in the cabin. While the dwarf and the gyerian searched for shelter, the others rescued their belongings and gathered driftwood for a fire. Dav was surprised to discover the sacks were watertight until Leanna told him Serdic had put a shielding spell on them to keep them dry.

"We owe him our thanks," Dav said, glad he would have dry clothing and charcoal to make a fire.

"We owe him nothing," Leanna snapped. "He hasn't done anything that didn't benefit him as well as us."

Dav picked the leaves of a pale green plant struggling to grow in the salt-rimed vegetation that edged the sand. He held them up for her to see. "This is canredwaith. It reduces fever. It

115

doesn't grow in cold climates." He carefully tucked the leaves in the pouch at his waist.

"What do you think we should do now?" Leanna asked. "I'm afraid of taking passage on another ship. Even if we could hide the elves, we might be shipwrecked again."

"I know. I guess we go overland," Dav agreed. "If we can find a village or a town, maybe we can buy some horses." He saw her eyes flicker and laughed. "And, yes, you can pay me back."

"What about the others?" Leanna asked. "I don't want to share the reward."

"Is money all you ever think about?" Dav demanded, disgusted with her mercenary attitude.

"Yes, right now it is," she snapped. "You don't know what it means to be *owned*, for someone else to have the right to tell you when you get up, lie down, work, eat, breathe, to have no right to make a decision for yourself."

"No, I don't," Dav admitted. She stopped to pick up a board that had floated ashore, then caught up with him as he was adding wood to his pile.

"If you're not interested in the reward, why are you working so hard to get them home?"

"I suppose I'm doing it mostly because of Erian." He had also developed a fondness for Calenderi. The haughty princess was working as hard as the others, with fewer and fewer complaints. More he wasn't ready to say.

Withis had taught him to hate war. Men should fight evil and injustice, and there were too many wrongs in the world for them to waste time battling each other. Leanna had been brought up to view war as an occupation. He didn't know if she'd understand what he meant, and he didn't want to argue about it.

"But there's another reason we should return them," Dav said. "History hasn't been kind to the Shadow Elves. They were forced underground by a catastrophe, and when they tried to get to the surface, there wasn't a place for them. If you'd been shut away from your rightful place, you'd hate other races just as they do. Somewhere, someone has to begin to show them kindness so they'll begin to trust others. We have the opportunity to start with Calenderi and Erian. One day they might be the rulers of Aengmor and the City of Stars."

They carried their supplies and driftwood to the cave the dwarf and the gyerian had found, then changed into dry clothing.

Dav told the others of the decision he and Leanna had made. Serdic and Hoganvar nodded as if they had expected it.

"I've got business near Tavaro in Darokin," Hoganvar said, but he didn't elaborate.

"I'll trail along, since I'm not welcome in Thyatis." Serdic smiled, and Dav saw Leanna's eyes flash. "I think that's where we've landed. There should be a road somewhere around here circling north around the mountains and turning west through the foothills."

"Danger walking," HeyYou announced. "Walk and trouble follows."

"You're trouble," Hoganvar told the gyerian.

"Said going on a boat was trouble," HeyYou announced. He shook his head and tilted it sideways, glaring at the dwarf with one eye. "Said it was trouble, and it was."

"You say that about everything," Hoganvar groused.

"Was trouble."

"All right!" The dwarf was getting impatient.

"Was."

"Does any one want *chicken for dinner?*" the dwarf demanded.

"You're suggesting we *walk?*" Calenderi stared at Dav as if he had lost his senses.

"I don't mind walking," Erian said, slipping his hand into Dav's. "Not if we're going home."

"You're outnumbered, teshalla." Dav grinned at the elf princess as he called her by her honorific title.

Dav had made light of the journey before them, but when he finally lay down, wrapped in one of the cat-skin furs, he stared at the flames, wondering what dangers they would face. They wouldn't have time to detour around the obstacles in their path. Too many lives depended upon returning the elf children before King Telemon could lead his warriors up from the deep caverns.

Chapter 9

The Army of the Dead

They spent two days in the cave resting, waiting out the storm, and sewing the cat-skin furs into coats. On the third morning, the sky remained cloudy, but the rain had stopped. They shouldered the makeshift backpacks they had made of the provision sacks and left the cave, heading west. The three humans and three demihumans wore their cat-skin coats with the fur on the outside, hoping the natural camouflage would help keep them from being noticed. HeyYou's garment was a cape, since the feathers that draped from his arms prevented him from wearing a garment with sleeves.

They continued their trek until late in the afternoon, leaving the coastal plain behind and walking through the gently rolling hills. Directly in front of them, they could see mountain peaks, blue and shadowy in the distance.

Just as the sun set, they topped a rise and stared down at a road that ran north and south. To the southwest, they could see the towers of a fort.

"Zendrol," Hoganvar muttered, pulling at his beard.

"Can we make the fort before dark?" Leanna asked. She looked around as if she sensed danger.

"Must be five miles away," the dwarf replied.

"We're not taking the elves into that fort," Dav announced, leaving no room for argument. He hadn't brought them safely across an ocean through a storm just to lose them to a group of mercenary soldiers.

"We can't camp here," Leanna objected, but Serdic, who suffered most from their day-long trek, dropped his pack to the ground.

"Then let's find a sheltered valley where we can't be seen from the road," he said. "I'm tired and hungry, and I'm not going to be able to go much farther."

Erian tugged at Dav's coat, asking why they had stopped. Dav told him.

"I'm hungry, too," he complained. "You said we would have a fire tonight." The young prince had trudged all day without objecting, even about the small pack he carried, but his shoulders slumped and his voice was plaintive.

"The elves can't go much farther," Dav told the others. "Remember, they're just children. They're tired and hungry. We need to stop and make camp." The company had committed themselves to a cross-country trek, and they should have understood it meant camping in the wilds.

Leanna, Serdic, and the elves were unused to roughing it, so he had expected complaints from them, but not on the first night of the journey.

Hoganvar seemed as reluctant as Leanna. That surprised him. The dwarf had been strangely reticent about himself and his adventures, but Dav suspected he was a mercenary.

"We'll find a sheltered place and stop," Calenderi spoke up, looking around as if hers was the final word. She pointed to a hill across the road from where they stood. "Over there, on the other side of that hill, where our fire will not be seen from the road or the fort." She marched off in the direction she had indicated.

Erian and Serdic followed her without a word, and HeyYou trudged along at the side of the elf prince. They moved quickly across the road and into the valley between the two hills. Knowing they were at the end of their day's march, Serdic kept pace with the elf princess. By the time Dav reached the spot Calenderi had chosen, Serdic had lit a fire using the last of the charcoal.

"Don't like the dark." HeyYou squatted close to the fire. "Trouble in the dark."

"Quiet, you scrawny-necked beast," Hoganvar grumbled as he scanned the shadowy hillsides.

They gathered around the fire, ate a quiet meal, and sat resting after their day's travel. Suddenly Leanna jumped to her feet, staring out into the night. She pulled out her sword.

"What's the matter?" Dav didn't see anything, and Leanna didn't answer. She stood as if frozen. Hoganvar grabbed his axe, Serdic picked up a burning brand from the fire, and the elves and the gyerian stared fearfully into the night.

Dixie McKeone

Dav's years on the Great Escarpment had sharpened his senses. He knew there was nothing within several hundred yards of the camp, but he drew his sword and stepped away from the fire. He stood waiting for his eyes to adjust to the darkness. He expected to return to the fire after making a short search and reassuring the others. Unused to camping in the wilds, they were bothered by the dark, and they were affecting each other with their fears, he decided.

Dav had turned back toward the camp when he stopped and stared. Leanna swung her sword. It seemed to hit something he couldn't see. It bounced back suddenly, as if she had struck it against a sharp stone, but Dav could see nothing. She parried and thrust gain.

What was she fighting?

Hoganvar stood flat-footed, wielding his axe. Serdic jabbed awkwardly with his stick of wood, but as far as Dav could see, they were fighting thin air!

* * * * *

Leanna would have been outraged if she had known Dav thought she was afraid of the overland journey. She had looked forward to their first night on the trail, even though she expected to be tired and hungry. She knew the ground would be cold and damp. That was the way it always was in the wonderful adventure stories told by the soldiers in the mercenary camps.

Her happiest memories were of listening to those tales, and she had always wanted an adventure of her own. She had grown up dreaming of tramping in the wilds, walking through barren hills, searching through dark forests, and climbing towering mountains. She didn't worry about the dangers until she learned they were planning to camp in the hills near Fort Zendrol. She knew the fort, and she also knew that some of the surrounding area had been the site of a major battle in the late war. A deserted battlefield was a dangerous place at night. She had heard many stories of the spirits of dead warriors. They attacked the living who crossed the lands war and destruction had tainted.

She had suggested they spend the night at the fort, but Dav had been afraid the elves might be recognized. He had been right, of course.

At first, she had thought Hoganvar might share her concern, but he hadn't spoken out. None of the others seemed worried, so she assumed they were far enough way from the fort to be safe, and she wasn't willing to be the only one to voice her concerns. She didn't want to appear cowardly.

She continued to believe they were safe until she felt the horror creep into her mind. Mortal fear, she had been told, was what brought the ghostly warriors to mortal sight and gave the dead the strength to attack the living. But even when the terror crept over her, she hadn't been sure what caused it, not until she saw the camp surrounded by a host of glowing apparitions.

Dixie McKeone

She opened her mouth to scream, but fought it back. Her personal fear had caused her to see the horde and exposed her to danger. If the others didn't see the glowing warriors, then they were safe. According to the tales she had heard, she must fight her battle alone.

Dimly she heard a sound of a horn, and a warrior stepped out of the circling host, his eyes holding Leanna's in a personal challenge. The specter that advanced was a horror of fatal wounds. Its iron helmet had been cloven nearly in two, and the deep gash in its head must have killed it before some mage fire had burned away its clothing and part of its flesh on the left side of its body. Worse than the sight of its wounds was the smell of rotting flesh and the terror that radiated from it like heat from a fire.

The wounds that had taken the ghost's life didn't slow it in death. The apparition's blade came down to meet hers, and her fear was so strong she barely had the strength to turn aside the sword with her own. When she tried to dodge the dead warrior's second thrust, her feet seemed reluctant to obey her. She forced them to move just in time and felt the breeze as the blood-encrusted blade whistled past her throat.

Dav appeared at her side, staring at her as if she had lost her wits. He held his sword in his hand, but made no move to help her. His arrival had driven off the ghostly fighter, who stepped back into the shadows and stood waiting, shifting his feet as if impatient over the interruption.

"What were you fighting?" Dav demanded.

Leanna opened her mouth to tell him and then closed it abruptly. To tell him might bring danger to him, and if the tales were true, he couldn't help her. She resented his safety even as she made up her mind not to involve him in her peril. He repeated his question, but still she kept silent.

* * * * *

Dav's anger built, the only emotion left after his mind had shed its confusion and frustration. Leanna refused to tell him why she was battling air. Serdic, Hoganvar, and Calenderi were fighting as hard as Leanna as they formed a protective square around the fire. Inside the area of protection, Erian and HeyYou stood with burning torches, but they seemed too afraid to confront the unseen adversaries.

Suddenly Erian screamed and dashed between his sister and the mage, racing out into the dark. He threw a terrified glance over his shoulder as he fled the camp.

Dav ran after the elf boy and caught up with the child on the steep hillside. He grabbed the elf's arm and ducked as the child swung his torch at the human's head.

"Erian!" Dav shook him, trying to reach through the terror. "What is it?" The hair on Dav's neck tingled with the fear building in him, but he still couldn't see any danger.

"The godag," Erian sobbed and stared back over

Dav's shoulder. "A dead one—a dead warrior. He wants to kill me."

Dav turned but still saw nothing. At least now he understood what was happening. He had read about the curse of old deserted battlefields.

"Where is it?" Dav asked. "Where is this dead warrior?"

"There." Erian pointed. "He stopped when you caught me, but he is watching and waiting." Erian clutched the human with all his small strength and sobbed. "Don't let him kill me!"

"He won't kill you, Erian. You're with me now," Dav said as he held the trembling elf child. "He can't reach you because I'm not afraid of him. But you must fight him." The child trembled at his words. "You fight him by not being afraid. His only weapon is your fear. Turn around and shout at him. Tell him to go away, that you are not afraid of him. Tell him."

Erian looked at the human doubtfully, but he turned within the circle of Dav's arms.

"Tell him," Dav insisted.

"Go away," the elf child said, his voice trembling. Then he seemed to sense something more was needed. "Go away! I'm not afraid of you!" The child's face turned from a mask of fear to one of anger. He pushed loose from Dav's enclosing arms and stooped over, picking up a handful of small stones. He kept throwing the stones and shouting until suddenly he stopped and stared at Dav with wide eyes.

"He's gone! They're all gone," Erian said, looking

around in wonder.

"No, he's still there," Dav said. "But he can't come back unless you fear him. Fear is your enemy, a far worse danger than the ghost warrior. Always remember that."

Dav was leading Erian back toward the camp when HeyYou squawked and dashed out of the protective circle. Dav left Erian and ran to catch the gyerian. The elf boy ran behind him, and when they caught up with the bird-man, Dav stopped his flight.

"Ghosts is trouble," HeyYou said, trembling. He was even too terrified to sneeze.

"Where is the ghost warrior who threatens you?" Dav asked. The gyerian pointed behind him.

"Awk, there! Waiting to kill me—to kill me."

"Come back to camp," Dav said, pulling the gyerian's arm. Dav decided he was right; the ghosts couldn't approach people who didn't fear them. He would talk the gyerian out of his terror, but he wanted to do it within the hearing of the others, hoping his voice would help them overcome their fright.

They reached the camp as Serdic fell to his knees and lost his torch. Dav raced over to help him to his feet, still pulling HeyYou along with his left hand. He watched Serdic's eyes. They were focused on something Dav couldn't see.

"Don't be afraid. Shout at him to go away," Dav said. "Get angry, mad enough so you're not afraid anymore. That will keep him at bay."

"For you," Serdic snarled. "You're holding them

off with your own magic, not because you're un-afraid."

"But you can make them go away," Erian told the mage. "I did. I threw rocks at the one chasing me, and he disappeared."

"Throw rocks, throw rocks," HeyYou said and bent to pick up a handful of stones.

"Shout at him. Get mad at him," Erian was instructing the gyerian. "That's right, shout. Get mad!"

HeyYou made a feeble pretense and tossed a rock.

"More!" Erian shouted at the avian and threw a stone to show what he meant. In moments, the gyerian was putting more force behind his rocks and his shouts. His feathers ruffled in his anger until his body seemed to double in size.

"I don't fear you. You only exist in my head," Calenderi said, suddenly throwing her burning brand into the fire and staring into the darkness unarmed. Dav jumped across the fire to stand by her side, but after a moment of staring into the darkness, she turned.

"It's true. They do disappear when you no longer fear them." She turned and dashed to Leanna's side. "Begone, you spawn of evil!" she shouted, but she had to duck to avoid Leanna's blade.

"He's not listening to you," Leanna panted. "Get away before you get a sword stuck . . ." She screamed and fell to the ground.

Dav knelt by her side. She was still breathing. He picked her up in his arms.

"Serdic! Hoganvar! Let go of your fear! It's the only way to save your lives!"

"Your magic can save yours, but not ours," Serdic said, scrambling to pick up Leanna's dropped sword.

"Aye, the mage has the right of it," Hoganvar panted in a voice devoid of hope. "Save yourselves while we hold them off."

"Then we'll save ourselves," Dav said, hoping his gamble would work. If he took the others off the battlefield, Hoganvar and Serdic might follow. Leaving the cursed area was the only way he knew of to get them all to safety.

The gyerian was staring around in the night, his feathers sleek against his body, his fear gone. The elves were peering into the darkness. None of the three seemed to feel frightened.

"Grab the packs," Dav told them. "Pick up all you can carry. We'll move west, away from the road until we've left the battlefield behind." He knelt, still holding the unconscious Leanna as he slipped his arm through the strap of his own pack and another. He didn't take time to discover whose they were.

He rose awkwardly, the weight of the girl's body and the packs nearly throwing him off balance.

"Stay close to me," he instructed the laden elves and the gyerian. Hoganvar and Serdic could be right; he might be protecting the others, but if he was, he believed it was because of his lack of fear, not because of any magic.

"You coming? Awk, you coming?" HeyYou called

to the dwarf as Dav led the others away. The gyerian was lagging behind, looking back at the dwarf.

"Get along with you," the dwarf snarled. "I'll catch up."

"Trouble. Awk, trouble," HeyYou muttered as he reluctantly followed Dav.

Dav led the way west, carrying the packs and the unconscious Leanna, wondering if he had done the right thing. He had depended on the dwarf's affection for the gyerian to make him follow them from the battlefield, but Serdic and Hoganvar were still battling their demons by the fire.

Had he left them to their deaths?

Dav couldn't tell if Leanna was still breathing.

The load he carried made him feel off balance, and he stepped carefully to keep from falling. His load of guilt was even worse. He had allowed Calenderi to chose their campsite, though he knew Leanna and Hoganvar were unhappy with it. If the dwarf, the mage, and Leanna died, it would be his fault.

And how far did he need to travel to be away from the battlefield? Since he couldn't see the ghostly horde, he had no idea.

Chapter 10

Strange Rumors

Dav stumbled along in the darkness, carrying the unconscious Leanna and two heavy packs. The two elves flanked him, staying close to his side. Behind him, the gyerian squawked and gobbled, upset at leaving the dwarf behind to fight the ghostly warriors.

Dav kept to the valleys between the low hills, afraid to risk running into a rock scree where he might lose his balance. Their path twisted and turned, but they were heading steadily west.

Suddenly Erian screamed and clung to Dav's arm.

"What is it?" Dav asked, his voice hoarse. His fear wasn't for himself, but how could he protect four people from a ghostly horde he couldn't see—especially when one of them was unconscious?

"A snake," Erian said. "I almost stepped on it." The elf looked at the ground behind him and flinched as he raised his eyes. He pointed to the hill behind them. "I got scared and now I can see the godags again. They are standing on the top of that hill, watching us."

"Watching, awk, watching," HeyYou said, pointing up on the hill.

"You can see them, too?" Dav asked. He wasn't really surprised. The gyerian was easily frightened, and Erian's scream would have destroyed HeyYou's carefully nurtured bravado.

"They're not following us?"

"No," Erian said. "They are standing in a line on the hilltop. They do not approach."

"We have left the battlefield," Calenderi said. "The earth we walk upon is clean."

"Could you tell we were camping on ground where many had died?" Dav asked.

"I knew the soil had known great sadness," Calenderi said slowly. "The fear and pain of those killed upon it by magic arts drained into the soil with their blood. I had never felt such a place and did not understand it."

He strode over to a rock outcrop and gently laid Leanna on two large boulders, where she'd be up above the damp ground. He shifted his feet while he tried to make a decision.

"Calenderi, what do you hear?" he asked and waited while the elf princess turned her head slowly.

"The shuffle of feet—the dwarf and Serdic—the thumps of a rabbit to the west, the wind under a bird's wing as it hunts the rabbit . . . nothing else."

"Then take my sword and guard the others until I return." Dav gave her his blade. "I'm going back for Hoganvar and Serdic."

Freed of his burdens, he hurried straight up the hillside where the elf boy had said the ghost horde was waiting. His path was partly bravado, partly necessity. He needed to stand on the heights. From there, he'd be able to see the light of the campfire and go directly to it.

Without his sword, he felt vulnerable, and the hair on the back of his neck prickled. He turned slowly, half expecting to see the horde and a specter ready to attack, but to him, the night was empty.

He saw the fire glowing in the distance and raced toward it. When he reached it, he found two packs lying on the ground, but the dwarf and the mage were gone. By the tracks they had made, it appeared they had followed Dav's first trail.

He picked up the packs and ran after them. In the rays of moonlight that occasionally broke through the clouds, he saw scuffed patches of ground that indicated the two mortal fighters had faced opposition in their efforts to follow the others.

Dav rounded the spur of a hill and saw Serdic standing over the dwarf, who lay at his feet. Dav rushed forward, shouting to Serdic that he was coming. He didn't want to be spitted on the mage's blade.

"I came back as quickly as I could," he said as he stopped close to Serdic's side.

"Not quick enough for the dwarf," the mage snapped. "That was unfair. I don't fault you." He stared out into the darkness and lowered his blade. "Glad you're here. As I said, you can keep them at bay with your magic."

Dav was tired of arguing about magic he didn't have. He bent over the dwarf and noticed a faint rise and fall of his chest.

"He's not dead," Dav said. "I'll carry him. You stay close. If it's really my magic that keeps the dead at bay, take advantage of it."

"Thanks for the help," Serdic said, moving closer to Dav but still staring warily into the darkness. When they joined the others, Dav laid the dwarf on the rocks by the unconscious girl.

"Leanna moaned a few times," Calenderi said.

"Neither shows any wounds," Serdic said. "But then they wouldn't. The wounds inflicted by the swords of the ghosts don't draw mortal blood. If they strike a vital spot, their victims die. If the wound isn't fatal, it brings on unconsciousness. You protected Leanna after she fell, and I protected the dwarf, so maybe they'll live."

"Why didn't someone tell me we were on a battlefield?" Dav demanded.

Serdic shrugged. "I didn't know. I never claimed to be a warrior, and I wouldn't know a battlefield from a dead fish. Ask the dwarf when he wakes up. He and Leanna are your fighters."

"*If* he wakes up," Dav said, wondering what he could do to help the two who lay as still as death.

But Serdic had been right. While he and the elves gathered twigs and started another fire, Leanna stirred and sat up, looking around. She clutched her left arm as if it pained her. Two hours later, the dwarf regained consciousness and rubbed his right shoulder. Both complained of soreness, but neither had received a fatal wound.

Nothing bothered them during the night. Leanna was up at the first light of dawn, still favoring her arm but ready to continue the journey.

Hoganvar disagreed.

"The ghost warriors are limited to the area where they fought the battle," the dwarf told him. "They can't cross the top of that hill, but there's not much that has the courage to come close to where a ghost horde roams. You said you wanted to buy horses and supplies for the journey. There's probably no safer place for the others to wait than right here."

"Could we buy horses and supplies at Fort Zendrol?" Dav asked.

"We can't buy them directly from the soldiers," the dwarf said, "but there's usually some sort of settlement around a fort. But it could be a five-mile walk for nothing."

"Give me your opinion," Dav said. He had erred the evening before in not asking what caused Leanna's and the dwarf's hesitation about their campsite. He was determined he wouldn't make that mistake again.

He waited while Hoganvar tugged at his beard and resettled his helmet, a sign he was weighing their options.

"If I made the decisions, I'd chance the fort," Hoganvar said slowly. "A few months ago, the war swept through here. The locals may have rounded up spare mounts after the battle. If so, they should be glad to sell off a few so they don't have to feed them through the winter."

Dav looked out at the surrounding terrain. Only grass and small rocks topped the hills. Farther down the slopes, thick brush offered concealment from prying eyes. They were well away from the ghostly warriors, and the hills seemed devoid of all life but small animals. With sturdy steeds beneath them, they had a greater chance to prevent the deaths of the many elves and humans who would confront each other because of the theft of the children.

Leanna and Serdic grudgingly agreed to guard the camp. The gyerian babbled and moaned when he learned he would stay behind, but the dwarf insisted.

Dav and Hoganvar left their packs, taking only their weapons as they headed for the fort. When they topped the first rise, they saw they had less than three miles to walk.

"When you first came aboard the boat, I made it plain that taking the elves home was *my* venture," Dav said. "But I don't pretend to know everything. The next time it looks as if I'm leading us into a mess, take your axe to me."

"I'll do that," Hoganvar said, grinning broadly. "You'd be easier to handle than another ghost horde."

A mile south of the camp, they returned to the road, openly approaching the fort. As they strolled toward it, they concocted a story to explain their presence and decided Hoganvar should dicker for the horses and a few extra supplies.

The road topped a rise, and they could see the fort ahead. The soldiers were attempting to repair the ravages of war. The shattered walls were shored with thick timbers. The laborers had rigged two large catapults to handle the peacetime chore of raising broken blocks that sweating soldiers mortared in place.

Blackened timbers were all that remained of the wooden buildings outside the fort. Several work-men were re-roofing a large stone structure.

A stone barn, set well back from the rest of the village, still retained most of its roof. A makeshift sign advised the traveler that food, drink, and sup-plies could be purchased inside. A large corral with more than a score of horses abutted the rear of the building.

Hoganvar led the way inside and headed for the last of three long tables in the middle of the floor. Shelves, barrels, and wooden bins filled the stalls, all loaded with merchandise. The large room smelled of the animals that had lived in the stalls, mixed with the odors of beef jerky, apples, leather, spices, and ale. From a door at the end of the room came the aroma of roasting meat and fresh bread. It made Dav's mouth water. A scrawny little man with bulbous eyes hurried from behind a screen of stretched skins.

"Name's Likin. What's your pleasure?"

The dwarf ordered two mugs of ale and downed

his mug in one long draft. "Nothing like good Thyatian ale," he said, wiping a spot of foam from his beard. "Been hiding out in the mountains. Any news coming through worth hearing?"

"Got a new national holiday," Likin said. "You missed it by a week. We had a big celebration over whipping those Alphatian devils."

"Then the war is over?" Dav asked.

"Don't know as I'd say that." The Thyatian shook his head. "I heard the fleet's already sailed, meaning to take over the Alphatian colonies. And they say as the emperor has hired them Alphatian troops as was left here when the fighting stopped. First they're fighting us, then fighting for us . . . makes you wonder what's what."

"I'm beginning to wonder," Hoganvar muttered, his eyes gleaming. "Why did he do that?"

"Captain Framit here at the fort thinks they'll be used against that desert scum from the emirates that have taken over Biazzan and Fort Nikos to the west. And there's likely to be trouble with them Shadow Elves, but I guess you've heard about that."

Dav kept his eyes on his mug of ale and listened intently to the conversation.

"Nothing particular," Hoganvar replied, "but you don't expect anything else from that lot."

"Can't say as I blame old King Telemon much." Likin rubbed his jaw with the cloth he had been using on the tables. "I'd fight if some thief kidnapped my kids—that is, if I had any. Anyway, the rumor is he'll be bringing his army up from down below and there's trouble coming. Any more trouble and I guess I'll move down inside," he said, giving them a sly look.

"Inside?" Dav and Hoganvar traded puzzled looks.

The Thyatian laughed. "There's a woman from Karameikos—Claransa the Seer, they call her— she's stirring up folks with some tale she's published in a book. Claims there's a whole world down inside this one and says she went there. Figure that one out if you've got time to waste."

"Don't think I want to bother," the dwarf said. "Got more important things on my mind." He fixed the man with a stare. "You the shopkeeper, too? Want to sell a few of those horses?"

They picked out ten mounts, chose seven saddles, and heaped supplies on a table. Then Likin and Hoganvar bickered over the price of the horses, tack, arrows, quarrels, blankets, and a new sword to replace the one Serdic lost.

Dav wondered if they were about to come to blows, but the sparkle in their eyes told him they were enjoying themselves. When they finally struck a bargain, the shopkeeper brought out a baked ham, fresh bread, and more ale. He treated them to a meal, and then the dickering began all over again as Hoganvar bought the rest of the cooked meat, a sack of bread, and another of apples. The dwarf also bought a bright string of glass beads and a bracelet with cheap, gold-colored bangles.

"It's the only way I can keep that featherhead

from stealing, else he'd be scrambling in your pack," Hoganvar said gruffly, explaining the purchase. The dwarf paid for all his own supplies and three of the animals and led the way on their return.

They were still a mile from where they left the others when Leanna hailed them. Dav wondered why she hadn't waited for them at the camp, but he held back any questions until he showed off the horses.

"We'll be able to ride now," he told her as he led a string of mounts forward while Hoganvar guided the rest. "A horse for each of us and three to carry the supplies. We won't have to go near another town or settlement for most of the trip. Not at all if we can hunt some game on the way."

The elves had come running at the sound of Dav's voice, but they drew back when they saw the horses. HeyYou squawked about having to ride, but Hoganvar bribed him with the bracelet and promised him the necklace after he had ridden the horse for a week.

Leanna stood silent, watching. Dav could see the anger snapping in her eyes.

"We did the best we could," he said, defending himself without knowing why. "It took a while to get the supplies and come back without causing suspicion."

"You bought one horse too many," she snapped. "You bought seven saddles, and we only need six."

"But there are seven of us."

"Not anymore. I told you not to trust Serdic. He

left us right after you did. By now he's at the fort, getting a reward for information about the elves."

"He left you without saying anything?" Dav had begun to like and trust the mage.

"He took the water flasks down to the creek," Leanna told them. "I was on watch, and the elves and HeyYou were asleep. Two hours later, when Calenderi woke up, I went looking for him. I found the flasks but no Serdic."

Dav understood why she had moved the camp. If she was right about Serdic, he could be bringing back soldiers from the fort. They could be arriving anytime.

"I found more of this," Leanna said, holding out the leaf of an herb Dav had shown her that morning. "What did you call it?"

"Lavera," Hoganvar said. "Don't know why you'd want it."

"It's good for healing inflammations," Dav replied automatically, thinking Leanna learned quickly, but his mind lingered on their possible danger. So did hers.

"If we have to fight our way to Aengmor, we might need it," Leanna said.

"We'd better leave right away," Dav said, not wanting to believe Serdic had sold them out yet not daring to deny it. The mage had boasted about his exploits. He had never pretended to honesty and integrity, so why should Dav expect it of him?

They rode north through the hills, paralleling the road but staying well away from it for safety's sake. They rode on until dark, making good time.

Dixie McKeone

When it grew too dark to ride, Dav dismounted and led his mount, and the others traveled in single file behind him. They continued into the night and were at the base of the mountains before he called a halt. They camped on a smooth, dry shelf of rock. Hoganvar took the first watch, and as Dav drifted off to sleep, he remembered the ham, bread, and apples they had brought for the others. They had been so tired they went to sleep without eating.

The food would keep until morning, he decided. He just hoped no one followed them through the night.

Chapter 11

The Construct

Struth hated the continent of Brun, his weakened arm, the winter, and having to live in caves. He especially hated this cave in the mountains of Thyatis, some ten miles northeast of Fort Zendrol.

Still, he wouldn't be there much longer, no longer than it took for the construct to locate the elf children. He had been astounded to learn the young elves the orcs had captured were the children of King Telemon, who ruled the City of Stars. The brats were royal! He could hardly believe his good fortune.

He fingered the two silken capes that lay across one end of the table. No wonder he had felt the aura of magic so strongly when he first touched the clothing that had been taken from the captured elves. The elven wizards had obviously given them protection to keep them safe.

He had periodically used a sensing spell to be sure they were still captives. Then, just over two weeks before, the children had lost their fear suddenly and become filled with hope. He had still felt the rocking of the boat, and it seemed to be drawing steadily nearer to Brun.

He had teleported to Karameikos, close to the shore, sending his spell across the water to locate the elves, but he had been sensed in turn by Terari, an old enemy.

Terari—Master Terari, he called himself—had taken in most of the stranded Alphatian wizards and lived in Karameikos, where they planned to start a school. Luckily Struth had felt the probing of the master wizard and left the country before Terari could identify the new arrival.

Struth found a cave close to the southeastern tip of the mountains in Thyatis to make it easier to detect the elves.

Using the cloaks, he sensed the storm that had given wings to the boat and swept them ashore somewhere on the eastern coast of Brun. For some reason, he hadn't been able to pinpoint their location. His sensing spell provided only vague information. If they were as close as he believed, he should know exactly where they were.

He decided he had been driving himself too hard. He had finally healed his left arm, though it was still weak. Teleporting was a strain, and he needed to keep a constant eye on the orcs.

The orcs he had subjugated in the mountains of Thyatis irritated him and gave him a good deal of trouble, but their stupidity had served him better than he expected. When they told him they had seen seven travelers in invisible cloaks, he hadn't believed them. No one *saw* invisible coats, and if a magic strong enough to bring on invisibility had been used within a hundred miles, he would have sensed it immediately.

He threatened to punish the orcs for lying, but they persisted in their story until his curiosity was roused, and he ordered them to bring him one of the garments. The coat wasn't magic. Instead, it was made of mottled cat-skin that blended so well with the natural terrain that it was hard to see. He forgave the error of the stupid orcs because the coat they brought him had an occupant, a young mage by the name of Serdic. When he put the captive under a truth spell, he discovered two of the mage's former companions were the royal elves!

Why hadn't his sensing spell warned him they were so close?

What sort of magic was preventing him from discovering their exact location? It must be some magic given them by the elf wizards, he decided. Serdic hadn't been protecting them. The young mage lacked the skill to hold off Struth's power.

Struth immediately sent out the construct to find the travelers' trail. He could see through its eyes as it searched the ground for the trail of the humans and the dwarf. When it found them, he'd send the orcs after the elves; they could do what they wished with the others.

But first a celebration was in order. He reached for his wine flask with his right hand and the cup with his left. It was a mistake. The barely healed nerves in his left arm jerked spasmodically; the cup went flying from the table, along with the clay figure of the construct.

He couldn't lose the construct now! In a flash, he cast a spell that freed the little creature from the clay figure.

The second spell in a day exhausted him. His bones felt like water, and his muscles refused to move him. He lowered his head to the rough table-top and immediately fell asleep.

* * * * *

It flew, the creature that was meant to be the distant eyes, ears, and the extension of the mind of Struth the Shaker. Distantly it felt the pain of the wounded arm and the fatigue of its master.

It had detected the camp where the enemies had waited for most of the day and had seen the faint marks of the orcs' boots when they had captured Serdic. Other tracks came from the south, bringing horses, and they had ridden north through the hills.

The tiny creature tracked them through the night. Less than an hour past dawn, it found them. Hovering high above the small group of beings, it watched. Soon the orcs would come and kill these foolish humans who interfered.

A distant pain flashed through the right arm of Struth, the larger part of itself. Rage and frustration welled up, and it saw the clay *obeah* tumble from the table. Then an emptiness, as sharp and as sudden as a blow, tore away the knowledge of that

146

larger mind.

Its greater identity was suddenly ripped away.

It was suddenly a creature apart from its master, an identity, Self.

The change came so suddenly Self momentarily lost the ability to control his mind or his wings. He fell, tumbling, out of the sky. Self struck the hard surface of flat rock, and a terrible pain shot through his left wing before he lost consciousness.

As the mind-fogging pain receded, he realized that some enormous hand, a strange human hand, was holding him. Self struggled, but pain shot through him when he tried to move his left wing.

"Let Self go! Let Self go!" he demanded.

"It can move its wing, so maybe it's not badly injured," said the man who held it. His speech seemed impossibly slow to the construct.

"Don't be afraid. I won't hurt you," the voice said softly. "Easy . . . stop fighting me. I'll turn you loose if you'll stop struggling."

"I wonder what it is," said another man-thing, smaller than the first, with a higher voice and long, golden hair. "Did your studies ever describe anything like that, Dav?"

"No," said the man-thing that held the creature. "But by its expression, I think it must be intelligent." The face came down closer. "Can you understand me?"

"Of course I can understand you, you monster! Let Self go!"

"I wish you could tell us what you are," the man said, proving he had not understood.

But his question had left Self's mouth agape in wonder. What and who was he? Self had come into being in that tearing emptiness that had separated him from his larger identity when the clay figure fell and broke. He was his own thing and could have a name of his own. But what was he, and how did he get a name?

And what about that huge part of himself that had been torn away? Separated from it, he suddenly felt frightened. He didn't want to return to it, even though his freedom terrified him.

As if to ease the tiny creature's worries, the man's finger touched him again, gently rubbing the back of his head, his neck, and down the center of his spine, between his wings. The stroking eased his fears and made him feel safe. He ceased his struggles, suddenly as anxious to stay with his captor as he had been to escape.

"Are you hungry?" the man asked. He reached for a slice of meat.

Self nodded, carefully folded his wings, and sat up on the man's hand. He wouldn't be able to eat all of that huge slab of meat that dangled between the man's two fingers, but he munched on it, staring up at the smiling face while he chewed.

"You're hurt," the man said. "You can't fly with that wing."

Self shook his head.

"Do you want to travel with us until you're fit to fly again?"

Self nodded energetically. He knew he couldn't survive in the hills alone and hurt.

Dixie McKeone

"I'll stay with you," he said, knowing he wouldn't be understood. He gripped the man's thumb with one greasy hand as he nodded.

"You'll need a name," the man-thing said. "I once had a bird I called Wherann. Do you like that name?"

Self nodded. Any name would suit him. It made him whole.

* * * * *

Dav liked the little creature. Wherann stood just over a foot tall, and except for his bat ears and wings and dark gray skin, his appearance was that of a human in miniature.

Hoganvar and HeyYou and the elves had walked down to a nearby stream to wash and fill the water flasks. When they came back to camp, the dwarf stomped over and stared at Wherann, who was sitting on Dav's outstretched leg.

"What is *that?*" he demanded, his beard bristling with suspicion. "What's it doing here?"

"I don't know, but it's hurt and hungry. I call it Wherann," Dav said.

"Humph! If you mean to pick up every stray we encounter, we'll need more horses," he grumbled.

"Can I touch it?" Erian asked. He had the fabled elvish instinct about dumb creatures.

Later, as they rode through the hills, Hoganvar led the way. HeyYou and Leanna followed. Each of the elves led two packhorses, while Dav brought up the rear with Wherann riding on his shoulder. Like the dwarf in the lead, Dav needed to be free to fight instantly. But they rode through empty lands, with the sun warming them, and Dav enjoyed being on a horse again.

* * * * *

The two orcs crouched by the wall in terror as Struth Florig paced up and down the cave.

Struth had lost the construct! In trying to protect it from destruction when he knocked the clay image off the table, he had inadvertently freed it, not only from the cantrip but from his influence. He had given it life with his own blood and wasn't sure how much of himself was in it, so it would have to be destroyed.

In accordance with Struth's orders, while the wizard slept, the orcs had slipped into Fort Zendrol and stolen four horses so they could ride with him after the elves. Without the construct to control them, however, they also took a small keg of ale. Drunk and careless, they had let Serdic escape on one of the mounts.

"Saddle the horses," Struth shouted.

When he had the elves, he would think of a suitable punishment for the stupid orcs that served him. Meanwhile, he would use the time on horseback to form a plan. He would also need a plan for the humans who traveled with the elves.

Chapter 12

Betrayed!

Wherann crouched on Leanna's shoulder and trembled in fear. He wished she'd stop trying to comfort him, stop telling him Dav would return soon, that his friend had only gone hunting.

Leanna didn't understand. Neither did Dav, or he wouldn't have left Wherann.

Away from Dav, the construct felt the terrible anger of Struth's probing mind. Wherann knew he had once been a part of that consciousness, but once he was away from it, he began to fear it. He was dimly aware of Struth's hatred and cruelty.

"I didn't try to run away," he squeaked, instinctively needing to explain his failure to the searching mind of the wizard. He shut his eyes and pictured following the trail and finding the humans. He showed Struth that he had found them by showing him the image of their camp on the flat shelf of rock. He pictured his fall and his injury. He had to make the wizard understand he hadn't been able to return.

But while Struth could feel Wherann's mind, the construct could also sense the thoughts of the wizard. Struth had received the projected images and believed Wherann and the others were still at the camp at the base of the mountains.

Wherann kept projecting the image of the first camp until Struth's mind turned away. Then the little construct relaxed. He had not deliberately communicated a lie; he hadn't known he could, but he would remember it in the future.

* * * * *

Struth the Shaker pulled himself upright in the saddle and called a halt. Behind him rode a score of orcs from a small band that lived in the mountains of Thyatis.

He had finally made mental contact with the construct, and it had given him an image of the humans, still camped at the base of the mountains on the flat rock shelf. Why hadn't they continued their journey? he wondered.

He reached behind him and pulled out the smaller of the two elven cloaks from his saddlebags and cast a sensing spell. His magic told him the elves were west of him, not back in the mountains. Then something passed between him and the elves, something he couldn't identify.

That something or someone was trying to make a fool of him, he decided. That unknown power was trying to send him on ahead, searching fruitless territory while it and the elves followed along behind at their leisure. Luckily he had the construct, who had told him they were still in the mountains north of Fort Zendrol. He had passed by the encampment, but he could return and reach it within half a day.

Then the elves would be his, and his plans would proceed on schedule. He turned back into the hills and urged the orcs to greater speed.

* * * * *

Dav was enjoying the journey. The magical climate of Ylaruam spilled over onto the great western trade route, and the days were warm and sunny. The political friction between Thyatis and Ylaruam discouraged travel in the area, and for Dav's small group, the danger had proven a boon. The dwarf had ridden on ahead of the others, watching for travelers, but for five days, they hadn't seen another traveler on the road.

Then, during the afternoon of the fifth day, the dwarf held up his hand, signaling the others to leave the road and circle behind the nearest hill. Dav rode forward to meet the dwarf. Hoganvar tugged at his beard, either angry or puzzled.

"Ylari?" Dav asked.

"No, it's one rider on a lame horse. He's slumped over like he's hurt or asleep, but it could be a trap of some kind."

"Then let's only risk one person," Dav replied. The mere suggestion of a trap had to be explored. Dav hoped it wasn't an injured traveler. They had no time to aid victims of the road. Still, he was unwilling to leave a man in need of help.

While Hoganvar led the others around the hill to the south, Dav took the road, whistling a tune as he approached the rider, careful not to startle the man he was overtaking. He forgot the tune as he rode close enough to recognize the rider.

"Serdic!" he cried, urging his horse to a gallop.

Serdic was slumped in the saddle, barely conscious. He hadn't fallen off the horse because he was tied to the saddle with a length of rope. His mare favored her right foreleg, and dried lather caked her sides.

Dav gave a shrill whistle to let Hoganvar know he hadn't ridden into a trap, then led the exhausted mare off the road.

"His fever's nearly high enough to boil," Hoganvar said after he inspected the wound to Serdic's leg. "He can't go much farther, and he's nearly ridden that horse to death."

"Find us a place to camp," Dav suggested. "I'll follow behind slowly."

By the time Dav, leading the exhausted mare, caught up with the others, Hoganvar had located a spot in a small meadow with a stream running through it. Dav took note of the eroded earthen bank in the hillside, partially roofed over with matted roots of tough grass. The bank would shelter the wounded mage from the wind.

Serdic roused as Dav helped him off the tired horse. "It would be you," he muttered.

"Rest now," Dav told him. "Don't try to talk. All

you need to do is rest."

Serdic shook his head impatiently, but his eyes lost focus and then closed. He kept muttering, but the fever had caught up with him.

"Now's the time to see if the herbs you've been gathering will do their job," Hoganvar said as he fanned a small fire to life. Dav got out two small metal bowls they used for cooking and eating. In the first, he crushed lavera and canredwaith, and in the second, he carefully placed three whole leaves of tothiel. He poured water in both while Leanna looked on.

"Those whole leaves are the ones for drawing out poisons," she said, as if reciting a lesson.

"You can remember tothiel another way," Dav said. "See how the five lobes resemble a hand? It's called the healing hand of Chardastes.

> *In time of strife and wounds and pain*
> *Seek the Immortal's hand.*
> *Health to the sick will come again*
> *As from the mage's wand.*

"It sounds better in the old tongue."

The others gathered grass to make a bed for Serdic. Even Wherann helped, staggering along under a load that would have been only a handful for Dav. By the time the medicine had boiled and cooled, they had gathered a thick pile of dry grass.

With Hoganvar's help, Dav forced the mage to drink the greenish liquid from the first bowl. They moved him into the shelter beneath the bank before attempting to clean his wounds.

Dav used the liquid from the tothiel to bathe the cuts and scrapes on Serdic's face and the deep wound on his leg. After Dav wrapped it in the tothiel leaves and bandaged it, they built a second fire close to the overhang to keep the mage warm.

"That's all we can do right now," he said when the others returned from gathering more firewood.

"I wonder if we're far enough away from the road," Leanna asked. "We crossed the tracks of a Ylari herd on the way here."

Calenderi raised her head. Her eyes lost focus. "For miles around, the breeze blows lonely across the hilltops and in the hollows. The slow thump of a rabbit . . . the bound of a deer . . . the wind does not speak of horses nor of booted footsteps."

"Where's the deer?" Dav asked. His mouth watered at the thought of fresh venison. Calenderi indicated the general direction, and Dav returned an hour later with the deer's carcass tied across the rump of the horse.

They spent the rest of the afternoon roasting meat and filling their stomachs with hot food. Hey-You found a clump of bushes loaded with wild ardor berries, a favorite of gyerians, and spent the afternoon filling his pack with the delicacies.

During the next two days, Dav used most of his supply of herbs on the mage, but it wasn't until the following afternoon that Serdic finally awoke. His eyes were clear.

Over Dav's objections, he sat up and looked around. "How long have I been here?" he asked.

When Dav told him, he shook his head as if he didn't believe him.

"Your fever is down, and HeyYou has had time to gather all the berries off the bushes. You ready to ride now?" The dwarf grinned, making a joke. The mage could barely sit up.

"No, but I must if I plan to stay alive," Serdic said. "So must you."

"Don't forget he sold information about our location," Leanna snapped.

"I didn't *sell* anything," Serdic objected. "I was waylaid by three orcs. I woke up in a cave, staring up at Struth the Shaker."

"By all the Immortals!" Hoganvar exploded. He had paled noticeably at mention of the name.

"Who's Struth the Shaker?" Leanna asked. Dav wanted to know, too.

"A very powerful wizard," Serdic replied.

"And as blackhearted as his birthplace," Hoganvar said. "You told him about the elves?"

"I probably did."

"Probably?" Leanna glared at him.

"I don't know. I don't know if he asked me anything, but if he did, I must have told him. He's one of the most powerful wizards around."

"There aren't many full-fledged wizards that could stand against Struth," Hoganvar agreed.

"As I said, I regained consciousness to see Struth staring down at me. Then I blanked out, probably under the influence of a spell. Later, when I awoke again, I was in another cave with three drunken orcs. I got this trying to escape." He indicated his wounded leg. His eyes darkened with anger as he touched the bandage.

"I'm surprised you came back," said Leanna.

"I didn't," he snapped. "This time, taking me in was your idea."

"Enough talk," Dav said. "You can't ride, so you need to eat, rest, and get your strength back."

"He's coming after you," Serdic warned.

"I don't suppose you can cast a spell to heal yourself," Dav said.

Serdic shook his head and grinned weakly. "I don't have the power or the knowledge, but Struth could do it if he happened to be in the mood."

"We'll stay here one more day," Dav said, "so get plenty of rest."

Leanna stared at him in disbelief. "He put this wizard named Struth on our trail, and we're just going to sit here and wait for him to catch up with us?"

"Awk, no wizards, no wizards! Wizards is trouble!" HeyYou squatted on the ground by Hoganvar and peered anxiously at the sunlit hills.

"Quiet," the dwarf ordered. The gyerian hunched himself into a feathered ball and gobbled quietly to himself.

"Maybe he told Struth about us and maybe he didn't," Dav said, "but we can't leave him here, and he can't ride. We'll wait another day while Serdic gets some rest."

Serdic slept most of the next thirty hours. Just after sunset of his third evening in camp, he limped over to the fire, using the crutch Hoganvar had carved for him.

"What's that?" Serdic demanded as he stared at Wherann, who sat on a stone by the fire, eating the meat off a rib bone.

The startled construct jumped to his feet and dropped his bone. He dashed over to Dav and sat on the ground close beside him, staying out of the mage's line of vision.

"That's Wherann." Dav reached for a small strip of meat and gave it to the construct to replace the food he had dropped in the dirt.

"We thought you knew. Dav gathers up every stray he can find," Leanna said as she turned the meat cooking for their evening meal. "We don't know what it is."

"It's a magical construct," Serdic said. "I've seen its *obeah*."

"A what?" Hoganvar grunted.

"Its what?" Dav puzzled over the unfamiliar word.

"Its *obeah* . . . its cantrip figure, a clay replica. I saw it on Struth's worktable. That little monster is Struth's tool. As long as he's with you, the wizard knows exactly where you are."

Wherann gave a shriek and dropped the meat. His wings opened as he climbed Dav's leg and grabbed the doeskin shirt with both tiny hands. He gibbered as he shook his head in energetic little jerks. Dav caught him around the waist and sat the construct on his knee.

"Did Struth the Shaker make you?" he asked, staring into the little face.

"If it's true, he won't admit it," Hoganvar cautioned, but the construct was already nodding. Then he gibbered urgently again.

"Have you told Struth where we are?" Dav asked and watched as Wherann shook his head in denial.

"Get rid of that thing," Serdic said. "As long as it's with you, Struth knows every move you make."

"He's right," Hoganvar agreed. "If it's a wizard's tool, it's best to kill it and be done with it."

Dav stared at Wherann. He could fight orcs and men, hydras and other monsters, but killing something as small and trusting as the construct filled him with a disgust close to horror.

"Around you, magic has no effect," Calenderi reminded Dav when Serdic explained the creation of magical beings. "Can this Alphatian wizard reach Wherann when he's close to you?"

Wherann chittered and shook his little head vigorously.

"Dav might stand against your spells or mine," Serdic answered her, "but Struth is one of the most powerful wizards on Brun. Dav could never hold out against him."

Dav wanted to deny the possibility that Wherann could betray them, but he knew his opinion was influenced by his affection for the little creature. Before he could voice his objection, Calenderi reached out and clutched his arm. She raised her head and listened to the night. Her eyes widened with fear.

"The breeze speaks of booted feet, more than a score, approaching from all directions."

"Who are they?" Hoganvar asked. His knowledge of Shiye-Lawr allowed him to understand a little of the Shadow Elf dialect, and he had learned more.

"Mostly orcs. I can hear their foul tongue, though they speak softly. One human . . . he is not as loud as the orcs."

"Get back under that overhang," Dav ordered Serdic. Leanna jumped to her feet and kicked dirt over the fire. The thin cycle of the new moon slid behind a cloud, giving them added darkness.

"Go to your master!" Dav tossed the construct into the air. He still couldn't kill Wherann, but he wanted the little creature gone from his sight. Wherann squeaked pitifully as he fluttered to the ground. Unable to fly, he trotted along behind Dav. Dav had buckled on his sword belt and was grabbing his bow and quiver when Wherann caught up with him.

"Get away from me," Dav snarled and drew back his foot as if to kick the construct. He was disgusted with himself for his inability to kill the wizard's tool, but he wouldn't allow it near him. Wherann backed off, still gibbering, holding out his tiny hands in supplication.

Dav turned away to locate the elves. While he went for his weapons, they fled the light of the fire, disappearing into the protection of the darkness. He cursed himself for letting them out of his sight. How could he protect them if he didn't know where they were?

If they ever reached their home again, it wouldn't be because of his efforts, he told himself. He had endangered their lives twice, first by bringing along the construct and again by delaying their journey while he waited for Serdic to heal. He didn't know what else he could have done, but the guilt still weighed him down. When an orc spear flew over his head and struck the ground two paces away, he had no more time for self-recriminations.

HeyYou gobbled in fear, and Hoganvar snarled at the gyerian to shut up. Dav moved away from the dwarf and his noisy companion. He wanted to protect the elves, but they had disappeared. Leanna had melted into the night as well, and Serdic, who had no weapons and was too weakened by fever to use his magic, had taken shelter under the grassy overhang.

What a mess, Dav thought as he watched for any sign of movement. If he saw a shadow, would he be shooting at an enemy or a friend? The dwarf had succeeded in quieting the gyerian, but Wherann still followed Dav, whimpering piteously.

Then suddenly he could see everything and everyone. Ten balls of light arced up into the sky. More than a score of orcs stood on the surrounding hillsides, with their spears raised high above their heads.

Chapter 13
Secret Weapon

Dav squinted against the sudden glaring illumi-
nation of the bright balls of light, but he knew he
could see as well as their orc attackers. The wizard
had overdone his spell. Or had he?

The orcs were carefully choosing their targets.
Struth would not want them to kill the Shadow
Elves. Dav took advantage of their momentary
indecision to put an arrow through the chest of the
closest orc. It fell, with its spear still raised. Dav's
bow sang again, and a second fell with an arrow
through its throat, but not before it had launched
its spear. It flew in Dav's direction, but the construct seemed to be the intended target.

Wherann squeaked in fear and leapt into the air.
The rusty spearhead plowed into the earth in the
exact spot where he had stood. His awkward flight
took him just out of the path of a second spear. Were
they trying to kill the construct? Dav wondered.

He heard the twang of Leanna's bow. She sent
one orc retreating back over the hill with an arrow

in its arm. The *thrip-thrip* of Hoganvar's crossbow had dropped one orc with a fatal shot and caught another in the thigh. Several ill-made spears landed harmlessly in the clearing at the bottom of the slope. Even the muscular arms of the orcs couldn't match the range of skilled bowmen. To get any closer meant death. The rest of the attackers dove for the shelter of the bushes, unwilling to face any more arrows.

A tiny storm of snow and ice shards rose in the air and consumed two of the balls of light before it dissipated. Calenderi had used one of her two charms.

Dav's third arrow caught another orc in the side as it scrambled for a clump of bushes. He nocked another arrow and waited for an orc to show itself. Erian's song broke the silence. The horses reared as if trained, pulled their tether stakes from the ground, and galloped off down the creek. An orc stood, spear raised, but an arrow in its chest from Leanna dropped it on the spot. The horses fled into the darkness.

Dav's gaze followed the sound and saw the elf boy crouched beside Serdic in the shelter beneath the earthen bank. A large orc had also seen them and dashed in their direction. Dav raced after him, unwilling to risk an arrow, since he might miss and hit Serdic or Erian. Hoganvar was better placed and sent a quarrel into the orc's back. The burly creature stumbled and fell against an invisible wall. Erian had used his magic to protect himself and the wounded mage.

Dixie McKeone

Dav, Leanna, and Hoganvar formed a triangle about twenty paces apart, each facing in a different direction, covering the hillsides. Not far from Hoganvar, HeyYou crouched fearfully. The waiting silence wore him down, and he started to gabble and cry again. In the dim light, Dav could see Wherann, crouching close to him. All the construct's attention centered on Dav.

The gyrating fireballs wheeled above them, making the shadows of the defenders and the bushes on the hill spin dizzily. The night seemed to gyrate with their movement, but the orcs had taken cover. In the silence, Dav could hear the soft wind.

The fireballs whirled faster, circling over the defenders. One left the circle and arced toward Dav. He ducked, but once again the construct seemed to be the target. Wherann shrieked and leapt into the air, dodging the first fireball, but as he fluttered to the ground, the glowing missile changed direction. A second streaked toward him. The construct leapt behind Dav, who felt a small thump at the small of his back.

The fireballs converged on Dav but suddenly disappeared when they were less than three feet away. He blinked in surprise, wondering what had happened. A soft chirp behind him reminded him of the construct clinging to his belt. The wizard's tool had used him for protection. What protection? Why had the fireballs disappeared?

Six fireballs still circled overhead. For a long moment, they continued in their whirling pattern, and then three flashed toward Dav, coming at him from different directions.

Calenderi gave a small scream, and her hand shot up over her mouth as she watched. Leanna shot an arrow at one fireball. Her shaft passed straight through it and fell to the ground, burning.

Dav tried to duck the first two flaming missiles, then turned and saw another streaking toward him. He froze in horror, far more willing to face a spear than risk being burned to death, but when the flaming balls were mere feet from him, they suddenly disappeared, just like the first.

On the hillside the orcs muttered in disbelief.

"Now we know," Hoganvar muttered. Dav saw the dwarf looking in his direction, his eyes reflecting the glow of the last three fireballs.

"Yes, now we know," Serdic shouted at Dav. The mage's voice sounded strangely hollow as it penetrated Erian's protective wall. "Use whatever you've got, Dav! Struth can't stop you!"

Dav bit his lip in frustration. Great! What did he have? The fireballs hadn't reached him. Did that mean none of the wizard's spells would work on him? Impossible. Who was he that he could hold off a wizard's power?

"Dav, lend a hand here," Hoganvar called out. The dwarf pulled a small pouch from beneath his tunic. As Dav reached the dwarf, Hoganvar stuck two fingers in the leather bag and tossed some white flakes in the face of the gyerian.

"Help me hold on to him," the dwarf said. He grabbed one of HeyYou's arms, and Dav caught the other one as the gyerian gasped, filling his lungs. Then he sneezed.

The force of the sneeze knocked the gyerian, the dwarf, and Dav off their feet. Dry grass, whole bushes, and even a few saplings were torn out by their roots and blew across the hill. The orcs rolled on the ground, buffeted by the gale of HeyYou's sneeze. Dav and Hoganvar scrambled to their knees as the gyerian started to gasp again. They each caught one of HeyYou's arms and turned him around. His second sneeze sent another storm against the hill to the south, blowing away the cover of the orcs.

On the third slope to the east, the orcs broke cover and fled rather than face the gyerian's potent weapon.

Dav, Hoganvar, and the gyerian struggled to their feet.

"Hate that, hate that," HeyYou squawked.

"He'd be great at clearing farmland," Dav said, awed by the force that had come from the gyerian's thin chest. His bow sang as he dropped the nearest orc. Hoganvar sent a crossbow quarrel after another, but the rest fled over the hilltop. Leanna and Calenderi ran up the hillside in hot pursuit. The elf had found the sword Dav had bought for Serdic at Fort Zendrol.

"Wait a minute!" he shouted at them. "What's the use of getting rid of the orcs if you go after them?" he called after them.

"Who can understand females?" Hoganvar muttered as he sprinted up the hill after Dav.

Leanna and Calenderi stopped just before they reached the top, crouching as they peered over the bank to the other side. Dav skidded to a halt when he reached them. Halfway down the far slope, they saw seven orcs, their backs to the defenders as they faced a tall, slender man in long, dark robes. By his gestures, he was ordering the orcs back up the hill, but they had lost their taste for the fight. He pointed a finger at the largest, who shook its head as it backed away.

"They're afraid of you," Calenderi said.

Dav had already come to the same conclusion. It filled him with heady excitement. He was also enraged. On the Great Escarpment, he had chosen his opponents. Ever since he left home, someone or something had been chasing him, attacking him, or interfering with his plans. He had had enough.

"So they think I'm a wizard. Suppose I give them something to be afraid of," he said, handing his bow to Calenderi and picking up an orc spear. He raced across the top of the hill, the spear in his right hand, his sword in his left.

Behind him, he heard the cries of objection from the others, and the construct's squeak of fear. He felt something bounce against his back and realized the construct still clutched his belt. He would have shaken it off, but his hands were full of weapons.

"Hisamor! Akin! Awan!" he shouted, choosing syllables at random. That should confuse them. It confused him. He wouldn't be able to repeat it if he tried.

The first orc turned to meet him and caught his thrown spear in its chest as Dav's momentum behind the throw drove it between the metal disks attached to the orc's heavy leather coat. The others jabbered in fear and backed away, seeking shelter behind the wizard.

The tall robed man raised his hand and muttered an incantation.

"Cafadra errus," he called, pointing his finger at Dav.

Since he had thrown the spear, Dav's right hand was empty. He hadn't had time to transfer his sword. He pointed a finger at the wizard and repeated the words that still seemed to hang in the air.

"Cafadra errus," he shouted back at the wizard.

Struth the Shaker was knocked into the air and fell ten feet away, as if some giant fist had struck him. He tumbled into the orcs who stood behind him.

Dav skidded to a halt and stared, stunned by his own success.

Struth heaved himself to his feet, his hands weaving in front of him. One of the fireballs came down to hang in the air between them. He stared at Dav.

"You!" he shouted, apparently as surprised as Dav. The wizard's hands and lips moved again, but he kept his voice low so Dav couldn't hear his incantation. Then he disappeared. The fireball died, falling to the ground in a puddle of white ash.

The orcs babbled in fear, then ran down the hill

and disappeared into the night. They shouted to their comrades, and Dav heard the sound of heavy boots receding into the distance.

When they were gone, Dav turned and walked back up the hill, his mind roiling with questions. The orcs he understood. They were fierce fighters, but stupid and frightened by anything they couldn't understand.

But the *wizard!*

Dav's knees weakened and his hands trembled as he returned to the others. How could he have been fool enough to challenge a wizard? And how had he succeeded? Dav recalled that Struth thought he had recognized him. Why? Did the wizard see a resemblance to Dav's real father?

He ignored the questions of the others as he led the way back to the campsite. Erian and Serdic left the shelter of the small grass and earthen overhang and joined them as Hoganvar raked away the dirt and exposed a few glowing coals.

"Is it safe to start the fire again?" the dwarf asked Calenderi.

She listened a moment and nodded. "The wind travels across empty hills. It brings word only of the few that are still fleeing."

"And Struth?" Dav asked.

"He is heard by other breezes in other regions," the elf princess replied.

Leanna added more wood to the fire. Calenderi pulled the sticks of partially roasted meat out of the ground and took them to the stream to wash away the dirt Leanna had kicked on them when she covered the fire. Hoganvar picked up his own pack and HeyYou's, which had been kicked away in the excitement, and shook out his and the gyerian's cat-skin cloaks.

Dav sat staring into the fire. Hoganvar told Serdic about Dav's encounter with the wizard while Calenderi explained it to Erian. Dav listened, hoping they might have noticed something that would give him a clue to understanding what had happened. When Hoganvar finished his story, Serdic eyed Dav with a twinkle in his eye.

"I think it's time you told us who you are," he said evenly.

"I thought I'd given you enough hints by now," Dav replied, his nonchalance disguising his irritation at the question. His anger was not at Serdic for asking, but at his own lack of understanding. "I'm Lake Amsorak at the moment. Next month I'll be the Streel River."

"We need to know the truth." Leanna had no time for jokes. "With a wizard on our trail, knowing what to expect could save our lives. He recognized you."

"He did not recognize me," Dav said slowly, pronouncing each syllable with exaggerated care. "He has never even seen me before now. I don't know what he thought." Dav still wasn't ready to admit Struth might have recognized a resemblance between him and his real father. "And for the last time, I have no magical training. I wouldn't know an incantation if I fell over it! I just repeated what Struth said and pointed my finger at him."

Dixie McKeone

"Why?" Serdic asked. "Why did you do it?"

"Foolish bravado," Dav admitted. "He didn't touch me with his spell, and I just repeated it . . . making fun of him, I suppose. The result probably scared me more than it did him." Dav stared into the fire, which crackled and sizzled as the grease from the meat dripped into the flames.

"The only magic I've ever used is this light charm." Dav pulled the white metallic disk from beneath his tunic and looked at it. "And you said I had used up all its power." He had decided to keep the charm even if it no longer served any real purpose. He rubbed a spot of dirt from its smooth surface, wishing it still held some of its power. The light flashed out as brightly as ever, causing the elves to flinch and cover their eyes.

A squeak of fear behind him startled Dav. He turned in time to see Wherann scuttle away, frightened by the brilliance.

"So much for my ability to detect magic," Serdic said, still speaking of the charm as Dav hastily tucked it back inside his shirt.

He had turned and was gazing at Wherann. The construct had shown a desperate desire to stay with his human friend. Even when Dav had threatened him, the little creature had continued to follow him.

"I'm sorry, Wherann," he said, holding out his hand. "I think we've been blaming you for something you didn't do."

Wherann approached cautiously, his wings half open and quivering, ready to take instant flight.

174

Hesitantly he touched one finger of Dav's outstretched hand, curled his tiny fingers around it, and allowed himself to be led close to the fire.

"I don't believe you're Struth's servant any longer," Dav said. "He wouldn't have tried to kill you if you were. Friends again?"

Wherann nodded emphatically and seemed to forget all the unpleasantness. The construct walked closer to the fire and stood looking up at the sizzling meat on the stick. When he turned and chittered at Leanna, she laughed.

"For him, everything is back to normal," she said.

Before long the meat was ready. They put aside the discussion to eat.

Dav sat thinking. Struth had mistaken him for someone. He wished he could have asked who.

He still had no idea what protected him from magic, but he believed he had only reflected Struth's own power. If he was right, the wizard would be too smart to let him do it again. And they *would* meet again. Dav was sure of it.

* * * * *

Hugin and Mugin, the two ravens, flew about Odin's head as he paced. They were sensitive to the moods of the Immortal, and their agitation matched his.

Every time Reddican's charm had been used, the Immortals had sensed it. Its owner sometimes used it for minor magic, but a tremor had gone

through the foundations of Pandius when its
owner threw a stronger spell.

Then, less than an hour later, the Immortals had
sensed a minor use of the charm again. It had been
used three times within a matter of weeks.

Someone was learning to use the magic. Was the
carrier of Reddican's charm preparing to challenge
the Immortals?

Chapter 14

The Bones of the World

"We should move on now, before Struth can gather up his orcs," Leanna suggested when they had finished their meal. No one disagreed.

Dav was never adverse to traveling. In fact, he begrudged every stop, counting the minutes until they were on the trail again. He could never forget the cloud of war and death that hung over Aengmor and Darokin.

In less than an hour, they were back in their saddles. Calenderi led, using her ability to see in the dark to choose a safe trail, and her wind hearing to listen for danger. Hoganvar followed her. Dav, with Wherann on his shoulder, rode at the end of the column as usual.

Hoganvar thought they had made their three-day camp directly south of the Ylari city of Hedjazi. They rode through the next four nights, resting during the day. On the second night, they crossed the trade route that ran from Ctesiphon in Ylaruam to Fort Nikos in the mountains of Thyatis.

On the fifth night, it rained, so they took inadequate shelter on the leeward side of a hill and began their journey during the day. They traveled during daylight for six more days, and had traveled halfway through the seventh when Calenderi raised a hand for quiet.

"The wind speaks of hard-ridden horses," she said. "Only orcs treat their mounts so cruelly. They are still a great distance back."

Dav looked around, wondering whether they should try to outdistance their pursuers, hide, or take up a defensible position.

"Not much cover ahead." Hoganvar tugged at his beard. "The hills are mighty barren and empty hereabouts."

Dav turned his head to the left, eying the mountains.

"Be easier to defend ourselves up there." The dwarf understood his gaze and agreed with his unspoken assessment.

"Mountains is trouble," HeyYou gobbled.

Dav agreed, but the only other option was the barren hills where they could be surrounded as they had been when they first encountered Struth and his orcs. The ploy they had used to drive the orcs off the first time might not work again. He stroked Wherann's head. The construct's wing had healed, and he was able to fly again.

"Find us a safe path into the mountains," he told the construct. He ordered Calenderi to take the lead and listen for danger ahead. Erian followed her, singing to the pack animals to keep them moving. HeyYou and Serdic rode with them while the dwarf, Leanna, and Dav brought up the rear.

They rode on at full gallop until they reached the end of the long valley. Ahead, the slopes were steep, leading into the mountains. By the time Dav and Hoganvar caught up with the rest of the group, Calenderi had jumped off her horse and was leading it up the side of a cliff that rounded a break in the hill. Erian and the packhorses followed her, but HeyYou stood in his stirrups, hauling back on the reigns with all his strength. Leanna's horse had caught the tension of her anger, sidling and bucking.

"Tell her to come back," the girl shouted at Dav. "If she gets trapped up there, there's no room for the horses to turn around."

Dav shivered as he looked at the elves walking the horses along the cliff path, but he saw something Leanna had missed.

"She won't get trapped." He pointed at the large tracks on the open soil at the base of the cliff. They all led to the cliff path.

"That's the print of a giant elk." Hoganvar had also recognized it.

"If a beast that large went up that ledge, then we can make it," Serdic agreed. "Sorry I didn't notice it. Had a few other things on my mind."

"I wonder why," Hoganvar muttered with a grin as he dismounted and shouted to HeyYou. "Get down, you feather-necked beast, and haul that horse up after the elves."

"Serdic, you'd better ride as long as you can," Dav said as he dismounted. The moment he freed his mount, it started up the trail after the singing elf boy. The other horses seemed eager for the climb as well. Serdic's went last, carrying the mage since he was unable to walk. Behind him, the others ascended on foot, glad they didn't have to worry about the horses if Struth and the orcs caught up with them.

Hoganvar stamped on the rock and patted the cliff wall. "Good sound stone," he said. "Bones of the world. Dwarves were made from stone."

Serdic, riding just ahead of them, looked back over his shoulder. "I always thought dwarves were made of bluster and blow."

"And mages and displacer beasts come from the same place," Leanna retorted. "You never know where you are with either one."

They continued to climb throughout the dwindling afternoon. The string of horses separated them from the elves in the lead, so Dav couldn't tell how Calenderi and Erian were faring. And where was Wherann? The construct had been gone a long time.

Another half hour passed before he saw a dark speck in the sky. As it flew nearer, he saw tiny legs and arms dangling from beneath the wide, dark gray wings. Wherann darted toward them and pulled up suddenly in front of Dav, hovering as he chittered and waved them back, indicating they should return the way they came.

"What is it? Is it a blind trail?" Hoganvar asked.

"Told you it was trouble," HeyYou announced triumphantly. "Told you."

"Keep your beak shut!" the dwarf groused.

Dav ignored them. Wherann had understood the dwarf and shook his head.

"Where are the elves? Can they reach the top?" Dav asked and watched as Wherann nodded.

"It's trouble, it's trouble," HeyYou said, and Wherann nodded energetically.

"Then let's get up this cliff," Leanna urged. She pulled her sword and hurried after the horses. "I'm not losing my reward now," she called back, as if needing to explain her haste.

They were all puffing by the time they reached the top of their climb, but they hadn't reached the end of the narrow cliff path yet. It wound its way down for several hundred feet before giving out onto a stony slope. Calenderi and Erian were sitting on a boulder waiting for the others. The horses were placidly cropping at the dry grass.

"But there's nothing here," Leanna complained to Wherann, who lit on Dav's shoulder as they reached the elves. He sat with his wings half extended, as if ready to take flight.

"Something frightened him," Dav said, but if any danger threatened, Calenderi's acute hearing would have warned her.

Serdic stiffly climbed down from his horse and limped a few paces, stretching his injured leg. He frowned at the blade in Dav's hand.

"You're forgetting one thing. Wherann can feel threatened by creatures we'd totally ignore. Under the right circumstances, a rabbit could be a danger to him."

Dixie McKeone

Wherann squeaked an angry denial, but Dav reluctantly sheathed his sword.

Hoganvar tucked his axe back in his belt. "Going back means running into Struth. Besides, we'd never get down that trail by nightfall."

"No, we can't go back," Dav agreed.

"We need to find shelter before dark." Serdic climbed painfully back into the saddle. The others mounted their horses, and Dav led the way down the trail.

Their only possible path led west through a narrow defile between two peaks. Dav's worries increased with every step the horse took. The narrow trail became a narrow rocky gorge.

They had left behind the magically induced warmth of Ylaruam and were feeling the bite of the winter winds. Behind Dav, the Shadow Elves were huddled in their saddles in little humps of misery. Wherann crept down from Dav's shoulder and crawled inside his cat-skin coat. He kept chittering, his small face with its large eyes raised to look at the human.

"I wish you could talk," Dav said, wondering what the little fellow would say if he could. He looked down, watching the construct as it listened. Wherann's movements were so quick his moments of stillness were more noticeable than they would be in a larger being. So very quick. Impossibly quick for most species.

Was it possible . . . ?

"Try to say my name, but say it very slowly. D-a-v." He watched as the construct's mouth moved more slowly than before, but the squeak was still unintelligible.

"Try it again. This time drag the word out very, very slowly. D-D-D-a-a-a-a-v-v."

"Dv."

"You *can* talk, can't you?" Dav exclaimed. "You just speak so quickly we couldn't understand you."

Wherann nodded, chittered, and tried again to slow his words.

"Dgn. Dgn. Dgn-dgn-drgn."

Dav had been looking down at Wherann, trying to understand what the construct was trying to say. The trail turned sharply, and suddenly he understood the warning.

Dragon!

A blue dragon stood right in front of him.

Chapter 15

Messing with Dragons

Dav's horse reared, nearly throwing him from the saddle. Wherann sprang from beneath Dav's coat and tumbled, spreading his wings just before he hit the ground.

Caught by surprise, Dav's left foot parted with the stirrup, and he slid to the ground, clutching the reins in one hand while he pulled out his sword with the other. For a moment, he stood eye-to-eye with the monster while the horse shied back and tried to free itself.

Some odd part of his mind seemed to laugh at him. As a child, he had played games in which he killed dragons in his imagination. See where it got you? his mind teased.

The monster had been asleep, but the noise of the frightened horse startled it. It stared at Dav. A deep rumble started in the dragon's chest and came out its mouth as the deepest, longest whine Dav had ever heard.

The dragon definitely whined.

Dav stared at the creature. When he had first seen it, his panic caused it to loom huge in his mind. Once he brought his fear under control, he realized it was less than fifteen feet long. Its head and feet were disproportionately large in comparison to its body—a very young blue dragon.

It crouched close to the rock wall. The crisp, clean break in the stone of the mountain showed a fresh slide. The dragon's left forefoot was caught somewhere beneath the tumble of rock.

Just beyond the dragon sprawled two huge bodies. Frost giants, Dav decided by their pale skins and yellow hair. One was half buried, and all that could be seen of it was its head and one arm. The other had been thrown partially clear, but the odd angle of its head showed its neck had been broken in the fall. Both wore fur clothing and heavy armor. Among the rocks of the slide were the remains of two huge spears.

The dragon whined again. Like any young, frightened creature, it begged for help.

"You're a brave little fellow if you took on those two," Dav said to the dragon. Both giants were nearly twenty feet tall. "And you got yourself in quite a fix." He sheathed his sword.

Erian had quieted the horses. Leanna and Hoganvar squeezed past the others and stopped just inside the narrow rock passage, their weapons drawn. Serdic eased his horse forward to see what was happening without dismounting.

"His foot is caught," Dav explained. "It looks as if he tried to climb after the frost giants. You can see their trail up there at the top of the break. The rock wall couldn't hold his weight, I guess."

Leanna and Hoganvar stared from Dav to the dragon and back again. Serdic, still astride his horse, shook his head.

"No, Dav."

"What do you mean, no?"

"Absolutely not!" Hoganvar glared at him.

"What are you talking about?"

"You've picked up every stray on our trail," Leanna said, standing on tiptoe in an attempt to meet him eye-to-eye. "But I draw the line at a dragon. *No dragons!*"

"Thank you." Hoganvar bowed to Leanna. She suddenly remembered the dwarf and the gyerian had been two of the strays they had rescued and reddened in embarrassment.

"I didn't mean you, Hoganvar. I didn't mean . . ." She threw a dissatisfied look at Serdic but didn't mention him. "But Dav *can't* have a *dragon*."

"Dragons is trouble," HeyYou squawked. He poked his head out from behind one of the horses but stayed well back, out of danger.

"I'd give a couple of silver pieces to see Struth's face if we did have one with us." Hoganvar grinned and then seemed to realize what he was saying. He lowered his brows and glowered at Dav. "But nobody has any business messing around with dragons."

Dav realized they understood him better than he knew himself. He had been wondering how to free the creature.

"I didn't say a word about taking it with us," he objected. "But if we leave it trapped, it will starve." He walked closer, inspecting the rubble around the monster's foot. "Besides, I was taught that blue dragons aren't necessarily evil, but frost giants always are. If it hunts frost giants, it's really doing a service to people. . . ."

"Stop pulling my leg until it heals," Serdic said.

"Don't you think we've got troubles enough?" Leanna demanded.

"Not nearly enough." Hoganvar sheathed his battle-axe and stumped forward, inspecting the slide. "We've only got a wizard and his orcs after us and all of Brun trying to find the elves. Besides, there's nothing we can do." He pointed up at two huge slabs of stone leaning against each other. They were precariously balanced against a third smaller, but still immense, boulder that disappeared into the rubble.

"Move any one of those three masses of stone and the others will fall and crush your friend before he can get out of the way."

"There has to be something we can do," Dav persisted.

"It's a hard world," Hoganvar said, shaking his head.

"There's nothing we can do, so let's move on," Serdic advised. Dav glared at him, ready to retort, but stopped himself when he saw the pain and fatigue in the mage's face.

"The elves need shelter from this wind. They're not used to the cold," Leanna reminded him.

Dixie McKeone

"Then go on," Dav snapped. Frustration over the young trapped dragon made him angry. They were right; he had no business messing around with dragons, but magic couldn't have held him any tighter than his sympathy. He sighed.

"I'll catch up with you, but I'm not leaving without trying to do something." He turned his back on the others and walked over to the dragon as they led the horses out of the defile and into the small valley.

"I'm going to move a few rocks and see if there's anything I can do," he told the small blue. He picked up a stone and carried it away. As he turned back, Wherann flew to the ground, picked up a pebble barely over an inch in diameter, and went trudging off with it. Dav stifled a laugh, yet when he considered the difference in their sizes, Wherann carried a similar load.

"Together we'll manage to get it done, won't we, little fellow?"

Wherann nodded and the dragon rumbled, turned its head, and picked up a boulder with its mouth. Then it gave a sharp twist of its neck and hurled it across the small valley.

Hoganvar gave a yelp, and Dav jerked around to see the dwarf dodging the rock the dragon had tossed. At the far side of the cliff wall, Leanna removed the saddles and the packs. Erian, Calenderi, and HeyYou gathered wood and brush.

"Got to camp somewhere," Hoganvar grumbled. He eyed the dragon with distrust, but helped Dav to remove rocks. Wherann labored in the spirit of

188

the task, and the dragon moved as many of the larger boulders as it could reach.

In a few minutes, the fire burned merrily, but after a short time warming themselves, Leanna, Calenderi, and HeyYou came trudging over. After Calenderi removed her third rock, she stopped and stared up at the darkening sky.

"The wind sings of giant wings," she said, and almost immediately a huge shadow darkened the little valley and a giant dragon descended.

"I think mama has arrived," Hoganvar said as he stared up at the monster. His black beard contrasted sharply with his pale face. Leanna, Hey-You, and Calenderi backed up against the sheer rock wall beyond the pile of rubble.

Dav considered dropping his rock and pulling his sword, but to what purpose? It took a magical weapon to hold off a creature that size.

As he watched the giant blue descend, he saw three long scars that crossed her breast. He felt the awe of a legend taking on reality. The smaller dragon raised its head and caroled to its arriving parent. It extended its right wing, covering Dav and Hoganvar. Leanna, Calenderi, and the gyerian rushed behind the protective wing while Wherann flew up on Dav's shoulder.

Both dragons rumbled deep in their chests, and Dav knew the great beasts were speaking to each other. The younger one was doing most of the talking. Then the wing was withdrawn, and one great, slitted eye of the big female dragon stared at the company.

"You assist the foolish youngling of my lair, human?" The dragon spoke in Thyatian.

Dav gulped and bowed. "We make an honest attempt, Great Bletinferelth, most magnificent of creatures," he said, remembering that dragons liked to be complimented. "It is our wish to assist him, though we lack your great strength."

Bletinferelth inspected him closely. "It is long since my name traveled on the wind. You are a master of dragon lore, human?"

"Your name is still spoken among us," Dav replied. "The Battle of Many Days, in which the evil shamans of Akkila-Kahn trapped you and tried to bring about your death, is a story often told. Though the lives of humans are short, many still tell of your brave fight and the shameful way you were tricked." The others were staring at him with strange expressions, but he ignored them.

"I was then only young," Bletinferelth rumbled.

"If our small strength can help to free your young one, we hope it will soften your mind to those who tread lawfully in this land."

She stared at him for a tense moment that seemed to stretch painfully before she turned her attention to Hoganvar. "Dwarves are knowing about the movement of stone."

The dwarf explained the dangers of trying to move the huge balanced slabs of rock. "The trick is to keep both those big slabs from falling while we raise the bottom stone so he can remove his foot. I don't yet see a way to do it."

"My foot was caught in the tree," HeyYou spoke

up suddenly. "My foot was caught in the tree."
Everyone stared at the gyerian as if HeyYou had
lost his wits.

"Quiet," Hoganvar snapped, still considering the
problem.

"One hand wouldn't free my foot. One hand
wouldn't do it," the gyerian chattered.

"I told you to shut up!" Hoganvar shouted at the
gyerian. "If we don't think of something, she might
make a meal of us."

"Took two hands, awk, *two* hands. Took *two*
spells to knock the wizard down, *two* spells. . . ."

Hoganvar lost patience with his companion. He
whirled and advanced on the bird creature. "I
mean it. . . ."

Leanna jumped between them. "HeyYou is right!
Two levitation spells will lift the two slabs." She
turned to Dav, her face shining with her idea.
"When Struth used that incantation to try to knock
you down, all you did was repeat his words and you
got a stronger spell," Leanna said. "We could do the
same thing here. Calenderi can levitate. You repeat
her words, and together the two of you can raise
the slabs."

"You want me to raise one stone while Dav re-
peats the spell and raises a second?" asked Calenderi. "I don't know if it would work."

"There's still the smaller boulder trapping his
foot," Hoganvar reminded them as he tugged at his
beard.

"And I could not lift one of the slabs," Calenderi
said. "My power isn't great enough."

"But there's a third power here—the physical strength of Bletinferelth," Hoganvar said. "She could hold the left slab in place while Dav raises the right one. Then if you could raise the small bottom boulder until the youngling can just get his foot out and get away from the slide . . ."

Up on the mountain, a rock broke free and tumbled down, narrowly missing the young dragon.

Bletinferelth ended the discussion. "We will do this thing you have said. You will all stand out away from the cliff wall."

"But I don't know what to do after I repeat the words," Dav told Calenderi as they backed away from the slide. "There has to be more to a levitation spell than just repeating words."

"Just think where you wish the slab to be," Calenderi said. "Use your hands as if you were holding it. That might help your concentration."

"I don't like this," Dav muttered, but Bletinferelth had made the decision, and Dav knew better than to argue. The large dragon crept closer to the cliff, rising to brace one foot against the stone wall, the other one poised to grab the slab on the left.

Dav and Calenderi stood just inside the narrow upper entrance of the valley, where they both had a view of the stones they would attempt to levitate. The others grouped behind them.

Calenderi stood for a moment composing herself and then held out her hands, palms up. Dav mimicked her actions. She began to speak slowly and clearly, and he repeated her words sound for sound.

He felt a weight on his mind, as if the giant slab of rock were slowly crushing it. The pressure seemed to darken his vision. He was afraid of raising his hands, afraid the movement would smash his mind to powder, but Calenderi moved hers. Her slender wrists and hands seemed to be straining in the effort.

He raised his hands slightly, testing. The weight was no worse on his mind, but a shower of pebbles bounced down from the huge slab as it moved. Bletinferelth grasped the second slab and rumbled deep in her chest as she held it steady.

Calenderi's hands came up, and the young dragon, Bluenstrinel, cautiously pulled his foot free. He scrambled away as Bletinferelth lost her grip on her slab and it came crashing down, breaking into huge hunks that bounced down to the valley floor.

The elf princess jerked her hands away and covered her sensitive ears. Dav held his slab for a moment before he let go, adding another giant crash to the echoing noises.

A hunk of rock broke loose and came hurtling in their direction. Dav grabbed Calenderi and jerked her back into the narrow defile. Over the noise, he heard HeyYou squawking and the dwarf shouting. The horses were squealing in fear. Then Bluenstrinel roared in pain.

When the rocks stopped bouncing, they saw the young dragon curled in a knot, licking his tail. Bletinferelth sat by the wall of the valley, watching her offspring moaning over his injury.

"He should consider himself fortunate that his disobedience didn't cause him greater harm," she told Dav. He wondered if the youngling would be punished when he returned to the lair, but he had something else on his mind.

"You spoke of gratitude," Dav said and paused as Bletinferelth drew back her head warily, her eyes lit with a terrible glow.

"I don't speak of your treasure hoard," he added quickly, afraid she might burn him to ash. The dangerous glow died out of her eyes, and her head came down close to him.

"You do not seek treasure?"

"We seek the quickest, safest way into Aengmor," Dav told her. "You fly wide and see much."

"I do you no service to help you to reach the Forest Canolbarth," the dragon said, turning her head to the west as if she could see through solid rock. "The people of the twisted trees prepare for war, as do the ones from the city to the west of the blighted wood. Already the humans of the river plains are marching. Yet to turn back on your trail is unwise. A wizard and his minions are even now climbing the ledge to reach this place."

"We must escape this wizard and reach the blighted forest," Dav said. "Our coming will stop the war before it begins."

"The battles of restless, short-lived people do not interest me," she said, "but if you seek the shortest route, you could travel the path of Iscranin, the greatest of the annelids."

"Trouble, awk, trouble," HeyYou gobbled from

the shadows, and Dav realized the others had drawn closer to listen.

"We don't want to be eaten," Dav objected.

"Iscranin exists no more. Few of your kind walked this land when he traveled beneath these mountains, leaving passages greater, wider, and straighter than your puny roads. The hills trembled and peaks fell when he burrowed into the lair of Yealeletherveri, the great red dragon. Neither survived the battle." Her eyes glittered with the avarice of dragonkind. "Do not waste your time searching for the red one's hoard."

"The treasure we seek is peace and trust among peoples," Dav said. "We must reach Aengmor. What dangers would we find in those tunnels?"

"The sounds of annelids tunneling no longer echo from these mountains," she said. "What other creatures you may find, I do not know. It is long since I walked those dark regions, but there is less life below than above. A break in the roof of a tunnel lies just beyond those rocks." She turned her great head to look at a huge tumble of boulders. "Through it, you can reach the darkened wood. No path will be straighter. Now I must take the youngling back to my lair." She scratched the ground, seemingly unwilling to leave. She lowered her head and gazed into Dav's eyes. "You will from this time forth call yourself friend of Bletinferelth and Bluenstrinel." She sprang into the air. The young dragon followed her. The force of air under their wings knocked the party to the ground. They got to their feet, coughing in the dust. Hoganvar was the first to clear his throat.

"Underground . . . now, that's the way to travel."

"But we could lose our way," Leanna objected. "We could get lost and never find our way out."

"With two Shadow Elves and a dwarf?" Hoganvar's look suggested she had lost her mind. "And you heard the dragon say there were no more annelids below these mountains."

"But what else might be down there?" Dav asked softly.

* * * * *

Hundreds of miles to the southeast, the merits of traveling underground were on the mind of Korshnid Hatelight. He, too, was making plans for a journey and trying to decide on his course.

Korshnid's orc-elven blood was diluted with the ale he had been drinking, so he thought lazily about his options as he watched his band of twenty-three outlaws caper drunkenly around the natural cavern. Three trolls danced awkwardly, singing a slow, ponderous song in their own foul tongue. They lost the thread and started over from the beginning. The fourth troll tended the wide beds of live coals, where two whole ponies were being roasted.

Korshnid frowned. The theft of the ponies from the nearby town of Threshold would bring the soldiers of Karameikos down on them before long. Well, no matter. The ale would be running out soon, and they would be on their way to Aengmor.

Dixie McKeone

The six kobolds watched the trolls, hoping for a share of the meat. The trolls were not generous, but Ackvig, the kobold shaman, would change their minds with a spell. Too much ale weakened the little dog-faced kobolds, and they hadn't been able to hunt for several days.

Neither the eight orcs nor the five goblins were bothered by the drink, though the sixth goblin had fallen off a cliff when he tried to hunt in bright sunlight.

Goblins were fools, Korshnid thought as he watched them caper around their fire, where a wild boar was roasting. They should only hunt at night, since the glare of the sun made them half blind.

Korshnid suffered from the same weakness. He hated it because it pointed out his half-breed ancestry. But the day-blindness was his only physical drawback. He could outwalk all but the eight-foot-tall trolls without tiring. He could see better in the deep caverns than even the goblins, and his quick mind found all the humanoid races, particularly the orcs, to be slow and stupid.

His big mistake had been in showing his intelligence too blatantly before he had followers. If he had waited, matured, and gathered a little more wisdom, he might be sitting on the throne in Oenkmar instead of that fat lout, Thar.

Instead, he was sitting in a natural cavern, watching his drunken troop enjoy themselves. Their party had started several weeks ago when they had sold the Shadow Elves to the Hattian, Gorval.

Son of Dawn

Just thinking of the sale enraged him, and he jerked in his impatience, spilling some of his ale. He had sold them for slaves, when he could have gotten a hundred times the price for them as hostages, but he hadn't known they were royal. Gorval hadn't known it either.

Still, there was more money to be had. Gorval had told him he would take any of the pale elves the half-orc could capture. There were mine owners in the islands who would pay well for elves, who could live in the darkness where humans often died from lack of light and fresh air.

Korshnid shifted as he thought pleasantly of the battles awaiting them when they raided the dark forest to the north. No need to go underground for the elves. There were enough on the surface. He'd fill the Hattian's boat with captives.

There would be fine battles, he'd be killing or selling into slavery the hated Shadow Elves, and he would be paid for it.

They'd start north in a few days, just as soon as the ale ran out.

Chapter 16

Split Company

"Told them how to do it, I did." HeyYou stretched his neck and puffed out his chest feathers. "Told them."

"That you did, old featherbrain," Hoganvar replied as they resaddled the horses. "If you hadn't thought of it, we might be filling old Bletinferelth's stomach right now." He glanced at the others and hurrumphed. "Of course, I'll never hear the end of it now that I've admitted he was right," he said gruffly.

They had decided to take the tunnel of the annelids to avoid the mountain's winter storms and hopefully avoid another meeting with the wizard, Struth.

"What I don't understand," Serdic spoke up as he sat on a stone and wound dry grass around a length of tree limb for a torch, "is why you let that dragon off so easily. You could have demanded a payment large enough to make us all wealthy."

"A fortune doesn't interest him," Leanna said,

her disgust plain as she threw the saddle on her horse. "It's against his morals to be paid for his efforts, or ours either."

"We should have had a say in that decision," Hoganvar agreed, glaring at Dav. "Dragons have more than they can count, and it wouldn't have hurt to increase our purses."

"And how much gold could you carry with a wizard on your trail?" Dav asked, refusing to admit Bletinferelth's malevolent stare when he mentioned a reward had scared him into backing down.

Calenderi raised her head to listen. "Many voices travel on the wind," she said softly. "The neighs of frightened horses who do not like being lifted. Orcs muttering in fear."

"Sounds as if Struth is doing some levitating of his own," Serdic said, painfully scrambling to his feet and drawing his sword. Dav rose but left his weapons sheathed.

"Let's move," he said.

They followed Hoganvar, who led the way to the partially hidden mouth of the cave he had found while the others were breaking camp. Erian followed the dwarf, singing to the horses as they picked their way down a boulder-strewn passage. Serdic lit two torches and gave Hoganvar one. Leanna and Dav brought up the rear, walking in the darkness as they listened for following footsteps.

They had been traveling for half an hour through natural caverns when they entered the huge passage created by the annelid. The tunnel was round, at least thirty feet in diameter and nearly a complete circle. It was slightly broader near the floor. It stretched away into the darkness.

"We can mount up now," the dwarf called, striding back for his horse. "Luck is with us. This part of the tunnel runs to the northwest, straight toward Aengmor."

Calenderi rode by the dwarf to listen for danger, while Leanna and Dav brought up the rear again. Leanna kept turning her head, looking over her shoulder.

"That light of yours would help," she said.

"Rk, rk," Wherann squeaked, warning Dav of a large rock in their path.

"The elves and Wherann can see in the dark," he said as he guided the horse around a small boulder and scattering of stones. He didn't tell her he was also afraid the light might help Struth find them.

They rode on for another three hours, but the horses were tiring. Hoganvar paused at a small passage and dismounted to pass under the low ceiling. The rest followed. Dav helped Serdic until they had rounded two sharp bends. The dwarf stopped by a narrow stream that had cut a shallow channel in the floor.

"At least the horses can drink," he said.

Calenderi appeared out of the darkness ahead and leapt across the little stream. She carried a chunk of what looked like gray stone, but it broke easily in her hands. When she offered it to her mount, the horse sniffed and then bit into it with obvious relish.

"It's mungan," she told Dav. "It's a fungus that grows in mounds on cavern floors. The orcs that captured us brought their beasts down into the tunnels and fed them on mungan." She gazed at the horse with wonder. "Our people have always thought it was useless, but we have no horses in the deep caverns."

Calenderi led her mount across the shallow stream, and the others followed. Dav helped Serdic as he struggled to keep up.

Around the next bend, the tunnel ended in a large natural cavern. The floor glistened with moisture. A forest of stalactites and stalagmites grew to meet each other, reminding Dav of an open mouth with sharp teeth.

Several types of fungus covered large areas of the floor and grew on the stone pillars. Several areas of the floor were covered with mungan, an uneven growth that rose in three-foot peaks and resembled miniature hill country. The outer surface of the fungus formed a tough, leatherlike covering, but beneath it, the crisp gray, porous meat gave off a fresh scent that lightened the air of the cavern. The horses happily chomped on it.

While the others hacked at the mungan, Erian led HeyYou over to a small forest of tall dry fungus, and they pulled off dry sticks of strider wood.

"We can make a fire from this," he said, his voice traveling across the cavern. "Then we can get warm. You'll like this, HeyYou. It's good for torches, too."

They were still feeding the animals when Calenderi suddenly grabbed Dav's arm.

"The orcs follow," she said.

"How close?" Dav asked. "How many?"

"Not far, but I don't know their number. The air does not move here, so it cannot speak of all that passes."

While Erian kept the horses quiet, the others drew their weapons and waited. Before long, they heard the sound of heavy boots and the curse of an orc as the creatures traveled along the narrow passage that led to the large, natural cavern.

Serdic leaned against a stalagmite with his sword in his hand. "Whatever Struth says, repeat it," the mage said.

"Great," Dav muttered. "If he casts a spell to drop a stalactite on you, I'll bring down the roof."

"Risk it," Leanna advised. "You're our only hope."

Dav thought they should put their reliance on their weapons. Calenderi doused the torches. As the last light was extinguished, Dav saw Hoganvar's and Leanna's bows trained on the entrance to the cavern.

They waited in complete darkness for several minutes. The echoes of the heavy booted footsteps made it seem as if their enemies were all around them. Dav was growing desperate and reaching for his light charm when Wherann tugged at his hair.

"Sth, wz, wz," Wherann hissed.

Six fireballs whizzed down the passage and flew into the chamber. More than a dozen orcs charged in behind the lights. The first three fell to Dav's, Hoganvar's, and Leanna's arrows. The others took shelter behind stalagmites. To Dav's right and left, Hoganvar and Leanna spread out to keep the orcs from flanking them. Dav held his position near the entrance to the cavern, waiting for Struth.

A pig-nosed orc peered out from around a column near the entrance and ducked back as Dav's arrow missed its head by less than an inch. Once more the orc's spearpoint came in sight, followed by its head. Dav was ready for it; his arrow grazed the metal-trimmed leather helmet. The orc's head popped out again. It was drawing back to cast its spear when Dav tried the third time to stop it with an arrow. The shaft caught the orc in the shoulder. But even as the arrow flew, Dav realized the orc had been deliberately diverting his attention. Another hulking brute had worked its way from column to column, closing the distance. Its charge came too suddenly for Dav to do more than drop his bow and grab for the hilt of his sword. It was still in his scabbard when he sidestepped to avoid the slashing knife. The orc's heavy shoulder crashed into him, and they both fell on the slick floor.

The orc's heavy body knocked the wind out of him. Squirming to free himself from the attacker's weight, Dav grabbed at the orc's thick arm as the knife plunged for his throat.

He felt the blade against his skin. He braced his elbows on the floor as he held back the force of the orc's arm. They locked in a contest of strength, Dav's two arms against the orc's one, and Dav knew he was tiring. The effort made his ears ring.

Dixie McKeone

Around him, he could hear the sounds of metal on metal.

He heard a whisper he recognized as the wizard's voice from the direction of the entrance, but Struth was taking care not to speak loud enough for Dav to hear him.

But the wizard hadn't allowed for the keen hearing of the elf princess. She shouted the words so Dav could hear them. As her voice rang across the chamber, Wherann flew into the orc's face, startling it enough break its concentration. Dav jerked, arced his body, and rolled, throwing the orc into a thin stone column with a force that cracked the stone.

Dav repeated the spell.

The fireballs blinked out, and the sounds of battle died as quickly. All Dav could hear was cracking, falling stone. A chunk hit his shoulder and knocked him off his feet. He rolled down the side of a mound of mungan and came to a stop in a depression between two small hills of fungus. Then he felt a blinding flash of pain as he was struck on the head by falling rock.

The blackness of the cavern filled his mind.

* * * * *

Erian liked some things about the surface world. He liked singing to the animals, but the bright sun hurt his eyes, and the wind and rain frightened him. When they entered the passage of the annelid, he felt safe at last.

Then the wizard attacked, and he tried to keep the horses calm, but they bolted. When he ran after them, he stumbled, fell, and scraped his hand on a sharp rock. HeyYou rushed over to him to help him up, but by the time he remembered to sing again, the horses had fled into the darkness.

Then, across the cavern, he had seen the wizard as he cast a spell. Calenderi shouted the words at Dav, and he repeated them. Suddenly Erian found himself in a terrible nothingness that seemed to last for hours before the blackness left his mind and he was himself again.

He called out to the others, but no one answered him. He searched through the cavern, but he couldn't find anyone, only a few dead orcs. Huddled by a rock in the darkness, he was crying when he heard the gyerian gobbling.

"HeyYou?" He stood up, wiped his eyes, and circled the rock to see the funny bird-man crouching between two stalagmites.

"All gone, all dark," HeyYou gobbled. "All gone, all dark." The gyerian seemed even more frightened than Erian, so he took the gyerian's hand and convinced HeyYou to get up off the cold stone floor.

"They must have been captured by the wizard," Erian said. "They're all gone. There's nothing left but dead orcs."

"Wizard didn't find us? Awk, didn't find us?" HeyYou asked the obvious question. "Wizard wanted you and Calenderi, Hoganvar said. Told me so."

"I don't know what happened," Erian said.

Dixie McKeone

"They're all gone, so Struth must have taken them."
He shook with cold, so he crept over to where they
had left their packs and put on his coat. He
wrapped HeyYou's cloak around the avian's shoulders and found their packs, but the gyerian kept
gobbling in fear.

"What you need is something to eat," he said.
"And some light. We have these strider-wood
sticks, but I don't know how to make a fire.

"Fire, awk, fire," HeyYou gobbled and scrambled
for something in his pack. He brought out a small,
cunning dwarf-made tinderbox and lit the stick of
dry fungus.

"We should save the others," Erian told him. "We
must go after the wizard and help them to escape."

"Awk, afraid of wizards. Wizards are trouble,"
HeyYou said, shaking his head.

"I know." Erian looked out into the darkness and
shivered, thinking of going back to the surface
again. "But the wizard has Calenderi and Hoganvar and our friends, and we must save them."

"Big trouble," HeyYou gobbled. "Told them wizards was trouble," he said as he shouldered his
pack and followed the elf boy out of the cavern.
They retraced their path, walking through the rest
of the night and reaching the surface as the sun
rose.

"Tired, so tired," HeyYou said, and Erian agreed.
They had spent the day before climbing the ledge
into the mountains and the night traveling in the
caverns. He looked around and spotted a shallow
opening, just a narrow fissure in the rocks.

"We can rest in here," he said, leading the way. "I'll keep first watch, just the way Dav always does." He tried, but the gyerian slept, and bundled in the warm fur, he soon became drowsy. Before long, his eyes closed.

Neither heard the hooves of horses as Struth and his orcs emerged from the cave and rode back down the mountain.

* * * * *

Leanna noticed a change in the blackness. She smelled the musty odor of the cave and felt the bow and arrow in her hand. She stepped sideways, feeling a little off balance, and fell. She dropped her bow and her arrow and muttered as she banged her shoulder on a rock.

"Leanna?" Calenderi called to her.

"Where are you?" Leanna sat up and fumbled for her weapons. Carrying one of her mushroom-stick torches, the elf princess walked around a thick column of stone.

"Put that light out!" Leanna hissed, jumping for the shelter of a stalagmite. "You're making us a target!"

"There's no one to see," Calenderi replied. "Struth got the rest."

"Did you see him take them away? Were they still alive?" Leanna took the torch and began to search the cavern.

"I didn't see anything." Calenderi sat on a stone and hung her head. "I've searched the cavern, and

209

everyone is gone but a few dead orcs and us. Struth must have captured them. They wouldn't have left us unless they were forced to."

"No, they wouldn't," Leanna said. She broke off her search and picked up her pack and coat. "Let's take what we can and get moving. Struth may send his orcs back for us when he discovers he has only one elf. We should be long gone."

Calenderi stared at Leanna in dismay. "But surely we will follow the wizard and try to help them escape."

"We'll get you back to your people," Leanna said, transferring more food and a few essentials into her pack. She felt Calenderi's stillness and looked up to face the elf's contempt.

"I forgot for a moment. Nothing must interfere with your reward," Calenderi said.

Leanna stood, eyes blazing. "Are all Shadow Elves as stupid as you are?" she demanded and saw the shock register on the princess. "You don't know how to fight, and your two spells would be useless against Struth. I may know how to fight, but I can't save them alone."

"We're not even going to try?"

"We'll do better than try. We'll succeed, but we'll do it by getting help from your people. At least I assume you have wizards and warriors . . . right?"

Calenderi raised her head, her eyes sparkling. "The children of Rafiel are the greatest warriors and wizards in the world." The elf princess picked up her own pack.

In minutes, they were on the way. They used the

small tunnel to reach the wider path, setting a grueling pace. Whether they traveled underground or on the surface, they needed to move as rapidly as possible.

* * * * *

Slowly Dav regained consciousness. When his vision cleared, he looked up to see Hoganvar, holding a torch. Serdic wiped Dav's face with a wet cloth. Wherann sat near his shoulder, pulling at the collar of his shirt.

"By the Immortals, boy, you scared the life out of us," the dwarf said.

Dav pushed Serdic's hand away and sat up. His head spun.

"What happened? Is everyone safe?" he asked. The simple act of speaking set off a hundred hammers in his skull.

"You knocked an orc into that slender column, and it broke under his weight. You caught a good blow on the head from falling rock."

"When you said you might bring the roof down, you sure said a mouthful," Serdic said. "When Struth threw his spell at you and you threw it back, everything seemed to disappear. I can only speak for myself, but I felt like my mind was hanging in a black void."

"A black void." Hoganvar nodded. "That's just what it was. Never felt anything like it." He told Dav how he had come out of the spell and looked around, but he hadn't seen anyone. Thinking the

Dixie McKeone

others had been captured by Struth, he had found his torch, lit it, and sprinted up the tunnel. In the distance, he had seen the wizard and the surviving orcs.

"Struth was using one of his magical fireballs to light their way, and they didn't have any prisoners. That I'm sure of. I came back here and searched for a short time. Then Serdic appeared right in front of me."

"I thought he'd jump out of his boots," Serdic said. The dwarf glared at him. "We think Leanna, the elves, and HeyYou came out of the spell before we did. They couldn't find us, assumed Struth had captured us, and set out on their own. The orcs wouldn't have taken their belongings and left ours. I imagine Struth searched, too, but his orcs were probably terrified, and he didn't wait around to run into you again."

"Why didn't they find me? I wouldn't have been invisible if magic doesn't work on me."

"But you were unconscious from the blow on your head and mostly covered with small rocks. You were lying between two mounds of that mungan fungus. We didn't find you until Wherann came out of the spell and set up a fuss."

"If Leanna and the others left first, how far could they get?" Dav asked. "How long have I been unconscious?"

"No way to tell where they are. I came out of the spell more an hour before Serdic did, and we didn't find you for an hour after that," the dwarf replied. "I have no idea how long we were under the spell or when the others came out of it."

Serdic nodded. "At least Leanna is with them. There's her footprint."

Serdic was only half right.

Chapter 17

Trouble

Who is he? Who is he? Who is he?

The question echoed in Struth's mind in time with the clip-clop of the horses' hooves as he rode back down the narrow ledge that led down the side of the mountain. Below him spread the foothills of Ylaruam.

Dav, the girl had called him. It wasn't an Alphatian name, but he closely resembled someone Struth had known. He couldn't place the face, but somehow he felt as if he were facing an old adversary. Struth was sure of only one thing: He had to kill this upstart called Dav and all his companions. No one who had seen him flee from the youth's power could be allowed to live to tell the story.

Something was strange about the boy. No youth could overcome Struth's power unless he used some trick. Belgroth the Lamer, Solclow, and Verchan, the most powerful wizards of Blackheart, might best Struth, but they had been lost with Alphatia. Only two others had ever stood up against Struth in a contest, but they were dead, both killed in Castle Qain nearly seventeen years before. The boy was obviously too young to have learned his power from either Melina or Reddican.

Reddican!

That's who he resembled! Not the older Reddican of Castle Qain, but Reddican the youth, the young mage who began his apprenticeship when Struth was in his second year of study.

Dav was the son of Reddican! But how had he developed his powers so young? Possibly he had inherited some of the wizard's spellbooks. Still, at his tender age, the boy couldn't have developed enough discipline to be so proficient.

Struth needed to rest and rebuild his strength before he faced the youth again. He urged his horse to greater speed, anxious to reach the bottom of the cliff. It would take Dav and the elves days to reach Aengmor. If he could use part of that time resting, rebuilding his strength . . .

Behind him, the orcs urged their mounts to keep up. They were terrified of the "spotted wizard," as they called Dav, naming him for the mottled deer- and cat-skin clothing he wore.

Orcs were inept riders, habitually jerking at the reins and shifting in their saddles, throwing the horses off stride. The clatter of scrambling hooves and the terrified screams from a horse and rider warned the wizard that one of his minions' mounts had lost its footing on the narrow ledge.

The screams had frightened the other beasts. Two horses reared, one throwing its rider. Both horse and rider plummeted toward the valley floor below. The orc's diminishing wail changed in pitch as Struth cast a levitation spell, caught the creature in midair, and deposited it on the trail below. Then, using the same spell, he caught the horse, remounted the rider, and lifted them back onto the upper trail.

Struth felt the strain of his magical exertion and asked himself why he bothered. Allowing these orcs to live would only cause him trouble. They would spread the word that Struth was up against a more powerful force, and that could cause King Thar to withdraw his support.

Struth cast an ice spell on the ledge behind him. He looked back to watch the horses scrambling to maintain footing on the slick surface. First one, then five, and then a dozen fell, horses and riders flailing in the air and screaming until they struck the rocks far below.

The horse Struth rode, maddened by fear, reared and lost its footing. The wizard cast a teleportation spell and let the horse tumble over the edge. By the time it hit the ground, Struth was in the mountains just south of Fort Hobart.

He'd rest, gather his strength, and find another band of orcs. He'd be ready when Dav and his group caught up with him.

* * * * *

Erian awoke to find HeyYou shaking his shoulder. The sun hung low in the sky; the wind had changed direction and now blew directly into their meager shelter.

"Must go, awk! Must go." The gyerian looked around, tilting his head in typical bird fashion as he eyed the area. His feathers stood up on his head in a crested disarray as the wind blew them. "Find warmer place, warmer place. Too much wind."

Yes, a place out of the wind would be more comfortable, Erian thought. He forced himself to move, thinking only of his discomfort. Then remembered why they had slept in the narrow fissure, why they were alone. They had slept when they should have been following the wizard! They must rescue their friends!

HeyYou searched the network of narrow gorges for another crevice or small cave out of the wind, but Erian looked for and found the trail of the wizard and the orcs. He hurried back to pick up his pack and shouted to HeyYou.

"This way," he called, starting up the trail, still determined to rescue his friends from the wizard. HeyYou caught up with him as he threaded his way among the scattered rocks and boulders in the small valley where they had freed the dragon.

"Trouble," he gobbled as he followed.

"Don't you want to rescue Hoganvar?" Erian demanded.

"We find Hoganvar," the gyerian agreed. "Maybe not with wizard," he said hopefully.

"They must be," Erian explained. "Dav would not leave us. They looked after us; now we must save them." He glanced impatiently at the feathered

Dixie McKeone

creature at his side. "Now hurry up. We must go
back up the trail and take the path down the cliffs,
and we can't do it after nightfall."

Erian would have preferred descending the cliffs
at night, but the gyerian would be afraid, gobbling
and crying out until every creature within miles
would hear them. The little elf stolidly led the way,
wondering if he would ever get home again.

* * * * *

Leanna's small torch did little to light the huge
annelid tunnel. For hours, the elf princess had set
a grueling pace. Leanna was tired, depressed, and
hopelessly lost.

Water, reflected in the light from her torch, glim-
mered at Leanna's feet, and she slowed, carefully
stepping through the cascade that ran down the
wall of the tunnel and across the floor in a shallow
sheet. A soft, slick moss beneath the water made
walking treacherous.

Ten paces into the water, Calenderi raised her
hand to her ear. Suddenly the elf put one finger to
her mouth in a gesture for quiet. She grabbed the
dried mushroom torch from Leanna, dousing it in
the stream.

Leanna's heart thumped against her chest. The
darkness closed in on her. Dimly she heard the
ring of metal against metal and what sounded like
shouts. The sounds were far away, only whispering
echoes, but she had spent too many years in mercenary camps not to know the sounds of battle.

"Orcs—orcs and dwarves, and they're coming this way," the elf princess whispered. "The air currents speak of another tunnel that may be safer. We should take it."

Leanna didn't argue. She allowed Calenderi to lead, pulling her gently off to the right. The floor slanted and the water swirled faster; she could feel it tugging against her boots.

"We'll never keep our feet," Leanna whispered, fighting to contain her panic.

The slope of the floor increased, and she started to slide. She lost her balance on the slick moss and fell, losing her grip n Calenderi's hand.

"Calenderi?" she called and heard a splash as the elf fell, too.

"I'm right behind you," the princess called as they slid along on the steepening slope.

Leanna bit her lip and stretched her arms wide, reaching for anything that might stop her slide into the black unknown. All she could feel was the slimy moss that came away in her hand when she snatched at it. The slope steepened, and she slid faster.

"Calenderi?" she called again, fearing she was also alone, as terrible a fate in the darkness as she could imagine.

"I'm just behind you," the elf replied, sounding as frightened as Leanna felt. None of the horrors she had ever imagined equaled sliding down a moss-covered tunnel in complete blackness, and the journey seemed without end. At times, the slope steepened, and she was sure she was traveling faster than a flying dragon. At other times, the slope leveled out, but before she could stop herself and get to her feet again, she slid onto another steep downgrade and took another wild ride. They continued on and on, down and down. Neither had any idea how far they had traveled.

Leanna called out periodically in fear, and Calenderi always answered her, always from about the same distance, she thought. Then she heard the elf princess whimper. Leanna didn't need to know the Shadow Elf language to understand fear.

"What is it?" she demanded, but before the elf could answer, Leanna could hear the roar of falling water. They were approaching a waterfall, caught in the speed of their slide and helpless to stop themselves. The noise grew to a roar, and suddenly Leanna shot out into the air and fell.

Leanna only fell three feet or so before she hit the surface of the water. Her pack and heavy coat pulled her under, but she felt her knee scrape against the stony bottom. She pushed against it with her feet, and her head popped to the surface. She stood just over waist-deep in water, straining to keep her balance against a strong current.

"Move off to your right," the elf shouted over the roar of the waterfall, and Leanna started forward at an angle.

"More to your right!" Calenderi ordered. "To the right!"

"Stop giving me orders!" Leanna snapped. "So far your advice hasn't been so wonderful."

"The roar you hear is not from the falls we came

over," Calenderi broke in. "We traveled in a small stream that feeds into the underground river we are now standing in. Just to your left the river falls into a deep chasm!"

Leanna swore at herself for not realizing the small stream in the tunnel couldn't account for the loud roar she heard. She stopped complaining and allowed the elf to lead her as they struggled out of the strong current. The floor rose, and soon they were out of the water. They sat on the tunnel floor and rested, heedless of the cold and damp.

"I accept the responsibility for leading you into danger," Calenderi said. Her voice, coming out of the darkness, seemed loaded with regret.

"I was wrong to blame you," Leanna answered. "I don't know how far we traveled on that slope, but I doubt we could have walked the distance in two days."

"Then we are two days closer to Aengmor. We continued in the same direction we were already traveling."

"But how far underground are we?" Leanna thought she could feel the weight of miles of rock pressing down on her.

Calenderi remained silent for a moment. "The air currents do not speak of surface winds," the elf said.

"Why don't you just admit your hearing is better than most? Why keep taking about the singing wind and whispering air currents?" Leanna was irritated with herself for her near panic and looking for any excuse to work it off.

"How else does sound travel but on the air?" the elf princess demanded. "Perhaps you do not want to hear that it carries odors as well?"

"Odors? What odors?" Leanna asked, immediately thinking of orcs.

"The scent of dead strider fungus and pearl dew. There is a grove cavern close by."

"Strider fungus—that's what we made the torches from."

"The air currents speak of a large grove cavern. We can build a fire to warm ourselves and dry our clothing."

"Lead the way." Leanna stooped, fumbling to find her pack and wet coat. "Being cold and wet is bad, but I really hate being blind."

Several varieties of giant mushrooms and fungus grew in the giant cavern. When they had built a fire, Calenderi insisted on taking the first watch while Leanna slept for a few hours.

When Leanna awakened, the fire had died to embers. Calenderi sat by a small stalagmite, sound asleep. Leanna added more strider wood to the fire. In the light of the flames, she noticed the dry clothing stacked on the packs. Her activities awakened Calenderi.

"I didn't mean to sleep," the elf apologized.

"What did you expect?" Leanna snapped. She was angry at herself for sleeping and leaving most of the work to the elf princess.

"Be satisfied that you slept safely. Nothing dangerous is in the tunnels that connect with this cave." Calenderi glared at her. "I didn't hope that you would be pleased. Gratitude is beyond the ability of humans, I suppose."

"That's not true," Leanna said. The elf's remarks reminded her of all the times she had truly been glad of Calenderi's efforts. But they had been constantly in conflict, and she had felt the admission would somehow weaken her. But fair was fair, and she owed the elven princess the truth.

"Thank you for drying my clothing. I also appreciated it when you cleaned the cabins of the boat," Leanna said. "And without your magic, we might not have escaped from the decapus, or the hydra, or the orcs. And you can certainly walk farther in a day than I can."

"But we would all have been dead without your sword," Calenderi said. "I have never seen such ability, not even among the greatest of our warriors."

"It's true that I want to get a reward for helping you to return home," Leanna said, "but I want it because it's the only way I can buy my freedom. If you were to tell me now that there will be no reward, I would still do everything I could to help you reach Aengmor."

Calenderi nodded. "I believe you. I find it strange that you would help us, but perhaps there is much for my people to learn about those who live on the surface of this world." She shook back her hair. "If we reach my homeland, I will beg of my father the reward you seek. I long ago ceased to think of you as a servant."

"And I stopped thinking of you as a princess," Leanna said. Then, realizing what she had said, she stared, her mouth hanging open.

Calenderi's eyes widened, and then she laughed.
"That is a strange compliment indeed."

"Humans can be strange," Leanna admitted, glad her unthinking remark had been accepted in the spirit she had made it.

"I will think on that while I sleep," Calenderi said and stretched out by the fire.

Leanna stood watching the elf for a moment and was surprised to realize that she not only respected the elf and admired her abilities, but she was also genuinely fond of her.

Hours later, Leanna folded the rest of their dry clothing, then turned the heavy coats and decided they would need a few more hours to dry. She tested her boots before slipping them on and went in search of more fuel for the fire.

As she passed a tall, lace-capped fungus, she noticed a fresh cut in the side of the stalk. A short, roughly carved stick of strider wood acted as a spout and the sap dripped down into one of the dishes they had brought on the trip and overflowed onto the floor. Another empty dish sat close by. Leanna stared at it. Calenderi was collecting the fluid for some reason. Leanna knelt and lifted the full dish, tilting it and spilling some of the sticky stuff on her hands and arms. Sap spread on the floor before she put the second one in place.

As she continued on toward the tall strider fungus, she saw two other slashed plants with sap puddling at their bases. She shrugged off the puzzle and continued on her way.

Dixie McKeone

She soon found a dead strider plant and was busy prying off long strips for the fire when she heard a movement behind her.

She turned to face the largest worm she had ever seen. There were plenty larger, but a creature three feet in diameter and fifteen feet long was big enough when she had left her sword back by the fire.

She backed away, but the monster was quicker. With a blur of movement, its mouth closed on her hand, and she screamed.

Chapter 18

Captured!

Dav and Serdic waited in the cavern where they had been attacked by Struth and his orcs while Hoganvar and Wherann went in search of the horses. Serdic could only hobble on his wounded leg, and Dav was still unsteady on his feet after being struck on the head by falling rock.

Hoganvar had been gone a long time, and Dav's impatience was giving way to concern when Serdic, who had been sitting on the stone floor, scratching at it with a sharp rock, looked up.

"I think I've figured out what happened with that spell," he said.

"Then explain it to me." Dav was grateful for any distraction.

"I think I've got the general shape of the cavern," the mage said, indicating a rough triangle he had drawn on the floor. It was barely discernible within a group of concentric circles.

"What are all the circles for?" Dav asked.

"Just wait." The mage's voice echoed Dav's impatience. Serdic pointed at the longest side of the triangle and the passage they had passed through. "Here's where we came in, and where Struth and his orcs were when they attacked." He had gathered a handful of pebbles and spaced them around the entrance to the cavern.

Dav tried to help him. He picked up several pebbles and estimated his own position first. "I was about here, Leanna here, and . . ."

Serdic swept away Dav's efforts and placed the pebbles himself. "Erian and HeyYou were the farthest away, trying to manage the horses." He placed two stones in the farthest corner. "Leanna stood about here; Calenderi wasn't far from her." Serdic continued to place the stones.

"Now, notice where we were in relation to the circles," Serdic said. "You were in the center—call it the center of a power vortex."

"Is that the way it works?" Dav stared at the diagram, needing to understand.

"Nothing you *do* is the way it works," Serdic said softly. "That's what makes you so interesting. Now pay attention. Wherann was the closest to you and the last to come out of the spell. I was closer to you than Hoganvar, and I was still caught in the spell for—what did he say? More than an hour after he came out of it? He just appeared. While I was caught in the spell, I was invisible to him."

"What about the others?" Dav prompted.

"They were farther away from you, so when the spell wore off and they searched for us, we were invisible. You were unconscious and hidden under that pile of rocks. I imagine they thought we were gone and they left the cavern. The same thing probably happened to Struth. He didn't find anyone and no trail to follow so he left, too."

"And no one knew what happened to anyone," Dav said thoughtfully.

"As I said, you do make life interesting," Serdic said as he used a stone to scratch out his drawing. He had just finished his explanation when Hoganvar returned to the cave, leading their horses.

"Then Leanna, the elves, and HeyYou are on foot," Dav said when he had counted the animals.

"They have to be," Hoganvar said. "Stupid animals got themselves lost in a side tunnel. Lucky Wherann's got good ears. I'd given up and was ready to turn back."

"Let's feed them, give them plenty to drink, and get on our way," Dav said. "By the time we catch up with the others, they'll be glad to mount up again." He didn't say he wanted to catch up with them before they ran into danger. It didn't need to be said.

"If we find them at all," Serdic said. He sat on a broken stalagmite, tying sticks of strider wood into a bundle while Dav and Hoganvar fed the horses and tied chunks of mungan on the backs of the pack animals.

The dwarf turned toward the mage, his face red with anger. "Keep your troublesome tongue to yourself," he shouted.

"Leanna will keep to the main passage," Dav said. "She heard Bletinferelth's instructions." Dav refused to think anything else.

They rode three of their mounts and led the others.

"Now we'll cover some distance," Hoganvar said when he climbed into his saddle. "Never thought I'd be glad to see one of these monsters again."

Though riding horseback did help, they found they were still limited in their speed. The light of the torches only lit the tunnel floor a few feet ahead of them, not far enough to let them bring the animals to more than a gentle trot.

Hoganvar suggested using the light charm, but Dav shook his head. All his instincts warned against it.

"We're limited by more than light," he finally said. "The horses can't travel fast on this stone floor. It's too hard on their hooves." If the dwarf thought there was more to his refusal, he didn't mention it.

The stone walls and ceilings echoed the sound of hoofbeats. Their heads ached after the first hour, and they gave up trying to make conversation. It sounded as if hundreds of people were traveling through the tunnel. It probably frightened away every creature within miles.

They changed horses frequently and rode on until Serdic nearly fell from his saddle. Then they dismounted and took turns sleeping, keeping the torches lit.

By the end of the second day, Dav struggled to maintain hope of finding the others. He kept reminding himself that they could be far ahead and could travel nearly as fast as the horses.

Halfway through the third day, the tunnel made a sharp descent, but off to their left, through a second passage, they noticed a growing light. They rode through a natural cave and out onto the upper slopes of a low mountain. The air smelled of a recent rain and sparkled with sunlight. They had reached the eastern limits of the mountains. Below, not five miles away, they saw a road cutting through the dwindling hills. In the distance, the green of the forest lost its color and faded to a deep gray—Aengmor.

"We must have missed the others somewhere in the tunnels," Dav said, ready to turn back and retrace their path.

"Not necessarily," Hoganvar said. "We felt the breezes of several openings as we came through. Maybe they ran out of torches and decided to travel on the surface."

"Remember, we don't know how long we were caught up in the spell," Serdic reminded Dav. "They could have come out this same entrance and be somewhere in the foothills. They could be traveling along the slopes of the mountains, avoiding the roads."

"And they may be traveling at night, hidden away and sleeping during the day," Dav added, agreeing that they had very little chance of finding the others without help.

Wherann had been sitting on the broad rump of Dav's horse. Now he chittered and flew up in the air.

Dixie McKeone

"Yes, you go look for them," Dav said, nodding. "We'll follow the road toward Aengmor. If you don't find them, we'll ask the Shadow Elves to help us search."

Since no one else had a better idea, they descended the slopes until they came to the road. Dav had worried about the effect of the fungus diet on the horses, but they seemed full of energy and as frisky as colts. Roads and daylight were things they understood, and they had no objection to a good gallop.

They rode on for part of the afternoon. Before long, they could see the Darokinian city of Selenica in the distance. At Dav's suggestion, they left the road and located a grassy meadow hidden from the eyes of chance travelers by a copse of trees.

While Serdic rested his leg and Dav kept a watch on the rest of the horses, Hoganvar rode into the city for news. The sun was setting when Wherann came in sight and wearily dropped onto Dav's shoulder. He brought no news of the others.

Two hours after dark, Hoganvar returned. He listed to one side in the saddle and smelled of ale, but his eyes were dark with worry.

"There's already been some skirmishing near the road to Tavaro between the Darokinians and Tanadaleyo's army," he said. "King Stefan of Karameikos has promised Darokin support and is sending his first and second militia. They set sail from Specularum for Athenos two days ago. They'll be traveling up the Streel River."

"Then we'll ride at dawn," Dav said. "I just hope

we can get the elves to believe us."

They spent a restless night, but at least the horses were well rested. At Dav's insistence, they saddled extra horses and carried only the supplies they needed for the next night. Two days, possibly only one if they switched mounts during the day, would take them into the Forest of Canolbarth.

His hope grew every time they topped a rise. Just at sunset, they rode under the eaves of the forest. They were forced to slow the horses, but they had reached their destination.

"Now what do we do?" Serdic asked. His face was drawn with fatigue and pain, but he had managed to stay in the saddle.

"It won't be easy to find the Shadow Elves at night," Hoganvar said.

"Let's go a little deeper into the woods and build a large fire," Dav said. "With war on their borders, they'll have scouts out. We'll let them find us."

"They may find us with their arrows," Serdic warned.

"I don't think they kill for the fun of it," Dav replied. "If they see we're not hiding from them, we'll be safe from their weapons long enough to talk." But how would they get the Shadow Elves to believe them? He decided to face that problem when it arose.

Dav dismounted and picked up fallen branches as he walked. Hoganvar helped him, and by the time they had traveled half a mile into the forest, they had gathered enough firewood to keep a large fire going well into the night.

Dav was tying another limb to his load when his horse whinnied in fright and shied, his eyes rolling in fear.

"Behind you!" shouted Serdic, who had stayed in the saddle. As Dav glanced at him, the mage was pulling his sword. Five feet away, Wherann, carrying an armful of twigs, dropped them and flew into the air.

Dav whirled just in time to duck a thick axe wielded by the largest orc he had ever seen. He jumped aside and heard the axe come down with a thump, severing a thick tree root by his foot. He pulled out his sword and swung wildly at the orc as he fought for footing among the tree roots. By luck rather than aim, his blade cut deep into the muscles of the orc's right arm.

The orc screamed, dropped its axe, and backed away. The creature was out of the fight, and Dav let it go. He paused and looked around as Serdic threw his lightning bolt. By the howl that quickly followed, Dav could tell that the mage had struck a creature hidden from Dav's sight behind a large tree. When it fell, Dav stared.

A troll, he thought, though he had never seen one. The monster had stood a good eight feet tall, with clawed fingers nearly as long as Dav's forearm. Its left shoulder and the side of its head were still smoking from Serdic's lightning bolt. The left forearm had been ripped off at the elbow, but even as Dav watched, the fingers moved, pulling the stump of the arm as it crept toward him.

Dav jumped forward, gorge filling his throat as

he kicked the arm away.

He heard a roar behind him and turned to see a second troll lumbering through the trees. Above him, Wherann squeaked, speaking too quickly for Dav to understand him. The construct dove for the ground, grabbed up two tiny handfuls of dirt, and flew at the second troll.

"Wherann, take care!" Dav shouted, but an arrow flew past him, and he raced to take cover behind a tree. Safe for the moment, he tried to put the ambush in some sort of perspective. He had been attacked by an orc and a troll. Neither of those races commonly used bows and arrows, nor was the arrow that struck the tree ten feet away made with elven fletching skills, so there was some other type of creature in the battle.

He was still trying to puzzle it out when the second troll roared and stumbled into sight, rubbing at its eyes. Wherann had hit his target. The little construct flitted about, darting at the monster, whose clawed hands raked the air, trying to reach its tormentor. Dav held his breath as Wherann dove for the face of the creature, then hovered until the troll made a grab for him. Wherann just managed to escape, and the troll raked its vicious claws across its own face.

Another arrow came flying out of the darkness. Serdic was the target, but he was ready with another spell and threw a fireball at the bowman. A small, dog-faced creature with brown, scaly skin staggered into sight, screaming as it was consumed by the flames, then fell dead. A kobold.

Dixie McKeone

"Take the horses back out on the plain," Dav called to Serdic. The wounded mage had used up his spells and would be nearly helpless facing regular weapons. Dav and Hoganvar stood a better chance of protecting themselves if Serdic were out of danger. They could move about in the shadows and had the advantage over the clumsy, noisy humanoids.

Off to the right, a dwarvish oath and the ring of Hoganvar's axe against metal sang in the air, followed by the scream of a dying creature. It appeared to be a goblin, the ancient enemies of the dwarves.

Dav hurried in the dwarf's direction, but he was still thirty feet away when a humanoid stepped out of the darkness and blocked his path. This was neither troll, goblin, kobold, nor orc. At first Dav thought he faced a well-muscled but graceful human. Its face was no wider than Dav's. It had the tusks of an orc, but they were short and only showed when it drew back its lips. In its eyes gleamed an intelligence he had never seen in a humanoid.

When the creature pulled its sword and attacked, Dav knew he was fighting a half-breed—part orc and part elf. His opponent moved with a speed and grace impossible for any orc and many humans.

"Korshnid," he spoke his thought aloud. The outlaw habitually traveled with a mixed group of humanoids. He had heard the half-breed lived in the mountains of Karameikos and Darokin and had been the one who sold Calenderi and Erian to the Hattians.

"You know me, human?" Korshnid swung his two-handed sword, and Dav backed away as he fended off the blade. "We have not met, or you would be dead."

"Or you," Dav said. "I plan to avenge a slight to some friends of mine." He made a thrust that Leanna had taught him and forced Korshnid back. The half-orc's face tightened in concentration, and Dav could discern his elvish features.

"And who would that be?" the half-orc asked as he waded in again, his blade slower and surer as he took time to measure his opponent.

Dav was too hard pressed to answer. His life on the Great Escarpment had made him quick and strong, and Leanna had taught him well during the long days aboard the boat, but he was beginning to think he was no match for the half-orc. The creature had the strength of his orcish blood, the quickness of his elven ancestry, and had far more experience with a blade than Dav could claim.

Korshnid wielded the sword in a smoothly arcing figure eight, crashing against Dav's blade from the right and then the left in a lightning-fast pattern that left the human no time to do anything but field the blows.

Dav knew the orc was trying to wear down his strength—and he would succeed if Dav couldn't find a way to break the orc's offensive pattern. He backed away slowly, and the orc followed.

Dav failed to see the creeping troll arm behind

him until he stepped on it and tripped, falling on his back. The half-orc was caught off balance when Dav fell, and he tripped over the human's feet. Korshnid crashed down on top of Dav, who just had time to twist to the side so the half-orc's body didn't knock the wind out of him.

Unfortunately, he couldn't prevent Korshnid from falling on his right arm, which was then trapped under the outlaw. But the half-breed had lost his own long blade. The half-orc's sword had fallen more than five feet away.

With his left hand, Dav reached up behind his neck, pulling his knife from its hidden sheath. He slashed at Korshnid, who grabbed Dav's knife hand in both of his hands, trying to turn the blade and force it into the human. Dav was loath to let go of his sword, but he couldn't use it effectively as long as his arm was pinned beneath the outlaw's chest. He let loose of the hilt, grabbed the half-orc's big, pointed ear, and jerked, pulling Korshnid's head back.

Dav arched his back and kicked with his feet, throwing himself sideways and onto the body of his foe, but the half-breed was responding even as Dav rolled. With an arch and an even stronger kick, Korshnid threw Dav over his head.

Dav rolled and came up on one knee with the outlaw's sword in his hand. Korshnid lunged backward, one arm reaching out for Dav's blade, but the half-orc's hand had only just closed on it when he gasped and his eyes widened. He dropped the blade and reached for his throat.

Korschnid had rolled back on the creeping arm of the troll, and the long, clawed fingers were closed on the humanoid's throat in a death grip.

Dav watched as the half-orc's eyes seemed to bulge from his head. Then the creature gurgled once before the loud snap of his neck put an end to his struggles.

Dav was backing away, feeling as if the flesh on his backbone were walking around on its own. The hair on the back of his neck tingled with the horror of that severed arm and hand seeking to mindlessly kill. He was so intent on the horror he had witnessed, that he forgot to watch for uneven ground and stumbled into a slight depression between two trees.

He nearly lost his balance, but his stumble saved his life. A small cloud of glowing, greenish smoke passed just over his head and struck a tree behind him, searing away the bark. He jumped aside as a second cloud passed by him, and then he heard screaming. He turned to see two figures writhing in the cloud. He was just in time to see that they had pale skin and white hair before their flesh melted from their bones.

Dav's first thought was that Struth had found them again, but he turned to see a small kobold dressed in long robes. A shaman, he decided as the small creature raised its hand again and spoke the uncouth words of a spell.

After his experience in the caverns, Dav had decided never to repeat another spell, but the destruction of the Shadow Elves had enraged him.

Dixie McKeone

He pointed his finger at the shaman and repeated the words even as the kobold shaman finished its incantation.

A huge dark cloud came down from the top of the trees. It swirled between Dav and the shaman as if it were gathering the darkness. It hovered for a moment, then turned on the kobold. The shaman had time only to shout a strangled objection before it consumed him. As the cloud rose, Dav could hear screams coming from it, but they died away and the cloud dispersed.

Dav stood, mesmerized, but a clash of metal and an uncouth curse reminded him there were still enemies in the forest, and the dwarf might need his help. He turned and discovered he was surrounded by a ghostly-looking group of elves with pale skin and white hair.

They stared at him in fear, but their bows were drawn, and their arrows were all pointed directly at his heart.

Chapter 19

The People of the Twisted Trees

Erian and HeyYou sat by the bush and picked berries, eating their fill. The fruit had long since dried on the bush, but there were still enough for him and HeyYou to make a meal, and the berries were a change from hard bread and dried meat. Erian had never liked the humans' food.

At least, sitting and eating was better than walking, and certainly better than trying to get the gyerian down the cliff in the dark. They hadn't reached the bottom before nightfall, and HeyYou had been terrified.

They had left the mountains behind and wandered in the hills for two days now. Erian's legs ached from walking, but the sun hurt his eyes and still rode high in the sky, and he knew they had to continue. He stood up and shouldered his pack. Then he gazed at the gyerian.

"This time you go first," he said.

"Go first, awk! Go first," HeyYou said, leading the way out of the shallow valley. He crossed a stream and paused on the opposite bank, staring down at the hoofprints of several horses.

"You found the trail," Erian said, pleased that they had at last discovered the path of the wizard.

"Find the trail, find the wizard, find trouble," HeyYou said, following the tracks.

Neither HeyYou nor Erian realized the oddly shaped horseshoe prints were peculiar to the tribes of the Ylaruam nomads, nor that they were leading northeast, into the desert.

* * * * *

When Leanna screamed, the monster drew back as if startled by the noise, but then it whipped forward and caught her hand again. She hadn't brought a weapon, so she slapped at it with her other hand, but even that brought a strange reaction from an unexpected source.

"Don't hit it," Calenderi shouted at her.

"No. I suppose I should just let it eat me," Leanna retorted. But through her fear, she was beginning to realize she hadn't been bitten. She managed to get her hand out of the creature's mouth, but she couldn't get away from it. When she tried backing away, she found two more of the monsters behind her, sniffing at her clothing. In the dim light of the fire, she could see Calenderi hurrying toward her with one of the bowls of sticky fluid in her hands. She dipped a hand into the bowl and held it out. The first creature immediately whipped around and seemed to swallow the elf's entire arm.

"They're giant slugs, and they love pearl dew," she told Leanna as she took another handful and fed the creature again. The others immediately lost interest in Leanna and turned toward Calenderi. "When I saw the lermon and the pearl dew, I thought we might find slugs here."

"Wonderful. And what are they going to do for us?" Leanna demanded, angry about being frightened by the creatures that were nosing against the elf princess.

"They will take us to Aengmor," Calenderi replied. "These and others like them. We'll feed them and give them plenty of the sap. It makes them thirsty, and we want them to drink their fill. They travel on their own fluid, you know."

She continued to feed them the sticky liquid, backing up a few steps at a time, leading them toward the puddles where the sap had drained out onto the floor through the slits in the stalks. While the slugs sucked up the sap, she returned to the fires and started refilling their packs with their supplies and dried clothing.

"Quite a coincidence, finding wood for a fire and fodder for the slugs all in one place," Leanna observed.

"It is, isn't it?" Calenderi replied. Her eyes sparkled, but she didn't allow herself to smile.

* * * * *

Dixie McKeone

While Dav faced several of his captors, a cloth whipped down over his face and he was gagged. His hands were tied behind his back.

"You will not cast your spells on us, human," said the elf who bound him.

As his captors led him through the woods, he saw the bodies of the orcs, goblins, kobolds, and four trolls, whose remains had been set afire. Other Shadow Elves were gathering their spent arrows. Many would need to be cleaned of orc blood. At the site of the first battle, Dav saw Hoganvar bound and sitting by a small fire, grumbling because the elves had taken his weapons and his iron helmet.

". . . and King Telemon's children would have been dead ten times over but for us!" The dwarf harangued a small, slender female elf dressed in a suit of glittering, cunningly worked chain mail.

"Why should I believe a dwarf and a human?" she asked, staring down at them.

Hoganvar told her what he knew of the kidnapping and where he, Dav, and Serdic had lost the royal elves, Leanna, and the gyerian. As the dwarf spoke, Wherann flew down and lit on Dav's shoulder. The construct raged impotently at the elves and attempted to loosen Dav's gag until an elf sword convinced him to stop.

"And why would you help any Shadow Elves to return to their people?" the elf leader demanded of the dwarf. "It is not to be believed that you help us because you love us."

"For the reward," Hoganvar spoke up quickly. "If

they mean so much to King Telemon that he'd go to war over them, he can spare a few gold pieces for their safe return."

The circle of guards continued to stare at them with contempt, but they nodded, accepting human and dwarvish greed.

"After seeing your princess, I thought the faces of all Shadow Elf females were decorated," Hoganvar observed and received the response he expected. They stared at him wide-eyed, obviously convinced he must have seen Calenderi.

"Your words may have sealed your fate, dwarf."

"Or convinced you that they really did travel with us. All their efforts to reach Aengmor, everything we tried to do, will be for nothing if you don't help us find them."

The female leader made no response. She was still gazing at them thoughtfully when a tall male elf strode through the gathering, glared at the captives, and drew her aside. They conferred for a few minutes, and then, at a barked order, the elves prodded Dav and Hoganvar to their feet. They were marched off through the woods.

They walked for more than an hour before the forest began to thin and they saw open hillsides. Hoganvar gazed about with interest. Then he gasped and stumbled as he stared ahead.

"By Kagyar's beard!" he muttered, pointing ahead. "I never believed they existed!"

Dav saw what he first thought were small, thin dragons lying at their ease in the shadows, but as one stood and rustled its wings, he recognized them—skinwings, the legendary mounts of the deep caverns. He hadn't heard that the elves had brought any to the surface.

Dav and Hoganvar were forced to mount the skinwings and tied to the saddles. Hoganvar shouted and argued against their fate. Dav was thrilled when the great beasts leapt into the air and soared high over the forest. Wherann crouched on the saddle in front of him, until the cold wind forced the little creature to take shelter inside Dav's cat-skin coat.

Twenty skinwings flew in perfect formation. The female in the chain mail led the group and flew far ahead of the prisoners. Dav's guards flanked him, the wingtips of the other skinwings nearly touching those of the creature he rode. Behind him came Hoganvar, similarly flanked. The rest of the escort brought up the rear.

Dav's major regret was not being able to see more of Aengmor in the darkness. When the sun rose, they were already descending. They had flown over the rolling hills of eastern Aengmor, and now they landed on a small plain that had once been farmland. When Dav's elven guards untied him and allowed him to alight from the skinwing, he noted that the regular mounded rows of the fields were hard. No plow had loosened the soil for several years.

In the distance, he caught a glimpse of a village built in the trees. Only a few of the wildly slanted buildings were visible. The giant limbs on which they had been built had been twisted out of shape.

Dav would have liked to see more, but the elves led him into a hut made of branches and twigs. One of the elves drew his sword and moved back out of Dav's vision.

The female leader stood in front of him.

"Know this, human. Two of our people died when you and your enemy cast your evil spells. You will be freed and allowed to eat, but if you attempt to speak, Silmarin's sword will find your heart before you can hope to cast a spell to kill more of us. The dwarf's life and also that creature's depend on you." She pointed at Wherann, who crouched on Dav's shoulder.

Dav nodded slowly, not willing to risk the lives of the dwarf and the construct.

* * * * *

"I just want to see the sun. I don't care what it shines on," Leanna said as she followed the elf princess up out of the tunnel. She had no idea where they were and doubted Calenderi's insistence that they had reached Aengmor.

They had spent days riding the slugs, much of the time in darkness so black only the slight motion of the creature told her they were moving. They had traveled from grove cavern to grove cavern, releasing their tired mounts and finding others. Once they had started riding, they rode almost constantly, only stopping when they were too tired to keep their seats on the slugs.

With no dawn or sunset to guide her, Leanna

had no idea how long the slugs had been ascending the gently sloped passages, but she thought it had been more than a day. The last time they had changed mounts, they had been in a series of large grove caverns. By the light of her torch, Leanna had seen close to a hundred of the slow-witted, amiable creatures.

Their new mounts had traveled more slowly, working their way up steeper grades. Leanna guessed it had been an hour or more since they dismounted and Calenderi had sent the slugs back down into the deeper caverns.

Moments later, Leanna followed the elf around a turn and saw daylight ahead. They stepped out of the entrance and onto the lower slope of a low, rocky hill. A few twisted oaks with dark, almost black leaves shaded the hillside above them, but two hundred yards away, the forest thickened. She couldn't see into the deep shadows.

"This has to be a nightmare. This can't be real," Leanna said, staring at a twisted tree with blackened leaves. The bole was more than thirty feet in diameter and rose straight for more than seventy feet before it twisted grotesquely. Where it bent, the bark had split, and the pale wood weeped like seeping wounds. The limbs grew at unnatural angles to spread their black leaves in an unbroken canopy, shutting out the sunlight. The gloom hung like a pall.

"Your people did this?" Leanna glared at Calenderi, who immediately took offense.

"And what would you have done, human? Would

you have won a place for yourself on the surface of the world with swords and death, when by making the land unfit for others you could reduce the killing? Or do you think we should have stayed forever imprisoned in the darkness to see fewer and fewer children born, many of them too weak and deformed to live?"

"I—I hadn't thought of it that way," Leanna admitted. "I suppose cursing the forest did save lives, since the elves of Alfhiem left without much of a fight. It's just that—"

"Think of the beautiful forests you have seen, and feel gratitude for your good fortune," Calenderi said softly as she looked around. "I, too, am blessed with such a memory. I pity many of my people who now live on the surface, yet have never seen a tree in its natural glory. But remember this: We are elves. It is our way to love nature as it was meant to be. What has been done by magic can one day be undone by magic, but that cannot come to pass until we are strong enough to defend our land."

"But it will happen," Leanna said, offering reassurance born of sympathy rather than knowledge. She could see the sorrow in the eyes of the elven princess, and she wished she could take back her criticism.

But Calenderi's mind had turned to other matters. "You must stay hidden in the mouth of the tunnel until I can find my people," she said. "You will be in danger until they know you are under my protection." The elf princess raised her head and whistled, trilling in what sounded like a bird's song, obviously a message. Then she led the way back down the hill.

Leanna followed, her sympathy lost under her resentment.

"Under *her* protection," she muttered as she stood in the shadows of the tunnel mouth and watched Calenderi disappear into the forest. "Where would she be now if I hadn't found her when she was locked belowdecks on that boat?" But even as she grumbled, Leanna knew the elf was right. The Shadow Elves hated and distrusted humans, and the last thing Leanna wanted was to anger them further. She needed their help to rescue Dav and the others.

She turned back into the tunnel and found a wide, low boulder that made a comfortable seat. While she rested and waited, she considered how she had expressed her desires.

"Dav and the others," she repeated to herself, realizing that was how she always thought of them. She was concerned about Hoganvar and the silly gyerian. Her anger flared as she considered any harm coming to little Wherann or Erian. She had never completely trusted Serdic, but she didn't wish him harm. She missed Dav dreadfully, and most of her fear was for him. He was like the brother she had always wanted and never had.

She realized she wasn't alone when the noise of a pebble turning under the foot of an elf caused her to look up. A male warrior stood staring at her. He held his sword in his hand.

Leanna stood slowly, keeping her hands away

from her weapons.

"Well met," she said in Thyatian. Tired by their long journey and startled by his sudden appearance, she couldn't recall one word of the Shadow Elf dialect.

He spoke to her, demanding an answer to a question, but "teshalla," ancient elven for princess, was all she understood. He continued talking, and Leanna thought he was making accusations, but she couldn't understand the rest.

"She's looking for you. She'll explain everything," Leanna said, still in Thyatian. She swore at herself for her mental lapse and moved behind the boulder, trying to keep its bulk between herself and the elf with his drawn sword.

"You will pay for the shame you have brought on our people," the elf said, also circling the huge rock. Leanna's mind had cleared, and she finally understood him.

"Pay for what?" she demanded, this time in the elven tongue, but she had seen her opportunity. They had been circling the stone, and the elf was behind it. She turned and sprinted out of the tunnel and down the hill, knowing she couldn't outrun him, but if she could reach the trees, she might be able to dodge him.

As she raced across the open ground, she heard his light footsteps behind her. She had just reached the shade of the first tree when she realized the fallacy in her plan. The darkness of the forest would aid him rather than her. She stopped, whirled around, and with no other recourse that she could see, she drew her sword.

"Die, evil one," he shouted and brought his blade down on hers. He was a skilled swordsman, but he hadn't had the benefit of her training. Their blades blurred into shining arcs of reflected light as Leanna parried his attack, holding him off but taking no advantage of the opportunities her greater ability allowed her.

His eyes opened wide as he recognized her superiority, but he fought desperately.

"One of us will die, human," he said as he tried to force her back among the trees. "Honor demands it."

Leanna was determined neither would suffer harm if she could prevent it. She needed the assistance of the elves to help rescue the others.

"Calenderi!" she shouted, pitching her voice high so it would carry through the forest. Her call startled the elf into what would have been a fatal mistake if his opponent had wanted him dead. His hand slowed, and Leanna caught the hilt of his sword with the tip of her blade and flipped it away. In one leap, she bounded sideways and put her foot on the quillons of his weapon.

"We will fight no more," she said in the Shadow Elf language, but it took time for her to mentally translate the words, and the elf was too quick. He pulled his knife from its sheath and charged her again.

"Stupid elf!" Leanna snapped and easily fended off the shorter blade, nicking his hand to force him to drop it. Then she stepped back, hoping the fight was over, but her abilities had shamed the elf, and his eyes flashed with ungoverned rage.

An arrow thudded into a tree at her left, and Leanna stepped back behind another tree to shield herself from her unseen opponent. But the warrior she had been fighting gave her no time to think about the archer.

"I will not surrender and die in dishonor," he said through a clenched jaw and charged her, even though he was unarmed. He would have run himself onto her blade if she hadn't hastily withdrawn it.

With a silent thank-you to the mercenary who had spent years training her in battle, Leanna dropped to one knee and caught the arm of the charging elf, flipping him over her shoulder. He fell on his back, and she heard a loud "Umph" as his fall knocked the breath out of him.

Another arrow dug into the ground by her right leg. She was just rising, ready to seek cover, when an elf dashed out of the trees.

"No!" Leanna recognized the voice. It was Calenderi! The elf princess dashed forward, throwing herself between Leanna and the hidden archer. But the assailant had already loosed a third arrow. It struck the princess in the chest.

"Calenderi!" Leanna screamed and rushed to catch the elf girl as she fell. She sank to the ground, her arms around the unconscious elf.

From the shadows, she heard excited whispers, and three elves appeared. They held bows, with arrows nocked in place. The sharp shafts pointed at the ground, as if they had forgotten their weapons. Leanna, looking through tear-blinded eyes, could hardly see them.

"She tried so hard to get home, and now you've killed her!" she sobbed.

* * * * *

The sun had set, turning the dunes into ghostly purple shapes. The terrible heat that had tortured HeyYou and Erian during the day blew away on the wind. The night would be cold, as cold as winter.

"Awk! Must go, must go!" the gyerian shook the elf boy's shoulder. "Must go back."

"I can't walk anymore," Erian said, his voice hoarse with thirst. He had tried hard to find the others, but the terrible desert burned his skin and sapped away his strength. He had lost his pack two nights ago, and HeyYou's berries were all gone. They had no water or food left.

"It's no use. I can't walk anymore," he wailed when HeyYou pulled him to his feet. Then, just as suddenly, the gyerian pushed him down again.

"Something comes, something comes," the birdman gobbled.

A huge black shadow drifted over them, hiding the moonlight.

Chapter 20

Flying Lessons

Dav hunched his shoulders, trying to keep the cat-skin coat closed against the freezing wind. He had been bound, gagged, and tied to the skinwing for four nights running. More than a score of guards were escorting them to the capitol, Rafielton.

Always they flew at night. During the day, when they landed to rest the beasts, Dav had been allowed to remove his gag to eat, but the elves still considered him a magician and would not let him speak.

Halfway through the fourth night of their journey, they were intercepted by a flyer hurrying east. The lone rider veered off his course long enough to pass a message to the leader of the escort before continuing on his way.

Dav's interest picked up as the elves turned north-northwest and flogged their beasts to greater speed. Beneath Dav, the beast he rode whined at the increased effort. Dav wondered what had happened to change their course.

Dixie McKeone

An hour later, Dav thought the darkness was playing tricks on his vision. He thought he saw the edge of the forest. Beyond it, he could see hills, their slopes standing out sharply against the shadows cast by the moonlight. If he was correct, the Darokin border wasn't far ahead.

He twisted his head frantically, trying to loosen the gag. After a few minutes, he could barely mumble, but Wherann heard him. The construct, who had been sheltering from the wind inside Dav's coat, climbed onto Dav's shoulder and squeaked a question.

"Try to untie my hands," Dav instructed, and Wherann climbed down his back. Dav pressed his wrists together, giving the little creature the advantage of slack ropes.

Every beat of the beast's wings took them closer to the border. His skinwing was being led in a long line, but the reins were permanently attached to a ring on the front of the saddle pad. If he could free his hands, he might be able to break away from their captors.

Behind him, he could feel Wherann's tiny hands as they occasionally touched him, but nothing seemed to be happening. He kept his wrists tightly together and tried not to let his impatience hamper the construct.

To the east, Dav saw several other skinwings, some circling to land. Several miles ahead, a fire licked through the tops of the trees. The wind carried the faint sounds of battle.

The elves shouted and pointed, then pulled their bows from their shoulders and broke their traveling formation, zooming down to join the fight. Obviously the two prisoners were not as important as helping their own people.

Dav's and Hoganvar's skinwings circled, squawking anxiously. They appeared to want to follow their companions, but the sounds of battle and the fire frightened them.

Then Dav felt the construct's hands as he pushed on the human's wrists, spreading them apart. The rope fell away.

Dav ignored the gag and leaned forward to take up the four impossibly thin silken lines of the skinwing's reins. The rope that had held him securely tied to the saddle slipped, and he grabbed for the saddle as he started to slide sideways. Wherann had untied both knots. Wherann climbed back on his shoulder and squeaked in his ear.

"All ntied, Dv free."

"Thank you," Dav mumbled through the gag, only marginally grateful. How was he to stay in the saddle and manage the ungainly flyer? The saddle was too large for him to use his knees as he would have gripped the sides of a horse, and the stirrups were no more than footrests.

Holding on to the saddle with his left hand, he reached for the four reins again and stared down their length, along the long neck to the head of the beast he rode. Two would turn the skinwing, one would make it rise, and the other would direct it to descend. The wind whipped the slender white lines about until Dav was unable to tell which one gave which command.

"Make a decision," he muttered into the gag and pulled hard against one line. The skinwing abruptly dove for the treetops, its change of direction bringing Dav up out of the saddle. Wherann squeaked and caught a handful of Dav's hair. Dav's feet left the stirrups. He slid completely out of the saddle onto the skinwing's back. He dropped the reins and grasped the saddle bow to keep from falling into the treetops.

While he fought to regain his seat, the skinwing squawked in alarm and leveled off just above the highest limbs. Dav heard the squawk of another skinwing. Hoganvar's beast had followed them down. Through the treetops came a shower of arrows, barely missing the dwarf's mount.

The arrows flew wildly, corkscrewing off at odd angles, but they were nonetheless dangerous. Hoganvar was jerking in the saddle, kicking his legs and struggling against his bonds. Dav could tell he was shouting, but not what he was saying.

Dav's own mount flew over a small clearing, and a second volley of arrows arced up. The skinwing veered sharply to the left. Dav lost the stirrups and slid again.

Below him, he heard shouts, harsh and guttural. Orcs, he thought, but he couldn't spare any time to think about them. His right leg dangled free over the dark forest below as he gripped the saddle bow with his right hand. He grabbed for the ornate backrest and had pulled himself halfway back into his seat before he realized he was gripping a strap fastened to the back of the saddle.

So that's how the elves secure themselves when they fly, he thought as he braced himself and fumbled with the straps. As he tried to fasten the two ends of the belt around himself, he understood why they hadn't used their customary method of securing him and the dwarf. The small strips of silk webbing weren't made for the thicker bodies of humans and dwarves. He slid back as far as he could, drew in the taut muscles of his stomach, and fastened the buckle. He could hardly breathe. Still, it was better than falling into the treetops and not breathing at all.

Once he was firmly secured in the saddle, he pulled down his gag before he grabbed the reins. The beast had been circling and was approaching the orcs in the clearing again. He pulled on one of the leads at random, thinking any direction was better than being a target for the orcs.

Any direction but down, he amended, but thankfully the skinwing was soaring up into the dark sky, out of range. When the beast was several hundred feet above the tops of the trees, Dav experimented with the reins. When he understood them, he guided the beast into a wide circle, trying to locate Hoganvar. At last he saw the dwarf's mount, circling just over the treetops, still within range of the orc arrows.

Dav guided the beast in a shallow dive, swooping down over Hoganvar's mount and then up again, hoping the second skinwing would follow the first. His plan was successful. He decided to fly under Hoganvar's mount and catch the long, trailing lead line. Then he would take both beasts and Hoganvar into Darokin.

He veered sharply to the right and down, but the second skinwing followed too closely for him to get under it. He tried a second and a third time, but Hoganvar's mount continued to stay right behind him. They swooped and dived, circled and dipped, but Hoganvar's skinwing wouldn't be left behind.

Then Dav realized his beast was shaking with fatigue. He could feel its labored breathing through his legs. The ugly beast was a faithful creature, attempting to obey his every command, and he knew he would kill it if he continued the aerial acrobatics. He pulled on the reins and turned his mount west, but the edge of the forest seemed far away. He had been veering to the east in his attempts to catch the lead line of Hoganvar's mount. Dav doubted the creatures could make it to the border. He continued to fly west until he spotted a small, empty meadow and guided the beast down to a landing.

There might be orcs around, but he decided he'd rather fight and walk out of Aengmor than kill the greathearted creature he rode. He was sure the second skinwing would follow. He had wasted their chance to fly into Darokin convincing himself of that.

He misjudged the area needed to land both creatures. By the time his own beast was down, Hoganvar's mount was forced to close his wings and dropped down in a jarring fall.

"Hoganvar? Are you still alive?" Dav called

softly as he unbuckled the flying strap that held him in the saddle.

"Remind me to ask the elves to give you flying lessons," the dwarf grumbled as he twisted in the saddle, trying to work himself loose.

"Flying lessons I've had," Dav said as he slid from his mount's back and hurried over to help the dwarf. "It's landing I need help with." His efforts to untie the ropes that bound the dwarf were hampered by Hoganvar's attempts to help. "Will you sit still?"

"If you hurry," Hoganvar grumbled. "This whole forest is crawling with orcs."

When Dav finished untying the knots, the dwarf slipped to the ground and stomped around, swinging his arms to bring back the circulation. Dav returned to his mount and pulled away the rope that had kept him tied to the saddle.

"My guess is we're near the western border of Aengmor," Hoganvar said, which verified Dav's opinion. He coiled the other rope and looped it over his shoulder.

They stood in the shadows of the skinwings for a minute, listening. To the northeast, they could hear shouts and the clang of metal.

"Best we get moving while they're busy," Hoganvar said, leading the way west.

Dav followed the dwarf, anxious to leave the dark forest behind. Somewhere in the mountains east of Aengmor, they had left Leanna, the elves, and the gyerian, and his entire mind centered on getting back to them.

The memory of Erian's arm around his waist in an effort to protect him from Leanna's teasing, the child's desire to sit close, needing the security of a strong arm. The little prince's trust had haunted him since they had been separated. As important as the elves' safety was their information. The tale of their kidnapping could prevent hundreds, possibly thousands of unnecessary deaths.

"Not more than a day's walk to the west is a fort, if I remember right," Hoganvar said. "At least we can get some weapons. . . ." He stopped, his chin up as he listened. Dav caught the sound of heavy footsteps and breaking branches.

"Quick, into the trees!" Dav hissed, hurrying to the side of the clearing nearest the approaching sounds. Orcs, he decided, since he knew of no noisier creatures in the forest.

He held one end of his rope and threw the rest of the coil over the lowest branch. He offered the rope to the dwarf, but Hoganvar shook his head.

"You climb," the dwarf said, picking up a sturdy tree limb. "Now that I've got my feet on the ground, that's where they're going to stay."

Dav shrugged and climbed, gripping both dangling lengths as he ascended hand over hand. When he reached the first limb, he pulled his rope up after him.

The landing of the skinwings had attracted the orcs' attention. They slowed their pace as they approached the clearing and circled to the right and left. None of the six came within twenty feet of the tree where Hoganvar waited in the shadows beneath Dav. If Hoganvar moved, he would be seen, but Dav crept along the thick limb and climbed onto another, moving along on the second tree until he stood directly above one of the orcs.

Or were they orcs? he wondered as he gazed down at them. The physical shape was right. They had the stocky, heavy bodies, huge, muscular arms, and thick necks and narrow heads of orcs, but he had never seen orcs dressed like the creatures below.

Or undressed, he thought, since three of the five wore nothing but loincloths and belts. The other two wore short, sleeveless leather vests open in the front. Most orcs kept their heads covered. These wore no helmets; their heads were shaved on the sides, and the short cap of hair that remained was decorated with feathers.

They carried small hatchets tucked in their belts instead of spears and axes. Each had a bow and a quiver of arrows suspended from its left shoulder. Dav had never known orcs to use bows and arrows.

The first two paused, and he heard their low, guttural speech as they argued. The dialect was strange, but he caught a few words, enough to tell him they were orcs, apparently scouts separated from a larger band that was attacking the Shadow Elf village to the southeast.

One moved away from the others and angled toward the clearing where the skinwings waited.

Dav knotted a sliding loop in the rope and dropped it off one side of the limb, over the head of the orc. With a good grip on the rope, he jumped off the other side, using his weight to jerk the noose tight. He heard the creature's neck snap before he reached the ground. Dav released the rope. The orc fell, and the silken rope of the Shadow Elves slid silently from the tree, looping itself over the orc's still-twitching body. None of the other orcs had paid any attention to the slight sounds.

Dav recoiled his rope and took the creature's bow, quiver of arrows, and three hatchets. All the weapons were poorly made, but at least he was armed again.

"Godish? Hulsfag?" a hoarse voice called softly, then waited a minute and called again. It came from off to Dav's right, and close by. He looked around and spotted the orc just as it saw him. With a snarl through its bared, tusklike teeth, the orc charged. In a quick move that was almost a blur of motion, it pulled one of its small hatchets from its belt and hurled it at Dav's head.

The blade bit into the bark of the tree behind Dav. He jerked one of the hatchets from his own belt and threw it at the orc. The badly balanced weapon arced up, twisted in the air, and plummeted downward. The handle struck the ground, but the hatchet bounced up and the blade dug into the orc's left thigh.

The orc gave a howl and backed off, dragging its wounded leg. Dav shrugged and let the creature go. He pulled the wounded orc's weapon from the tree and stuck it in his belt.

Dav slipped from shadow to shadow, searching for Hoganvar, until he heard the dwarf whisper his name. Hoganvar now carried an orc bow, a quiver of arrows, and a couple of hatchets. He spat on the ground, showing his disgust as he inspected one of the small axes.

"Pitiful," he said. "Almost better off fighting bare-handed."

"The bows aren't much better," Dav said as he inspected the one he carried. "I didn't know orcs used them."

"These are red orcs," Hoganvar told him. "Strange bunch, but no better than the others."

While Hoganvar was talking, Dav heard the snap of a branch. He gestured for the dwarf to be quiet. They moved into deeper shadows as a troop of more than twenty red orcs moved through the forest, traveling northeast, toward the battle at the village. This group ignored the skinwings, apparently intent on their destination.

Twenty was too many for Dav and Hoganvar to take on. They waited until the forest was silent again. They had their own problems, and by unspoken agreement, they decided to leave the elves to deal with their enemies.

"West?" Dav asked. To the west was Darokin, where the humans would be more hospitable to two wanderers. Darokin was reputed to be friendly to anyone with gold, and the Shadow Elves had not taken their purses. They could buy more horses and travel along the border of Aengmor to search for their lost companions.

"West," Hoganvar agreed. "I've had enough of elves."

They had been walking less than five minutes when, through a break in the trees, they saw a skinwing just above the treetops. An orc arrow arced toward it, catching the creature in the left wing. As it screamed and jerked in pain, the rider slipped from the saddle and fell.

"That elf will come down right in the middle of those orcs," Dav said, running across the clearing and into the woods on the other side. Hoganvar pounded after him, complaining all the way.

"Do we care? Even if we do, he probably died in the fall."

"Maybe not. His mount was close to the treetops." Since his capture, Dav had found little cause to like the Shadow Elves. On the other hand, he had no reason to hate them, but plenty to hate orcs. He might leave the elves and orcs to fight it out, but not when one elf was surrounded by a group of enemies.

They slipped from shadow to shadow and watched as the troop that had passed them massed around the base of a huge tree.

Up in the tree, the elf climbed down, staying to the shadows whenever possible, but her long, flowing white hair streamed in the wind, giving away her position. The orcs kept craning their necks, searching for her, though she was in plain sight. The orcs' actions were inexplicable.

At their leader's direction, the orcs made a ladder of their own bodies. One, two, and then three of them managed to climb to the first limb.

"She'll need help up there," Dav said. He tossed

the coil of his rope over the limb of the nearest tree and started to climb.

Gripping both descending lengths at once, he climbed up hand over hand till he reached the lowest limb of the huge tree. By pulling up the rope, recoiling it, and tossing it over a higher limb, Dav continued from limb to limb until he was nearly a hundred feet above the ground. He worked his way from limb to limb and approached the tree where the elf was alternately dodging from a barrage of orc arrows, then descending while the creatures nocked another round of arrows. None of the shafts had come close to her.

When he reached her, he stopped, making sure she understood he wasn't attacking. He kept the hatchets in his belt.

"I've got a rope," he said, taking care to use the Shadow Elf dialect he had learned from Erian and Calenderi. "We might need it if we have to keep to the trees."

She stared at him wide-eyed, her lips parted in surprise.

"How can you see me?" she asked him. She whipped out her sword and turned the point toward him.

Her surprising statement caused him to pause. Then he remembered he had also seen through Serdic's invisibility spell. Despite the danger from the orcs below, he was enjoying her surprise and confusion. Let her wonder.

"Oh, are you supposed to be invisible?" He raised his eyebrows, knowing she could see well enough to read his expression of mock surprise. "Sorry. I didn't know I was intruding on your spell. And you don't need that sword with me. I came to help."

The elf woman was a little over five feet tall, but she radiated confidence and authority. Her clothing was torn and dirty. A cunning suit of fine chain mail peeked from beneath a wide-sleeved tunic that was many sizes too large, with sleeves as threadbare and ragged as anything the Hattians had left behind on the boat. A cloak, heavy with charm runes woven into the fabric, hung from a cord around her neck and draped down her back. Golden charms decorated her belt and·scabbard. The quillons of her two-handed sword were gold, and the blade was inlaid with golden runes. On her person, he saw the wealth of a nation, mixed with the confusing tatters of her shirt and a pair of ragged, well-worn boots.

"You are a human," she said accusingly.

"Unless I've grown fangs," Dav answered, irritated by her distrust. "Yes, I'm a human, and if you want to stay an elf, we'd better get away from here," he said, pointing to four orcs who had given up trying to climb and were running along the thick limbs directly below them.

She sheathed her sword and whipped out a knife. "Walk in front of me, human. I will not kill you, but neither will I trust you until I have cause."

Dav turned and walked back along the limb, disgusted with himself for bothering with her. So much for saving the damsel, he thought.

A small hatchet arced up, struck the limb above

them, and fell within reach. Dav caught it and threw it back at their pursuers. The poorly made weapon corkscrewed down and stuck in the thick bark of the lower limb, directly in front of the orcs who were sprinting to catch up with Dav and the elf. The first pursuer tripped over the weapon and fell, landing on two others who were running along the ground, pacing their comrades. The three lay in an unmoving heap.

The female elf gave Dav a curious look. He wasn't about to admit the truth, that he would have considered it good luck to hit the ground with the badly balanced hatchet.

"I couldn't think of another way to bring down more than one with a single weapon," he explained and moved along the branch, leaving her to think it over until an arrow whizzed by, uncomfortably close to her. She paused and looked down at the orcs.

"Don't you think we should get moving?" Dav asked. "For a warrior, you sure don't know much about protecting yourself. And if you're counting on that invisibility spell, you should know it won't work with me around."

Two arrows sailed by close enough to prove Dav was telling the truth. The elf ignored the missiles as she stared at Dav.

"Just who are you?"

He was about to answer her when a moving shadow ahead alerted him to a new danger.

"Oops! Hold it." They stopped as, ahead of them, two orcs climbed onto the same limb. They turned to retrace their steps, but four orcs approached from the other direction.

Wherann shrieked and launched himself from Dav's shoulder, streaking for the ground.

"You won't take it personally if I help you hold them off?" Dav asked as he raised the weapon he was carrying.

"Back to back," she ordered and took a two-handed grip on her sword.

Dav sent three arrows into the shadows ahead. The first crooked shaft went wild. The second disappeared into the shadows, but he had hit a target. An orc fell with a scream. The third shaft struck the tree. When he reached for a fourth, he tugged at the feathered shaft, but somehow it was stuck in the quiver.

He was still tugging when a big brute with a bunch of feathers in its hair dashed out onto the limb and rushed at him with one of its small hatchets raised. The weapon looked lost in the big orc's hand.

Dav slipped the bow over his left shoulder and pulled two of the orc hatchets from his belt. He knew any attempt to throw one of the weapons would be a wasted effort. By experience, the orcs knew how to compensate for the imbalance, but Dav hadn't had time to experiment with them.

The orc threw its hatchet. Dav raised both his weapons and knocked the blade aside. He felt the air from the wooden handle ruffle his hair as he deflected it. A second hatchet whizzed by, this one coming from behind him. Then he heard the clang of metal against metal as the elf battled one of their pursuers.

He was dimly aware of a scream from the shadows on the ground and looked to see another orc stagger into a patch of moonlight with one of the small axes in its throat. Hoganvar dashed out of the shadows, retrieved the weapon, and disappeared again.

The orc facing Dav continued to approach. It had only one weapon left, and it carried the hatchet low as it advanced. When it was close enough for Dav to attempt a throw, he brought up the weapon in his right hand and stepped forward, putting his weight into his toss. The weapon wobbled slightly off course but caught the orc in the shoulder. It flinched and toppled from the limb.

Behind him, Dav heard the clang of metal on metal and a hurried invocation to Rafiel before another orc fell.

A second orc worked its way toward Dav and swung its hatchet. Dav fielded the blow, but the orc was strong and knew how to use its weapon.

Wherann tried to help, hovering over the orc with two small handfuls of dirt, but the orc raised its weapon and fended off the construct. Wherann darted away, the dirt falling harmlessly from his tiny hands.

Dav swung his weapon, but the orc's hatchet came down on his, nearly knocking it from his hands. His fingers went numb from the sting.

He stared into the creature's beady eyes and saw a grin spread on its cruel mouth, exposing another inch of the yellow tusklike teeth. The orc's next swing knocked the weapon from Dav's hand.

He backed toward the elf, who had troubles of her own. He was unarmed, and the orc came forward, its weapon swinging in long smooth arcs. The creature's pig eyes gleamed in triumph.

Dav thought of jumping, hoping to reach the next limb, but if he did, he'd leave the elf's back unprotected. And if he stayed to defend her, the next swing would finish him.

* * * * *

Struth the Shaker waited in an abandoned hut on the slope of a mountain above Fort Hobart on the eastern border of Darokin. From the doorway, he could look down on the black woods of Aengmor. He paced like a trapped animal. He was caught in the net of his own indecision.

His sensing spells were giving him conflicting information, telling him that the elves were out on the Ylari desert and also deep under the ground. The young wizard was to blame, he decided. Dav was trying to lead him in the wrong direction.

He was still stewing over the problem when Thar's messenger arrived, jabbering something nearly unintelligible.

"Red orcs attacking the Shadow Elves?" Struth demanded, and when the messenger nodded dumbly, his heavy orc jowls shaking in fear, Struth raised his hand and threw a fireball that consumed the hapless messenger in less time than it took to speak the spell.

This was the fault of stupidity and some orc braggart who had ambitions over another tribe. The wizard was tempted to teleport to Oenkmar and spread a rain of fire over the entire city.

Why wouldn't the stupid creatures do as he ordered? If Darokin and the elves turned on the orcs, the army Struth needed would be destroyed. He wanted the orcs to help hold the lands he took. If they hadn't been necessary to his plan, he wouldn't have cared how or when they risked their foolish necks.

At least the orcs of Oenkmar had stayed out of the fight, he thought. He would find a way to repair the damage. He would need a plan to further implicate Darokin.

He would have to think about it. . . .

Chapter 21
The Radiant Princess

Dav made his decision. He would have to jump. Staying and dying to protect the elf would only prolong her life for one stroke of a hatchet.

"I've lost my weapon. I'm going to make a jump for it," he said, giving her warning. "You'd better jump, too."

"Stay where you are," she said, throwing a corner of her cape over him.

"Lot of good that does," Dav said, stepping back and bumping into her as the orc took another step forward and swung his blade. Dav looked down, but below them half a dozen of the burly creatures were waiting, their arrows ready.

The orc brought its blade around again, but a thick arrow caught it in the arm with a force that raised it off the limb before it fell on its companions below.

Dav looked down into the shadows and saw an orc lying in a bloody heap. Nearby, Hoganvar nocked another arrow to his orc bow.

"Let's go," Dav said and rushed along the limb. He spared a glance over his shoulder and saw the elf running behind him. She soon outdistanced him, leading the way. When they left the orcs behind, she used his rope to lower herself to the ground, with Dav right behind her.

"I must get to Zorvallen," she said. "You can help me protect her from the orcs. I raised that skinwing from an egg, and I won't lose her to those vermin."

"Thanks just the same, but I have a dwarf friend around here somewhere," Dav replied. "He may need help."

"Human, you will do as I say. I allow you to live because you assisted me, but this is my land, and you were carrying a red orc hatchet. That does not earn my trust."

"Your people took my weapons. That doesn't make me like you either," Dav retorted. "I'm not leaving my friend to face an entire band of orcs alone."

"You won't be," Hoganvar spoke from the shadows. "But you two keep arguing, and you'll bring every monster in Canolbarth down on us. Saw you lose your weapon," he said, handing Dav another small axe.

The elf gave the dwarf a hard look and then trotted off through the woods. Since she was traveling west, they followed. Now that he knew Hoganvar was safe, Dav decided to help her protect her injured mount.

Her arrogance reminded him so much of Calenderi that he suspected she held a position of some

importance. If they helped her protect her skinwing, she might believe their story. The lives of
Leanna, the gyerian, and the elf children might
depend on it.

Their trail took them back to the small clearing
where their two mounts waited, along with a third
who stood licking its injured wing and mewling
pitifully. The other skinwings paced about the
clearing, dodging several orcs who tried to capture
them. A big, burly creature stood alongside a
smaller, thinner orc.

"A shaman," the elf woman hissed.

Dav understood. Most orcs would only be after a
kill, but a shaman would know the value of flying
mounts.

Though she was wounded, Zorvallen showed
more spirit than the other flyers. She lunged at the
orcs who were trying to catch her, thrusting her
head forward and snapping, her sharp teeth
gleaming in the moonlight. The two orcs hastily
retreated to the woods.

"Get away from her!" the elf woman screamed
and rushed into the clearing, leaving Dav and
Hoganvar gaping in the shadows.

"They *are* getting away—as fast as they can,"
Dav shouted, hoping to prevent her from getting
killed before they could help her. "Of all the stupid . . ." He raced after her. Behind him, Hoganvar
grumbled as he followed.

On the other side of the clearing, they saw more
orcs, who had been hidden from them by the bulk
of the skinwings. The elf's shout had alerted them.

Dixie McKeone

She charged into the meadow, and since her own mount was safe for the moment, she swerved to protect Hoganvar's skinwing. Her first swing cut down the orc on her right, and with her second thrust, she parried the axe of a large pig-faced creature, who grunted in gleeful snorts as it jumped away and drew back its weapon again. A third orc moved around behind the elf as she pressed her attack.

Dav raced into the fray. He threw the small hatchet Hoganvar had given him. The orc behind the elf swung its large axe, but missed her as Dav's weapon caught the creature in the neck. It would have been a perfect throw if he had been aiming for the neck, Dav thought. But he had been aiming for the middle of the creature's back, so he had missed by more than twelve inches on a fifteen-foot throw.

The elf made a sudden thrust with her sword, and her adversary doubled up and slumped to the ground. She dashed around the skinwing and out of sight as Dav hurried forward to pick up the larger axe.

Around him, he could hear the guttural shouts of the orcs. On the other side of the clearing, hidden from his sight by the skinwings, the elf let out a shout of triumph that blended with the scream of an orc.

A large orc with a fan of feathers stuck in its braided hair wandered into the light of the clearing, scrubbing at its eyes with one chunky fist. Wherann, carrying a large leaf, swooped down on it. The construct hovered, tilted his leaf, and dropped another load of loose dirt on the orc's face before darting back under the trees.

Hoganvar was nowhere in sight, so Dav retreated to the shadows, testing the weight of the axe. The double-edged iron head was very heavy. Since it wasn't a typical red orc weapon, it had probably been a trophy of its last owner. The wooden handle was new; the fresh, pale marks of whittling to fit the crooked handle to the head had not yet been darkened by age and dirt.

Dav heard a noise behind him and turned to see a big red orc raising its hatchet. Dav leapt forward, swinging his weapon, but the crooked handle and the weight of the heavy blade threw his aim off. The axe turned in his hands and caught the orc against the side of the head with the flat of the blade. The force of his blow slammed Dav into the nearest tree.

For half a second, he and the orc stood facing each other, the big humanoid half stunned and Dav with the wind knocked from him. The orc recovered first and charged. Dav ducked back against a tree, hoping the blade of the creature's hatchet would get caught in the bark, but the orc hadn't thrown its weapon. Seeing Dav's movement, it drew its weapon back it time.

Dav jumped away and realized he was flanked by two thick-boled trees that grew less than three feet apart. He brought his blade up over his head, knowing a downward swing would give him a smaller target area. He backed up, sure the orc would follow him. When the orc's snout appeared between the two tree trunks, he brought the axe down with a *swoosh*. The weapon's blade careened off a tree trunk and caught the orc in a ricochet, severing its head from its thick neck.

Dav stared at the twitching body and shook his head. He was still alive, but more by accident and luck than by his own skill. He looked around and saw Hoganvar dispatching one of the orcs who was trying to catch the other skinwings. The dwarf had somehow found a spear. He drove it into the creature and looked around for other foes, but a troop of elves had arrived. Dav couldn't see them in the forest, but three well-placed arrows brought down three orcs, and the others fled into the woods. The elf woman cleaned her bloodied sword on the fur vest of the second orc she had killed and strolled over toward him.

"You have helped me twice, human. I will remember."

"Then I ask for repayment now," Dav said. "Hear and believe my tale. . . ."

But before he could begin his story, they were surrounded by elves. Their gazes flicked from Dav to Hoganvar, but their attention was on the female elf.

"Praise to Rafiel for holding you in his hand, Radiant Princess."

"You're Tanadaleyo? Princess Tanadaleyo?" Dav stared at the elf. The hair rose on the back of his neck at the realization that this was the sister of Calenderi, who ruled Aengmor in the name of her father, King Telemon.

"That will make a difference in what you consider your reward?" The princess eyed him with suspicion.

"No, my request remains the same," Dav replied. "But my tale could save the lives of your sister and brother."

The red orcs had been driven off, and the immediate emergency was over, but with the Darokinian army massed on her borders, Tanadaleyo had no time to stand and listen. She mounted a fresh skinwing, and Dav rode behind her as she flew south again.

As they raced through the darkness, the princess heard him out, interrupting only once to ask a question. At her request, he described as best as he could the location of the grove cavern where he had thrown the spell that had caused their separation. For the rest of the ride, she remained silent and thoughtful. He had no idea whether she believed him or not.

For the rest of the night, they soared above the forest, heading south. Off to the right, Dav could see open lands in the distance. Not far behind them, other skinwings followed. Hoganvar rode behind another elf. Wherann stayed inside Dav's coat and slept.

Dawn brightened the eastern sky as they landed at the western edge of the forest. Ranks of pale elves stood sheltered from the light beneath the shadows of the trees. Beyond the edge of the woods, hundreds of campfires dotted the plain.

As the princess slid from the saddle and leapt

lightly to the ground, she was surrounded by elves, all talking at once.

While the Radiant Princess was thus occupied, an elf returned Dav's and Hoganvar's weapons.

"Enough of this babble!" she snapped, and Dav noticed how loud her voice seemed to be. Even when Calenderi had raged at Dav, her voice was always well modulated.

"Any word from my father?" Tanadaleyo demanded.

"King Telemon is nearing the surface with his forces," a tall elf told her. "We've learned nothing about Darokin's plans for battle."

"Draw our people back into the forest," she ordered. "If Darokin attacks, it will be during the day, hoping we will be blinded by the sunlight. Instead, let them venture into the shadows, where we have the advantage."

"But you shouldn't be fighting Darokin at all," Dav objected. "They didn't kidnap Calenderi and Erian!"

"That may be, if what you tell me is true, but believing they committed the outrage, we offered the challenge, and they are here to take it up." Tanadaleyo's smile showed the irony of the situation. "It's too late for either nation to withdraw without losing honor."

Dav was staring at her, wondering how to prevent the needless loss of life, when she was called aside by another elf. After a brief exchange of words, she returned to Dav. Her eyes were full of worry.

"Your tale was not entirely true," she told Dav. "The others did not all leave the cave together."

"You've heard something!" Dav's hope leaped.

"Is that fool gyerian safe?" Hoganvar demanded.

"We have learned nothing about my brother Erian or the gyerian," she said. "However, my sister and the female human have reached Aengmor. The human is unharmed. It is not known if a wizard will reach Calenderi in time to save her life with a healing spell. She shielded the human and took an arrow meant for her. Why would she do so?"

"People can care for each other even if they are different," Dav said, hoping the wizard arrived in time. His emotional pain when he learned Calenderi had been wounded was almost physical. But what could have happened to Erian and HeyYou? he wondered. How could they possibly survive on their own?

"Calenderi was able to send word. We now know Darokin and Karameikos were not to blame for the outrage." With one slender hand, she waved, indicating the fires among the sparse trees that grew on the plain. "But the war will be fought nevertheless. If we drew back now and did not face the Darokin forces, they would think we were too weak to defend our borders."

"But Darokin could withdraw if you told them it was a mistake. . . ." Dav's mind whirled, trying to come up with an explanation acceptable to the elf princess. "You could say you must and would avenge the outrage to your people, but to blame the guiltless was not the act of an honorable people. Then they could withdraw with dignity and so could you."

"Perhaps so, but they will not, and for the same reason we must defend the challenge. They were weakened by the recent war. If they leave the field without facing us, other nations will think they cannot defend themselves."

"They're already injured by war, so they must suffer more pain to prove they can defend themselves?" Dav cried. "Where's the sense in that?"

"Only the strong risk showing weakness," Tanadaleyo replied. "There are times when one person can back away with honor, but not a nation. And Aengmor cannot let the world see our vengeance go unsatisfied if we are to take our place on the surface." She walked off, leaving Dav no opportunity to argue. She nodded to three tall elves who approached the human and the dwarf.

"You will come with us," the first one said. Dav and Hoganvar were led east, into the darkness of the forest. "Consider your good fortune. This is not your war."

Dav didn't answer. But he didn't agree either.

Chapter 22

The Final Battle

As they walked deeper into the forest, Dav developed an idea. He slowed his steps little by little, trying to fall behind the others. His plan was hampered by Hoganvar's attempts to stay by his side. The guards urged them to move faster, but they kept their irritation in check. Dav suspected they had been ordered not to use force on the captives. He kept slowing his pace, staring up at the twisted trees, examining every strange bit of fungus until the dwarf and his escorts were nearly out of sight.

The largest of the elves heeded his instructions and stayed with the human, but in his impatience, he kept glancing ahead. When the guard's attention was thus diverted, Dav grabbed the elf by the arm, swung him around, and slammed him into the closest tree.

"Sorry," Dav said to the stunned warrior as he laid him on the ground, "but as Tanadaleyo said, sometimes one person can back down when a nation can't." Swiftly he slipped back through the forest until he reached the edge of the woods. When he sprinted toward the fires in the distance, arrows flew from the edge of the woods, but none really came close.

Before long he reached a company of Darokinian men-at-arms. The morning sun flashed off their wide-brimmed, spiked metal helmets. It gleamed off the sharpened edges of the wicked-looking pikes held by the first row of soldiers. Behind them, Dav could see the archers. They started forward as he approached. An officer rode up to him, blocking his way. Since he was unfamiliar with military ways, Dav had no idea what the insignia of rank meant.

"Are you the commanding general?" Dav asked. He knew he had made a mistake when he saw the smiles on the faces of the marching soldiers.

"I'm Captain Rippenwill. Consider yourself lucky you escaped those vermin with your life. The commander is occupied . . . a little matter of a war."

"But there's no need to fight," Dav panted. "It's all a mistake!"

The officer stared down at Dav for a moment before a wide grin showed his yellow teeth. "You're going to tell Commander Aswain he's wrong? I'd enjoy seeing that if I had the time."

"It isn't his fault . . ." Dav began, then realized he wasting his time talking to the captain. Commander Aswain was the only one who could stop the coming battle. "Where will I find him?"

The captain pointed down the line of soldiers.

"That's him with the white plumes on his helmet."

Dav didn't need to be told twice. He sprinted toward the commander, angling back toward the forest as he stayed in front of the line of marching men. They split ranks as they worked their way around the outlying trees. They were approaching the deeply shadowed woods by the time Dav reached their leader.

Commander Aswain was a large man, dressed in shining armor heavily embossed with gold runes. The white plumes on his helmet looped down his back. He rode a large white war-horse.

"Commander, there's been a mistake. This war is completely unnecessary," he shouted as he slowed his pace to walk by the prancing white horse. He swore at himself for not planning what he was going to say.

"Who are you?" Aswain glared down at him. "Do you lack all sense? Get back behind the lines."

"But this battle isn't necessary," Dav said. "Hundreds of men and elves will die to no purpose unless you stop it. The elves of Aengmor don't want to fight you."

"Then why did they offer a challenge and mass their troops on our borders?" the commander asked, but his question was rhetorical. He turned his head, watching the line of marching soldiers.

"Because of the royal children. The elves believe they must avenge the outrage, but your people had nothing to do with the kidnapping. The elves know that now. They don't want to fight you for something you didn't do."

"That was just an excuse," the commander said. "We're not even sure there are any royal children."

"But there are! And they *were* kidnapped. . . ." Dav paused. "The orcs made it look as if your people were to blame. Someone wants Darokin to fight Aengmor."

He had finally caught the commander's attention. "What are you talking about?"

"You're being used. You're serving the interests of someone who wants to weaken both nations. Tanadaleyo now knows Darokin wasn't at fault, so they have no need to avenge the insult in battle."

"It's too bad they didn't learn it earlier. But now they're massed on our borders. They think the last war weakened us. They'll learn better."

"And they'll fight to keep you from thinking they're too weak to keep you from invading them. You're both too weak to back down and just strong enough to hurt each other more. Can't you see how ridiculous this is?" Dav argued, nearly tripping over a tree root. "Hasn't there been enough killing?"

"Darokin cannot back down," the commander said. "Now, for the last time, get out of the way!"

"Let *me* do the backing down," Dav shouted. "Tanadaleyo has already said she doesn't want a war that serves no purpose! Agree with her, and we can stop it now!"

"It's already too late," Aswain said, pointing up the line. The left flank had reached the edge of the woods. The sound of clashing steel echoed in the distance.

"Stop it!" Dav shouted. "Call a retreat until you speak with Tanadaleyo! You owe your own men that much. You'll save countless lives. . . ." His pleas went unheard as the commander's mount leapt forward and met with a black horse that thundered out of the shadows. Dav recognized its rider as Colarsaran, Tanadaleyo's second-in-command. The elf held a lance upraised as he charged. Commander Aswain threw up his shield, but in deflecting the lance, he pushed it across his body, and it swept him from the saddle.

The effort of unseating the Darokin commander knocked Colarsaran off his horse. Dav reached him as he was getting to his feet and attempted to push the elf away.

"Don't do this!" he shouted into Colarsaran's sensitive ears. When the elf tried to force Dav out of the way, Dav knocked the elf down and then stood over him, fending off Aswain.

"You seem determined to get yourself killed," Aswain snarled, drawing his sword. "Well, if that's what you want . . ." He drew back his blade, but Dav leapt at him, knocking him sideways. By the time Dav and Aswain regained their balance, Colarsaran was on his feet again, his sword in his hand. His eyes burned with hatred.

"Well, Commander, it seems we must remove an obstacle from our path." He moved purposely toward Dav.

"If he won't remove himself from the field, let him suffer the consequences," Aswain answered. He approached Dav from the other side.

Dixie McKeone

"Then let's fight." Dav drew his blade, wondering if he had lost his mind. "But fight me rather than each other." Yes, he decided, he must be out of his mind. He'd addled his wits with too much flying. Both commanders moved toward him, two trained warriors, and what little skill he had, he'd gained at the instruction of a young girl.

Dav shifted his gaze from one hard-eyed warrior to the other. He wanted to say he was ready to forget the whole thing, but his mouth just wouldn't form the words.

Then he forgot one fear for another as a giant shadow darkened the sky.

"You will stop your foolish fighting!"

The deep, roaring voice rolled over the armies like thunder. Blades faltered. Arrows loosed by startled bowmen missed their marks. The battlefield grew eerily silent. Every head looked up into the sky at the huge blue dragon.

"Bletinferelth!" Dav shouted, overjoyed that the dragon had done what he could not. He felt the stares of Colarsaran and Aswain, but the explanations could wait. Bluenstrinel, the young blue dragon Dav and his friends had freed from the rockslide, hovered above his giant mother.

"Dav, friend of Bletinferelth," the dragon addressed him, "tell these puny humans to remove themselves from the clearing while Bluenstrinel lands. If any dares to shoot his foolish arrows, then all will die by dragon breath."

It was unnecessary for Dav to give the instruction. Colarsaran took one look at the descending

dragon and waved the elves back into the shadows of the trees. The soldiers of Darokin broke ranks and fled. Their commander made a more dignified but hasty retreat.

As the young dragon descended, Dav heard a familiar voice.

"Don't shoot arrows! Awk, don't shoot arrows! Arrows is trouble; arrows is trouble."

"HeyYou! You stupid featherhead!" Hoganvar roared from the shadows of the forest. "What do you mean by getting yourself lost and riding a dragon?"

"Awk, dwarf is trouble! Dwarf is trouble!" the gyerian gobbled as Bluenstrinel landed. HeyYou and Erian slid off the youngling's back and bowed to their mount before hurrying off toward the woods. They were still running across the field when the young dragon leapt into the sky.

Erian looked around fearfully, spotted Dav, and ran toward him, ignoring the elves gathered under the twisted trees.

"We tried to follow the wizard to rescue you, but we got lost on the desert, and Bluenstrinel found us," he shouted as he threw his arms around his human friend. In the silence, his high-pitched, childish voice rang in the air. "How did you get away from the wizard? Am I home now?"

"You're home." Dav laughed as he picked up the prince and swung him up on his shoulder. Erian's face and hands were blistered from the desert sun. His lips were cracked, but he laughed in delight. He sobered and nearly fell off Dav's shoulder as he attempted to bow to Tanadaleyo, who had left the forest and approached them.

"So there really were kidnapped children?" Commander Aswain said. He approached warily. "It wasn't a lie as we thought—an excuse to attack Darokin?"

"You see one of the children before you now," Dav answered. A small, dirty hand put pressure on the side of Dav's neck, and the elf child tensed at the arrival of the Darokinian commander.

Commander Aswain's eyes shifted from Dav to the child and then to Tanadaleyo. He raised his hand and slowly motioned his troops to withdraw.

* * * * *

High in one of the large trees that bordered the forest, Struth stood on a limb, watching the activities below. He was too far away to recognize any of the participants, but he could tell from the size of the child brought by the dragon that one of the elves had been returned.

The battle had to begin again before the child could tell his story. Once the total of the dead began to mount, the war would roll along on its own momentum, no matter if the children were believed or not.

But how to get them fighting again? . . . By the order of someone they dared not disobey, he decided.

* * * * *

"It was no lie that the youngest children of my father were taken from our lands," Tanadaleyo answered the question posed by the commander of the Darokinian forces. "Know you also that we found dead Darokinians in the lower passages where my brother and sister were captured and more Darokin dead on the path where they were taken from the forest. It seems we were meant to believe Darokin had committed the outrage."

"The humans fought with the orcs who took us away," Erian piped up. His voice took on a little tremor. "Korshnid's orcs killed them all."

"Korshnid was an outlaw even among the orcs," Dav said. "And I suspect Gorval, the Hattian who bought them from the orcs, was an outlaw, too. He sailed the shores of Brun and captured people to sell into slavery."

"Where do we find this Gorval?" Tanadaleyo's eyes flashed.

"Buried in the sands on the Isle of Dawn," Dav replied. "Leanna killed him and avenged your people as well as herself." Dav was stretching the truth a bit, since Gorval had fallen on his knife in the struggle, but he wanted Leanna to have the credit.

"Then we owe a debt to this human female," Tanadaleyo acknowledged. "And another to you for killing Korshnid, who sold my brother and sister to the Hattians, though it grieves me that others reap the revenge that should have been at the point of elven blades."

"Perhaps we can find a wizard who can make

them live again for you," Dav suggested, the softness in his voice belied by the gleam of anger in his eye.

"That will not be necessary." Tanadaleyo had turned away and did not catch the irony. "We will find a way to discharge our debts to you."

She gazed thoughtfully at Aswain, who met her look in return—two commanders trying to decide their future courses. The silence lasted for a full minute. From the edge of the forest, Dav could hear Hoganvar and HeyYou's voices as the dwarf and the gyerian argued.

"The time has not yet come for us to trust the peoples of the surface races," the Radiant Princess of the elves said slowly. "Still, it is the hope of my nation that we can live in peace under the stars and learn to love the bright light of day. I now believe we erred in thinking you committed the outrage. We have no cause to fight you, save that you are invading our land."

"If you have no cause to fight, then we do not invade," Aswain replied.

"There's not going to be any fighting?" Erian asked from his position on Dav's shoulder.

"No. Everyone is going to try to be friends," Dav said, grinning up at the elf boy who sat on his shoulder. He knew he was expressing his hope rather than fact, but he was also making a suggestion he hoped the two commanders would accept.

"Good," Erian said, smiling down at Commander Aswain. "When I'm big, I'm not going to fight anyone. I'm going to travel all around the world

and see all the different kinds of animals and
birds and . . ."

The elves and the humans smiled at the child's
excited chatter. Dav grinned up at him and sighed
with the relief he suspected they all felt. Then he
turned toward the forest and began strolling
toward the trees. By his side walked the Radiant
Princess, ruler of Aengmor. She was holding the
hand of her youngest brother, who still rode on
Dav's shoulder, when they heard a murmur rise
from the ranks of the Darokinians.

Tanadaleyo looked back over her shoulder.
"Someone comes, riding hard," she said. A moment
later Dav heard the hoofbeats. They stopped to
watch.

Commander Aswain was strolling back toward
his army's lines, so the rider rode out on the field to
meet him.

"Corwyn Mauntea, king of the merchants of
Darokin and president of their council," Tanadaleyo said.

Dav recognized the commander because he had
been close to him. The other figure was a tall man
in a dark, tattered cloak. The cloak looked vaguely
familiar. It wasn't a garment he would have
expected the ruler of a wealthy country like Darokin to wear. Every soldier on the field was dressed
better.

The newcomer was pointing at the forest and
exhorting the military commander while Aswain
shook his head and seemed to be explaining something.

A prickling of danger tickled the hair on the back of Dav's neck. He lifted the little prince from his shoulder and set him on the ground.

"Get back into the trees," he told Erian, who clung to his hand. "Go now," he insisted.

As Erian reluctantly headed for the trees, Dav started walking back across the field, toward the two who stood arguing.

"What is it?" Tanadaleyo demanded. She kept pace with him, her hand on her sword.

"What is Corwyn Mauntea wearing?" Dav asked, interrupting the radiant princess.

"A robe of deep blue trimmed with gold and white. His cap is blue. . . ." She gazed at Dav with narrowed eyes.

"Get back to the woods. You see an illusion," Dav told her. "If you have no magic to fight a wizard, leave now."

"What do you see?" she demanded. "I see Mauntea, and I can hear him now. He is ordering Aswain to attack, to rid Darokin of the threat the Shadow Elves represent. It seems we must fight to hold this land—"

"Struth!" Dav shouted, interrupting Tanadaleyo. He was close enough to recognize the cloak he had seen twice before. "Struth the Shaker, foul refugee of Alphatia," he shouted again. "You are not Corwyn Mauntea, and you have no influence here! Your illusion will not work on me! You will not drive these people to war."

The ranks of Darokinian soldiers were muttering dangerously, thinking Dav had insulted the president of their council. At his side, Tanadaleyo turned to stare at him as if he had lost his senses. Dav wondered how he could convince them that he could see the reality behind the wizard's illusion when Struth whirled to face him.

"You!" Struth's voice hissed across the field, reaching Dav as if the wizard were standing three feet away. Struth spurred his horse forward, riding out into the middle of the field to meet Dav. He was twenty feet away when he leapt from his horse.

The elves gathered in the shelter of the trees and the Darokinians all murmured at once and pointed to the wizard. Dav could see no reason for it, but Tanadaleyo gave a sharp hiss of indrawn breath.

"You were right. It's not Corwyn Mauntea," she said.

"Get away," Dav ordered. He knew he was the only one on the field who would be able to face Struth the Shaker and live. Both Darokin and Aengmor must have wizards close by, but they couldn't stand against Struth. Dav knew the only chance to best the Alphatian wizard lay with the strange power he carried.

Struth raised his arm as if to throw a spell. Dav raised his as if he were ready to counter it. The simple act of raising his hand seemed to call the wizard's bluff. Before Struth could make up his mind whether or not to risk a spell, Dav was on him. He balled his fist and struck the wizard on the jaw, knocking him off his feet. He waited, standing over Struth as the tall man sat up and wiped the blood from his lip. The wizard leapt to his feet and pulled a knife from his belt.

Dav bared his own knife. His sword had a longer reach, but Struth was armed with only a knife. He had to fight Struth on equal terms.

They crouched, circling each other. Struth lunged at Dav, who caught the wizard's blade with his own, forcing him back. They circled again, and suddenly Struth charged, grabbing Dav's right hand, while with his own blade, the wizard jabbed at his young opponent's midsection. Dav jerked aside, grabbing Struth's knife hand.

For a moment, they stood locked in a contest of equal strength. The wizard's eyes blazed into Dav's, scorching the younger man with hatred.

"So you think you can destroy Struth the Shaker, bastard spawn? Your father's power cannot save you."

The wizard's ploy worked better than he could have imagined. The hint of his ancestry broke Dav's concentration. He wavered, off balance, and Struth put all his strength into throwing the youth to the ground. As he fell, the wizard jerked away and pointed at Dav with the hand that still held the knife.

Struth spoke the words of a spell, and all around Dav, a fire roared into life. He stood in the middle of an inferno, staring at flames that terrified him with their intensity, but he could have been a world away, for all the heat he felt. He turned and pointed at Struth, throwing the wizard's words back at him, but he was too late. The mage had mumbled something and was shimmering into an insubstantial cloud. Suddenly he disappeared, and all Dav could see of him was the gleam of the knife he still held.

The fire around Dav died away, but the gleam of the wizard's knife still hung in the air like a disconnected glimmer of sunlight. Then it brightened, and the cold gleam turned from blue to amethyst, then purple, then red. Finally it flared into an orange flame.

Dav's spell was working after all!

An unearthly scream filled the air as Struth's burning arm appeared. Then Dav could see the wizard's entire body, orange with a fire too deep within to show the flicker of a flame. He brightened like an ember, and like an ember dimmed into gray ash that floated away on some nameless plane. Not a flake fell on the grass of the wide meadow between the armies that watched the confrontation.

* * * * *

In Pandius, the home of the Immortals, in the residential area of the Sphere of Thought, a parklike area was filled with trees of wondrous shapes never seen by mortals. Tall sprays from magnificent fountains rose in arcs and took unlikely courses in their fall, as if some magic wind whipped in many directions at once. Neither the shapes of the trees nor the fountains were meant to resemble anything from any plane. As the eyes of the beholder followed their curves, they helped to draw the mind into unaccustomed paths and provide new prospective.

Odin and Djaea walked among the trees and the fountains, seeking insight.

"He grows stronger every time he uses the disk," Odin said. "I begin to fear for Pandius." He looked toward the great dome, where a tiny crack had appeared after the last shaking it had received. Djaea's power had quickly mended the break in the dome, but no Immortal would ever forget where the rent had appeared.

"Who is to say it is not Easir who took it from Castle Qain?" Djaea asked. "We must not close our minds to any possibility. But you are right. The holder of the disk of Reddican must be found. We must make a plan before she destroys us, if it is indeed Easir. And we must be careful about it, since we won't be the only Immortals trying to find it."

Odin nodded. Reddican's charm was a danger in any hands—perhaps even his own.

Chapter 23

Chicken for Dinner

Just before sunset, Dav straightened his tunic, trying to make sure his sword belt had not creased it. Then he went to the table where Wherann chittered excitedly as he donned his new clothing, a gift from Erian and Calenderi.

The tiny trousers and boots were exact miniatures of elf clothing. The tunic had been designed with a panel in the back that came up from the waist, leaving his wings free. Tiny straps and buckles fastened it in front, just below his shoulders. Dav suspected the minute, perfect stitching and the intricate embroidery had required elven magic as well as elven skill.

"Prty, prty!" Wherann tied the little straps as he preened in his new finery.

Leanna entered the room and spun around, showing off her white skirt and tunic, embroidered in bright colors. She wore a pair of soft white elven boots. She and Calenderi, who had been healed by elven magic, had arrived three days ago.

Son of Dawn

Leanna, Dav, and Wherann left the upper floors of the inn, the Crafter's Rest, and joined Serdic and Hoganvar and HeyYou in the main room. Serdic had also been captured by the Shadow Elves when he had returned to the forest to search for his friends. He had been flown to Rafielton on a skinwing and had arrived the day after the battle.

The companions had been commanded to present themselves in the main square of the town just after sunset. Together they walked beneath wide linen canopies that shaded the street from sunlight and protected the sensitive eyes of the Shadow Elves.

Eight days had passed since Dav had fought and destroyed Struth the Shaker. A captured orc who had accompanied the wizard to the western border of the Canolbarth Forest had blurted out Struth's plan in exchange for his life. The war had been stopped before King Telemon and his forces had reached the surface of Mystara.

The companions had spent days exploring the city while they waited for the arrival of the king. Dav had been saddened to see the burned-out buildings near the western gate where the final battles for the city had taken place. Wizard's fire had left the timbers charred and twisted.

Many buildings in the city were falling into decay as the wood rotted in the dampness of the forest, and the efforts of the Shadow Elves, who had no experience in working with wood, were in some places pathetic attempts to shore up the structures. Still, they were learning, and some of

Dixie McKeone

their repairs could almost match the skill of the original work.

Much of the city was empty because the number of Shadow Elves that lived on the surface was still far fewer than the original occupants of the town.

Dav and Leanna led the way as the group turned onto the main east-west thoroughfare and entered Rafiel Square, where a thin forest of tall poles held up a linen canopy. The huge open space was filled with thousands of elves.

Only one small path was open through the crowds. It led toward the large building that had once been the Merchants' Brotherhood Hall but had since become the Radiant Princess Tanadaleyo's court. As they approached, they saw three tall thrones and two small seats on a hastily erected platform in front of the building.

To Dav's surprise, Commander Aswain was present, along with six Darokin officers, and stood just to the side of the dais.

The throne on the right was occupied by Tanadaleyo, who wore a silken embroidered robe of office. Between Tanadaleyo and the center throne sat Erian. He wore a sparkling white robe with a blue border on the hem and a blue sash. He smiled and waved enthusiastically.

On the throne to the left sat a beautiful elf woman whose face was as intricately marked as that of the princess. Her clothing was richly decorated, and from her came an aura of great power. As Dav gazed on the elf, he knew he was seeing the great Porphyriel, the radiant shaman and the high

priestess of Rafiel. Calenderi sat between Porphyriel and her father and wore the unadorned
white of an acolyte.

Before the center throne stood the tallest elf Dav
had ever seen. He knew it must be King Telemon of
the City of Stars. The king's face was neither young
nor old. He was dressed in a dusky blue robe that
blended with the evening. His eyes seemed weighted
with the cares of his people.

When the adventurers reached the edge of the
dais, a tall, stately elf led each of the companions
to a chosen spot on the pavement, placing Dav
slightly apart from the others. Even Wherann was
asked to stand apart from Dav, who wondered at
the placement.

When the elf stepped back and bowed to the
king, the small troop of adventurers followed his
example.

The king acknowledged them with a nod of his
head.

"You have done a great service for my house and
my people," he said. Dav thought his voice was too
soft to be heard more than a few feet, and yet it
echoed off the stone buildings around the square.

"You have returned my children, the hope of my
household. You have helped to avenge the slight on
our nation with the deaths of the Hattian outlaws,
Korshnid, who took them away, and the wizard,
who would destroy nations to serve his own ambition. You have prevented a needless war and saved
the lives of many of our people." He took a deep
breath and raised his voice. "And you have given us

a priceless gift. You have shown us that there are those on the surface who would be our friends."

He nodded at a robed elf, who stepped forward and handed Leanna, Hoganvar, HeyYou, and Serdic small silken bags about a foot square. A fifth bag, so small it seemed lost in the hand of the elf who carried it, was given to Wherann.

"It will be witnessed that Aengmor rewards those who do it service," King Telemon said, gazing down on Commander Aswain and the six Darokinian officers. The king waved his hand again. Five stalwart young elves stepped forward carrying larger bags, plus a sixth bearing a smaller one. At the command of the king, all the adventurers except Dav held their small bags open. Into each bag was poured a wealth of gold and platinum coins.

Dav was handed his reward in the sack in which it had been brought. He couldn't understand why he had not received one of the smaller bags until he realized the elves were pouring into them a greater volume than they should have been able to hold. The small sacks were magic bags of holding, great gifts in themselves, since they could contain huge quantities of wealth, supplies, and weapons. Furthermore, the weight of the contents of the bags would never be felt by their owners.

Dav hadn't been offered one of the marvelous bags because the power that traveled with him would negate its magic. The eyes of the adventurers and the Darokinians were wide with wonder by the time the large sacks were empty and the elves returned to stand by the dais.

Porphyriel rose, and as she stood, even the whisper of the wind in the linen canopies died to silence.

"The great Immortal Rafiel has seen your efforts to help our people. He names you friends, and he opens this land to you. Here you will find a home and safety if you choose to accept it. Our streams and trails are open to you in your journeys."

Porphyriel stepped back, and the king nodded to them again. He led the way off the dais, descending a stair at the rear. The others followed. Calenderi and Erian smiled at their friends before following the adults.

When the adventurers turned away from the dais, the path behind them had been filled in with elves, but another passage through the crowd had opened, and they followed it to a table heaped with food. Colarsaran waited for them.

"You have received the heartfelt thanks and reward of our king. Now celebrate with us, for ours are the lives you saved. Share this feast and our companionship, which is all our people can give in gratitude."

The celebration spread throughout the city, and before long they were walking down streets, taking food from table after table, sharing songs and learning dances from hundreds of elves.

They traveled in a group at first, but HeyYou stopped where a torch lit a large stone. They left him playing with his gold pieces, which glittered in the flickering light.

Dixie McKeone

Dav and Leanna left Hoganvar telling a tale to a group of warrior elves from the City of Stars. The elves' huge eyes opened even wider as he described his adventures.

Serdic opted to visit the great wizard Kanafasti, who had sent word he would use his magic to strengthen the mage's wounded leg. They later found the human mage dancing with Tanadaleyo, who had left the royal quarters and was enjoying the feasting in the streets.

The next morning dawn was paling the eastern sky when Dav and Serdic saddled the horses that had traveled from the eastern border on rafts moved by magic. The beasts were fresh and ready to travel.

None of the group really looked forward to leaving Rafielton, but Leanna was plagued with the need to return to Vorloi and buy back her certificate of bondage. Dav felt the weight of his promise to his dead stepfather that he would continue his studies with Amslothe Verdon in Luln. Neither Serdic, Hoganvar, or HeyYou had mentioned any destination.

They rode through the outskirts of Rafielton as pale faces watched from the shadows of doorways. Many others braved the light to step out and openly watch them leave. A delightful song hung in the air, preceding them and traveling along behind.

Leanna looked around as if trying to find the source. "What are they singing?"

Dav translated for her.

Son of Dawn

"Safe be the road,
Gentle your path,
And soft be your rest
In the night. . . ."

They rode until nearly sunset and made camp just west of the edge of the blighted forest so their animals could graze on the winter grass.

They sat around the campfire and relaxed, knowing they camped in safety, since they could see the Shadow Elves patrolling the edge of the forest. Their conversation was desultory. Dav felt a sense of loss and suspected the others felt the same. It took some time before he could come to terms with it. They had faced and won out over their dangers. They missed the elf children, but they could solace themselves with the thought that Erian and Calenderi were reunited with their people once more. Dav knew his own sense of loss was the dread of parting with the rest of the company.

HeyYou, Serdic, and Wherann seemed unaffected. The gyerian was playing with his glass necklaces, turning them this way and that in the light to watch their reflections. Wherann pulled out his gold pieces, which were as large as plates in his hands, and laboriously stacked them in piles.

Something seemed to be weighing on the mind of the dwarf, but his expression forbade any questions. Leanna also seemed to be worrying over something. Dav ventured a question.

"Once you've bought your freedom, what will you do?" Dav asked her.

"I don't know," she said softly, so the others couldn't hear. "All I could think of was buying back my certificate. I hadn't looked beyond that point. What do you do when you're alone?"

"For one thing, you need to learn how to read and write," Dav suggested, though he kept his voice low. She was sensitive about her lack of education. "If you don't, people will take advantage of you, and you won't keep your wealth very long."

"You mean go to school and sit with little children while they laugh at me for being there?"

"I was thinking about Luln," Dav said slowly. "You wouldn't have to go to school with little children. Amslothe Verdon would probably take you in. He won't be able to spend all his time with me. I'd have plenty of time to teach you."

Her face lit, and Dav felt a warmth inside himself. He wouldn't be losing all his companions after all.

"There's lots of things we can do," he said, suddenly full of high spirits again. "We won't spend all our time studying. There's probably wild country around Luln, and we can go hunting."

"If it's not too far from the coast, we could buy a boat and really learn to sail," Leanna said. Suddenly they couldn't talk fast enough to keep up with their ideas.

They were still making plans the next day when, as the road curved around a low hill, they saw a strange community of ramshackle structures made of mud-dabbed straw and branches built in a grove of trees.

For once, Dav's education failed him. He twisted
in the saddle, intending to ask Hoganvar what it
was. His question went unasked, however. The
dwarf's face had paled. He sat tense in the saddle,
staring straight ahead.

Then a feathered head peeked around one of the
huts and gobbled in alarm, and Dav understood.
He also knew the reason for the dwarf's moodi-
ness. They had reached a gyerian village. Hoganvar had brought HeyYou back to his people.

"We should stop and rest the horses." The
dwarf's voice was hoarse with unadmitted emotion. They had only been on the road for two hours,
but no one objected. Dav and Leanna exchanged
sorrowful looks and led the way off the road to an
open area where the animals could graze.

HeyYou had also caught sight of the gyerians,
who continued to peer at them from behind the hut
nests. He squawked in surprise and approached
them cautiously. Six curious gyerians came out
and stared at him.

"Looks like we'll be gathering our own firewood,"
Hoganvar said and stomped off. Dav, Leanna, and
Serdic unsaddled the animals, tethered them
where they could graze, and did their searching for
firewood well away from the dwarf.

Serdic made the fire and even helped Leanna
roast a rabbit Dav had shot that morning. They
spent the rest of the day and the evening in almost
complete silence, not wanting to intrude on the
dour dwarf. No one asked why they stayed. Hoganvar would want to make sure HeyYou was accepted

by his people before they moved on.

By the next morning, they had no doubts left. Their gyerian friend hadn't returned from the village. They saddled their horses in silence until Serdic asked about the extra horse and saddle.

"Leave 'em," Hoganvar snapped. "They belong to HeyYou."

At Serdic's questioning look, Dav nodded. Hoganvar had paid for three of the animals and their tack. If he chose to consider one the property of the gyerian, that was his business.

They rode away in silence, their numbers now reduced from eight to five, counting Wherann, who crouched on Dav's shoulder and kept up a steady line of questions.

"Hyu? Hyu? Hyu?"

"Shhh," Dav said, trying to quiet him.

Then, from behind them, they heard the hoofbeats of a galloping animal and the panicked squawking of a gyerian. They stopped and looked back. HeyYou clung to the horse's mane as the loosely cinched saddle slid around under his mount's belly. The stirrups swung wildly, terrifying the horse.

"Hyu! Hyu! Hyu!" Wherann launched himself from Dav's shoulder and flew in sweeping circles.

They spread out across the road and urged their horses into a trot and then a gallop as the gray horse approached. Serdic grabbed one side of the bridle and Dav the other, and they brought the gyerian's mount to a stop.

"Told you horses was trouble, awk, trouble,"

HeyYou said triumphantly as he slid to the ground. His head jutted forward as he glared at the dwarf. "Told you so."

"You stupid, three-toed featherhead," the dwarf roared, bouncing from the saddle. He grabbed the gyerian's left arm and jerked him around, inspecting his feathers and assuring himself that HeyYou was uninjured.

The others grinned at each other. While Serdic and Leanna checked the gray horse's legs to make sure he hadn't injured himself in his panic, Dav reset the saddle and tightened the cinch.

"I found you a place where you could be with your own people," the dwarf shouted at the gyerian. "If you're too stupid to stay there, that's your problem."

"Live in a mud house, a mud house?" HeyYou scrambled back into the saddle. "Eat snails? Eat snails?" He shuddered until his feathers fluffed and doubled his size. "And they *steal* things."

Hoganvar scrambled onto his mount, still glaring at the gyerian. "And you wouldn't know anything about that, would you?" He huffed and glared at HeyYou. "Well, you can come along. I can't stop you, but I'm not looking after you anymore. Get that into your feathered brain."

HeyYou glared back at the dwarf for a moment and then thrust out his beak again.

"*Chicken for dinner!* Awk! *Chicken for dinner!*" he shouted at the dwarf and urged the gray horse to a gallop as he headed down the road toward Tavaro.

Hoganvar sat stunned for a moment, then spurred

his own mount to a gallop and bounced in the saddle. "You listen to me, you scrawny-legged . . ."

Dav, Leanna, and Serdic slowed their horses to a walk until the dwarf and the gyerian were too far down the road to hear their laughter.